Take Time To Murder

Mystery
by
Jeanne Wilson

Kingston Publishers Limited

© 1996 by Jeanne Wilson
First edition 1997

All rights reserved. No part of this book may be reproduced in any form or by any means without the prior permission of the publishers, excepting brief quotes used in connection with a review written specifically for inclusion in a magazine or newspaper.

Published by Kingston Publishers Limited
LOJ Complex, Building #10, 7 Norman Road
Kingston CSO, Jamaica.

ISBN 976-625-094-4

Typeset by Hemmings'way Limited
Printed by Stephensons Litho Press Limited

Chapter 1
day 1 , Monday

The early morning tropical sun was quickly evaporating the heavy dew on the lawns, once so smooth and green, now brown and dry after a summer-long drought. The cheerful chorus of grass-quits and a chattering flock of black anis — sleek, glossy, hook-billed black birds — broke the silence outdoors, whilst on the shaded verandah only the occasional rustle of one of the island's two morning papers and the muted chink of china disturbed the ear.

Mr Justice Piers Smith-Watson put down the paper with a sigh and looked keenly across the table at his wife. He studied her for a few moments; she seemed quite unaware of his scrutiny. Her large, dark brown eyes, once so sparkling and full of life, now gazed in a dull, unseeing way at the brightness of the garden. She was still a beautiful woman in her early fifties, and once, not so very long ago, had been a noted beauty. Now there was a film across her beauty. Her bright eyes had dimmed, her skin was slack and seemed to have lost its moist elasticity. Her hair, of which she had been so vain and had cherished with loving care was — not neglected, but lifeless. She sat unblinking, breakfast untouched, even the coffee in the cup barely tasted.

"My dear," Piers said at last, "is something the matter? Are you not well?"

She started in alarm at this words, her eyes flared open wide, a slight colour flamed under her pale coffee-coloured skin.

"Matter? No...nothing. I...I'm tired, I...haven't been sleeping very well lately."

"Annabel," the judge's voice took on a slight asperity that was so well known in court. "I have spoken of this before, I have suggested that you see a doctor. You have done nothing about this — you have disregarded my wishes in the matter. You insist that you are well and yet — over the past two weeks your whole personality has changed."

Annabel bit her lip, there were threatening tears in her eyes. "I know," she said in a voice that was openly a little more than a whisper. "I...I'm sorry. I'm truly sorry, Piers. Maybe I should...see someone."

He got up abruptly; the chair made a harsh scraping sound on the verandah tiles. He folded the paper back into its original form, laid it carefully by the side of his plate, then bent and kissed Annabel lightly, unemotionally on the forehead. He noted that she clasped her hands tightly, that a slight tremor passed through her body at his touch. "Goodbye, my dear. Make that appointment early. Don't expect me for lunch, I'll be home at about six."

She nodded, then said in a low, intense voice, "Goodbye, Piers."

He went out briskly. A few moments later she heard the muted roar of his elderly Rover; then the engine settled to its usual sedate throb, wheels spun on the gravelled drive and silence descended on the house.

Annabel sat motionless where her husband had left her.

"Is it you finish, Miss Annabel? You want I should clear?"

She looked up as Clarice, plump, placid, widely smiling, came onto the verandah. Her dark face creased into worry lines as she saw the untouched food. "Eh-eh, Miss Annabel, you don't eat nothin'. You goin' quail away ma'am."

"It's all right, Clarice. I don't feel like eating."

"Let I fresh up the coffee, ma'am, I bring it to you room."

"All right, Clarice — just coffee, though."

Annabel walked slowly into the house, heels clicking on the tiled floor. She paused by a low table and took a cigarette from an inlaid mahoe box, then picked up the box and went to her room. The beds had been made by the efficient Clarice whilst they were at breakfast and the room's very tidiness struck a chilly, impersonal note. Four windows were shaded by vertical Venetian blinds. Long white frilly curtains fluttered at the side of each window and showed the sweep of the big garden.

As Annabel placed the cigarette box on her vanity dresser the telephone on the table between the twin double beds shrilled loudly. She straightened slowly, a look of fear in her eyes.

Oh God, she thought, not again. For two weeks — fearful dragging weeks — nothing. And now — when I begin to hope — not *again*.

She picked up the receiver, praying that it was a casual call, a wrong number — *anything* — but her hopes died as a soft silky voice said in her ear, "Mrs Smith-Watson? That is you, isn't it?"

"Yes." Her voice barely reached her own ears. "What do you want?"

A faint laugh came over the line. "What a question — as if you didn't know."

"But you said last time — you promised — that it was the end. I *cannot* give you any more."

"You have to. Bring it — to the usual place…"

"I tell you I can't. I have nothing left. Can't you understand?"

"Then you'd better get it from your husband. I think that he'd be glad to give it to you."

"I *can't*! Oh God, how can I make you realise…"

"Listen, my lovely Annabel, you'll pay — in person and in cash. Today. Or I'll be getting in touch with your husband — and the press." The soft voice had an underlying steely, menacing quality now. "At eleven — and don't be late. A case of love in the morning, eh?"

The line went dead and Annabel was still clutching the receiver when Clarice entered quietly, carrying a steaming cup on a tray.

"Lawd, Miss Annabel, you look sick fe true."

Annabel jerked her head up. She gazed at Clarice for a long moment then slowly put the receiver back in its cradle and reached out a steady hand for the cup and saucer. Her cigarette, burning down to a white ash, had spilled on the deep grey pile of the shag carpet.

"I'm all right, Clarice, thank you. Would you bring me — a glass of water?"

She sat quite still while she waited for Clarice to return.

Clarice handed her the glass and took up the empty cup, her dark eyes puzzled. She went out, padding silently on bare feet, a habit of which Annabel had never been able to break her. She opened her mouth to make her usual protest, then thought: It doesn't matter now. *Nothing* matters any more. She waited until she was sure that Clarice was safely back in the big kitchen, then went quickly into the square, grey-tiled bathroom that opened off the bedroom. She slid open the glass door of a built-in cupboard and took out a small dark brown bottle. Written on the label in careful small script was the injunction: *To be taken only by medical* prescription. *One tablet if necessary on retiring.* In red lettering across the top of the label were the words DO NOT EXCEED THE STATED DOSE.

She opened the bottle with steady fingers and poured a stream of small white tablets into the palm of her left hand. The bottle had held two hundred when full — she had taken no more than half a dozen — those remaining would surely be enough.

Resolutely she swallowed them, taking sips of water to help them down. Once she gagged as a tablet stuck at the back of her tongue and bitter acridity flooded her mouth— she fought back the resultant nausea and forced herself to swallow the remaining tablets.

At last her hand was empty.

She went back to the bedroom and sat down on one of the beds — it was Piers' but it didn't matter. She looked at the empty tablet bottle that she still held in her hand and a quick surge of fear welled up in her — she didn't want to die — was it too late? Could she still get help?

No — this *was* the better way.

Her hand moved towards the telephone— she could, just by lifting and dialling, undo the damage she had done — but was there time? Already she could feel the beginning of relaxation of muscles throughout her body, a heaviness that was fast spreading....

The telephone rang with startling clarity — it was with the greatest effort that she forced her hand, unwilling and leaden, to pick up the receiver.

"I must," she muttered aloud with a tongue already thickening, "before...Clarice...answers...downstairs."

She had the receiver off now and laboriously raised it to her ear. The same hated soft voice said, "You took your time, I must say. Make it eleven-thirty. Something came up." She was silent for so long that a question rasped in her ear. "Did you hear me? Eleven-thirty."

"Yes." Her voice was hoarse, slurred, almost unrecognisable. "I...hear. But you're...too late. I won't...be...there..." The receiver slipped from her fingers that had lost their power to hold it and clattered down between the beds, where it spun on its cord.

The voice came out of the earpiece, distorted, crackling, "Annabel? What in God's name do...Oh no, you *fool!* You..." The receiver bumped against the table leg, then the voice stopped.

Annabel Smith-Watson sank deeper and deeper into unconsciousness as the little tablets did their work. Her last coherent thought was: At least the phone can't ring again and bring Clarice too soon. She had difficulty in remembering the name — Clarice — and had to dredge it from the depths of receding consciousness.

Then deeper darkness, velvety and comforting, closed in — there were no more difficulties, no more troubles, no more decisions — nothing...just nothing.

She was left undisturbed and the minutes ticked away into hours. Then Clarice, made uneasy by the long silence in the large, lonely, cool house, went quietly into the bedroom to enquire what she should prepare for that night's dinner.

The beautiful antique grandfather clock that stood sedately in the judge's study began to strike eleven as Clarice dialled a number with shaking fingers, tears shining on her dark face.

* * *

Rachel Groome deftly parked her metallic-bronze Metro automatic in a seemingly impossibly small place. The little car was still — after two weeks of ownership — a source of joy to her. It had been a pre-wedding gift from Rowan Rodgers who, despite her protests, had insisted that she accept it. The white Starlet that she had before she went away over a year before had been sold.

"You need a car and you might change your mind again," Rowan had grinned, his black eyes smiling down at her. "This is just a form of insurance — your conscience won't let you go back on your word now."

She smiled at the memory of that moment as she switched off the ignition and swung slim coffee-brown legs to the roadway. She glanced at her watch. Eleven o'clock, right on time for her appointment at The Looking Glass.

The interior of the beauty salon was cool; the air-conditioning unit made a quiet, insistent hum. After the fierce heat of the morning sun outside — a sticky ninety and rising — the sudden drop in temperature made her shiver.

"Good morning, ma'am. Mrs Groome?"

The receptionist got up from behind a pale pink-painted desk. She was tall and svelte, black hair expertly braided and beaded to modern perfection. Her dark skin had a glowing satiny texture.

Her big brown eyes held a professional boredom. She moved with a sinuous easy grace, flaring hips swaying from a tiny waist. She regarded Rachel without any interest whatever.

"Michel will look after you. This way."

She led Rachel through an arched doorway which had a concertina-like fold of pink plastic in lieu of a conventional door. Rachel wrinkled her nose — this excessive pink, she thought. I hope that Michel, whoever he is, isn't garbed in a pink smock.

"Michel — your eleven o'clock appointment. Mrs Groome."

The girl, having done her duty, undulated back to the desk, exuding boredom and a faint contempt.

"Ah, Madame Groome."

The high, light voice, the accent and the gestures were very good copies of the Gallic, the features and colouring undeniably Jamaican. Michel was plump, dark, of medium height, urbane in manner and — repulsive, Rachel added mentally.

He had a — what is termed in the island vernacular — a *light* black complexion, a smooth round face, his hair was sculpted in the current cut. Dark brown eyes, small and set deeply in thick folds of flesh. A small full-lipped mouth, the edges raised, etched redly against his dark skin.

Rachel paused before she sat down, then shook herself mentally. Why had she taken such a violent dislike to the man she didn't know?

Man? Heavens only knew that she had had her hair done often enough in the past by one of his kind, so why this repugnance?

She gave a brief smile. "Good morning."

As he settled her in the chair and swathed her in a pink wrapper, he studied her small dark head with a speculative look. "What style does madam have in mind?" He affected a slight French accent.

"More or less the same."

"Ah, yes. The Vidal Sassoon. A flick here." He touched her cheek. "And high at the back of the crown?"

"Yes, please."

"Madam does realise that such a style is — how shall I say? — *passé*?"

"That doesn't matter — the style suits me."

"As madam wishes." He shot her a quick look in the mirror, Her small pointed face, flawless coffee-cream complexion, full sensuously shaped mouth and unexpected wide grey eyes gazed back at him somberly. Her silence disconcerted him; he was used to garrulity from his clients. As he worked she acknowledged his skill and relaxed a little, which he immediately noted.

"Madam is new in Kingston? I do not think that I have had the pleasure before?"

Good heavens, thought Rachel, where did he learn that approach. Aloud she said, "No, not new. I've been away. I always used to come here before..." She paused and glanced around the salon. "It's changed a lot."

"Ah, yes. The new owner made many changes. Madam said 'before'?" He looked up from his work and saw her expression in the mirror; she had become withdrawn again. "Ah, forgive me, madam, I have no right to ask questions — when you do not wish to..."

"It doesn't matter," she cut in shortly. "I was going to say before my husband died — I have to get used to it."

"Ah, madam, you will — and you will marry again. One so lovely, it is inevitable."

Despite herself, Rachel smiled. The man was such a phony — such a *practised* phony — and if he precedes another remark by "ah" I shall scream.

After her hair had been trimmed, and thoroughly shampooed, Michel himself attended to the set. When she had been settled under the dryer, large rollers hidden under the expected hood, a girl brought her coffee and magazines. Another new girl, Rachel noted. All the old ones gone in just a year. She idly studied the girl reflected in the big square mirror: she was slim almost to a point of being thin, quite tall with small pointed breasts that had the static quality which proclaimed padding — odd, Rachel thought, I'd understood that such bras were a thing of the past — and slim boyish hips. She was speaking in a low voice to Michel. She turned her head and looked at Rachel, then seemed to ask a question. Her words were completely drowned by the whirr of the dryer. Michel shook his head and spread his hands, the girl shrugged then reached into the pocket of her shift-like overall and took out a small box. She tossed a capsule into her mouth, then held out the box to Michel. He hesitated then took one.

Rachel turned back to her magazine, sipped her coffee and thought impatiently, tranquillisers, I suppose. Then some other drug to pep them up — and another to help them sleep. She sighed sharply, what a way to live. It had become the norm for far too many people.

She was pleased with the result of Michel's ministrations after he had brushed and coaxed into place and finally sprayed her fine black hair, thick, fine and springy but straight, a legacy from some unknown ancestor — European, Chinese or Indian? Who could tell in the island melting pot.

She smiled at Michel and said, "That's perfect — just how I like it. Next week at the same time?"

He bowed, a parody of his European counterpart, but Rachel had accepted him, her earlier revulsion overcome by his mastery of his art.

She checked at the pink desk about the next appointment on her way out. The thin girl was in attendance now and gave Rachel a keen appraising look from shrewd, brown eyes. It was a look that was reminiscent of that which she had seen in Michel's eyes as he had studied her mirrored face and it held a speculation that Rachel found in a vague way to be unnerving.

She dismissed the incident as unimportant and by the time she was weaving the little car through the lunch-time traffic at Constant Spring, had forgotten it entirely. As she turned at the complicated intersection near Manor Park Plaza, a car's horn hooted urgently and she glanced across at the stream of traffic on the other side of the road. Rowan Rodgers' pale grey Mercedes 250SL was just sliding to a halt at the traffic lights. She glimpsed his smile and the slight wave he gave her. She just had time to smile back and give an answering beep on her horn before she passed him. Despite the smile, she had time to notice that there was a worried look in his black eyes.

What's up now? she asked herself. Not another case to absorb all his time? The fact that if that were so their wedding might have to be postponed didn't disturb her as much as it should.

Chapter 2

The lights changed and Rowan Rodgers — Superintendent Rowan Rodgers of the Jamaica Constabulary Force, C.I.D. — swung the powerful Mercedes round the corner out of the main stream of traffic. Glimpsing Rachel had been the one bright spot in a gloomy morning.

"They've got the news already," he murmured to Sergeant Phillips, his aide, who sat solid, stolid and reliable beside him.

Two darting bare-footed urchins in ragged pants and shirts, each clutching a sheaf of newspapers under an arm, wove through the cars during a momentary pause in the traffic, pressing dark sweaty faces against closed windows, and shouting in the way of newspaper vendors the world over: "*Star! Starree. Judge wife foun' dead. Ssstaar!*"

Rodgers thrust some coins into a grubby outstretched hand and took a copy of the afternoon tabloid. He handed it to Phillips saying, "What does it say?"

Phillips looked with distaste at the two-inch high black type. "*Judge's Wife Found Dead in Bed. Suicide Suspected.*"

"All right, spare me the soap opera suspicions and speculations that I feel sure must follow," Rodgers said wearily.

His mind went back to the stunned look in Piers Smith-Watson's eyes as he had said in a bemused tone, "God knows why she did it, Rodgers. She hadn't been herself lately — but this..." He had gestured helplessly at the empty bottle, still untouched, by the now vacant bed.

"I hate to worry you, sir, at a time like this, but you know what has to be done," Rodgers had said.

The older man had nodded. "I know. Go ahead, ask your questions."

"You say that your wife had not been well — had she seen a doctor?"

"No — I'd advised strongly that she should. She — promised me — only this morning — that she would make the...appointment today."

"Were — you happily married?"

Smith-Watson had paused before replying, as if considering his words, then said, "We have always been happy. Not in the wild, delirious way one reads of in romantic fiction — and very rarely meets in real life — but in a quiet, steady wa., We...we were comfortable together." He had fallen silent, eyes turned inward, looking back at the past.

God, Rodgers had thought, he makes it sound dull as all hell. His thoughts had flickered briefly to the wild joy of loving and making love with Rachel — then he had switched his attention again to the older man.

"Maybe she wasn't happy — but I suppose we have proof of that. Maybe I was too practical in my approach to life." His voice had held a probing, introspective note, trying to find a reason where none seemed to be.

"I'm sorry, sir, for causing you pain with my questions. One last one — for the moment — would your wife have had reason to worry about money matters?"

The judge had jerked his head up. "No reason at all. She had a generous personal allowance — too generous she always said — over and above the house-keeping allowance. She always knew that she could come to me for whatever she wanted."

"I see," Rodgers had nodded then got slowly to his feet. He towered from his six foot three inch height over the seated man, who had seemed somehow to have shrunk in the last few hours. Smith-Watson had looked up. His opaque brown eyes were dull and lifeless, the whites red-veined. His hair, a greying caracul was ruffled from its usual well-groomed state, his dark skin had a yellowish pallor. He had spoken slowly. His normal clipped lawyer's voice with its nascent overlay of judicial dryness, had disappeared, "Thank you, Rodgers. You have to do your job I know. If anything comes to light, I'll call you."

"Thank you, sir. You realise that there will have to be a post mortem?"

The judge had nodded as Rodgers went on. "The tablets — where did they come from — originally?"

"Isn't it written on the bottle?"

"Yes, but I wondered if *you* knew."

"As far as I can remember they've been in the cupboard in the bathroom for ages."

"All right, sir, we'll check with her doctor."

Rodgers' thoughts were interrupted by a careering cyclist cutting out of a side street almost under the front bumper of the Mercedes. The inertia seat belts snapped into action as he applied the brakes. "Sorry," he said to Phillips. "I forgot I'd had new brakes."

Phillips' broad face broke into a smile. "Plenty power, Mr Rodgers, sir. Is one nice car — been one nice car a long, long time."

Rodgers grinned to himself. Phillips' ponderous return to any degree of patois from his usual correct speech always presaged a personal theory or observation.

He waited.

"Mr Rodgers — don't it funny, nice lady like that? Pretty house, nice furniture, own car, nice helper— what she want to kill herself for?" He didn't wait for or seem to expect an answer but went on, "She never leave no note. Most of them do that."

His last words seemed to hang in the air.

Rodgers could hear them repeated, over the soft purr of the engine, over the passing traffic, over the street vendors' cries.

Most of them do that. *Most of them do that.* MOST OF THEM DO THAT.

"Phillips." He said crisply, as he parked the Mercedes in the station yard, "I want all information available on recent suicides — going back — oh, about a year."

Phillips grinned broadly. "It just so happen, sir, I ask Goodbody and Pearson to start on the file — seemed like you might be needing it."

Rodgers laughed. "Why bother to think at all beats me. With you and those two around, I'm almost redundant."

* * *

Rachel parked the Metro in the big double garage. It looked very small and lonely. She remembered in sudden anguish how her first car used to park beside the bulk of Bill's Jaguar. She raised her hand to run it impatiently through her hair then in deference to the recent styling, she dropped it again without disturbing it. She *must* get over this constant thinking about Bill. The fact that he had died a murderer and that she had betrayed their marriage with Rowan Rodgers didn't negate the years of happiness they had known. And Bill had the exculpation of his mental sickness, whereas there was no extenuation for her act of adultery. Oh God, she thought, I must get over this. I'm falling into maudlin pity for my past acts and wallowing in mental objurgation. Then she laughed at her mental choice of words.

She picked up a cigarette and lit it with fingers that were steady again. These moments of self-vilification were becoming less frequent. In time they would pass altogether — but until they did, had she any right to marry Rowan?

The steady hum of the vacuum cleaner reached her from the bedroom then stopped abruptly as the telephone began to shrill in competition. She hurried towards it then heard Ruel, her male helper and security guard, say, "No ma'am. Mrs Groome is h'out. She wi' be back fe lunch."

"It's all right Ruel." Rachel took the receiver from him, noting again how his familiar gap-toothed smile had been changed by the acquisition of some startlingly white dentures.

"Hullo, Rachel Groome speaking."

"Rachel — I'm so glad that you're there. Your man said..." came a woman's voice, deep-toned, an unfamiliar note predominant as it greeted Rachel's ear.

"Margaret?" she queried, uncertain.

"Yes."

"Is there anything wrong? I hardly recognised your voice."

There was a short pause, then, "Yes, very wrong. Can you come and see me?"

"Yes, of course. This evening."

"No...that will be too...could you possibly come *now*?"

Rachel didn't answer for a moment. Margaret Cameron, retired Professor of Chemistry, the last member of one of the oldest families in the island. A mixture of Scots, island creole, pure Fulani, English and so down to pure Jamaican. From her Scots forebears she had retained her name, from her Fulani great-great-great grandmother she had inherited the long, high-bridged, aquiline nose and proud carriage. She had a fierce pride, an independence of spirit and a brilliant mind. Since her retirement, she had worked on research in sickle cell anaemia in conjunction with the current Professor of Chemistry at the University of the West Indies. She had her own well-equipped laboratory built on to her cottage high up in the hills.

Rachel wondered what had happened to occasion such an uncharacteristic call.

"Rachel?" the deep voice sounded again. "Are you there?"

"Yes, sorry. Yes, Margaret, I can be up, oh, in half an hour; make it three-quarters. I'll grab a sandwich; I haven't had lunch yet."

"Make it half an hour and eat here while we talk." Margaret Cameron's voice was lighter now, the worry note less.

"Ruel." Rachel hurried through the cool, shuttered house to the kitchen. "I have to go out. Put lunch up for supper. And give Bamboo some chicken. Cut it in very small pieces. Right?"

"Right, Miss Rachel."

The man looked disappointed. He was proud of his cooking and bewailed the fact that nowadays food meant so little to Rachel — she either didn't seem to notice what she was eating or else she dined out with that police superintendent.

Ruel had been general handyman in the Groome household for years until Rachel went away after Bill Groome died. She had paid him a large redundancy sum, but he was unable to get work with the growing unemployment problem. When she returned he'd begged for his old job back. "Please, Miss Rachel, ma'am, me wi' work in de 'ouse in de marnings an' keep guard at night. You cyan' stay so alone, Miss Rachel. Time 'ard an' them have plenty t'ief and gunman." And so it was agreed.

Now he watched her reverse smoothly out of the garage, his dark eyes thoughtful. Then he went in search of Bamboo, the six-month old successor to Li Po. She was asleep on the divan in the study, curled in a tight ball, her dark seal-point nose tucked into darkening paws, tail curved neatly round to meet her head. The soft cream of her back had just started to darken. Ruel watched her twitch her tail as she chased a dream-mouse. He was fond of cats, a not too common trait amongst youngmen of his generation.

"Mek I wait till you wake," he murmured. "Soon come cry fe food."

* * *

Rowan Rodgers accepted a fat file from Police Constable Emmanuel Goodbody, newly transferred to Kingston from the north coast on Rodgers' recommendation.

"This looks pretty comprehensive, Goodbody."

"Yes, sir," Goodbody agreed, stiffly at attention. He had no idea what the word meant, but from the approving note in his chief's voice he guessed that it meant something commendable. He made a mental note to look it up in his well-thumbed dictionary.

"You like the work in Kingston?" Rodgers asked.

"Yes, sir." Goodbody remained rigidly at attention but his eyes flashed their enthusiasm.

"Good. Keep it up, you're doing fine. Ask Sergeant Phillips to come in, please."

The young constable saluted with military precision and left the office in a glow of well-being. Praised by the super, eh-eh! Even the stolid Phillips noted with amusement the added zeal and correctness with which Goodbody conveyed Rodgers' request.

"That young Goodbody, sir," he remarked to Rodgers a few moments later, "he keen, you see, sir, keen, keen."

"Yes, a proper eager-beaver; he shows promise. He and Pearson work well together?"

"Yes, sir. They make a fine team."

"Good. Smoke if you want to," Rodgers said as he filled his pipe. Then they settled down to study the file.

* * *

Rachel gave a quick glance at her wrist watch as she turned onto the Papine Road. Five past one. She should be able to make it to the cottage in half an hour. The Metro could hold the road on that twisting hill climb with the utmost ease.

Margaret Cameron in her retirement, lived in a cottage high up above Mavis Bank. It was a delightful place of cut-stone walls, steep shingled roof, dark mahogany floors and panelled walls. The ceilings were of wood too, high and raftered. The scent of cedar pervaded the atmosphere pleasantly. The gloom of so much dark wood was lightened by bright curtains and gay upholstery. There was even a fireplace, rare in the tropical climate of the island, but a fire was often needed when in January or February the night temperature dropped to the low fifties on the old Fahrenheit scale. However high the temperature soared on the plains, it was always a good fifteen degrees cooler in the mountains.

The cottage stood on sloping grounds that extended over about ten acres. Tall pines surrounded it and added still further to its privacy; at the same time they kept up a constant soothing sough of sound, a lullaby at night, reminiscent of the surf on the shore. Further down the hillside was a clump of eucalyptus — not seen on the plains — near a grove of bamboo. There was the occasional mahoe, the solitary ebony. It was a peaceful place, far removed from the heat and turmoil of the busy city and its environs so far below, where the buildings had mushroomed, spreading ever further, encroaching to the very foothills.

Rachel felt as one with the little car as she climbed the hill road. The scenery was magnificent, ever changing. The deep vertical clefts and the sharpness of the corresponding high ridges made formal patterns, constantly reforming as the narrow toad swung round in continuous hair-pin bends, ever steeply upward.

A mountain which one moment was across a valley, at the next would be towering over her. The hills would unexpectedly fall away to show deep gorges and more half-revealed valleys. Abruptly the whole vista opened up as the Metro reached an even higher level and Kingston harbour could be seen three thousand feet below like a model of itself, all perfectly to scale. The harbour water was quite still as if it were made of glass or painted on the canvas of the plains. Rachel was barely aware of the beauty of the close-pressing hills or the panorama spread out below. Half of her mind was concentrating on the delight of handling the little car, its instant response to the controls; the other half puzzled and speculated on the reason for the sudden summons to the cottage.

Margaret Cameron was waiting on the steps of the cottage as Rachel slid the Metro to a standstill. Her ankle was heavily bandaged and she leant on a stout stick. Her figure was still upright and trim, her grey hair carefully styled, but there were lines around her eyes and mouth that had not been there on Rachel's last visit, six weeks before.

"Good of you to come, Rachel. I'm tied down here with this wretched sprain."

She preceded Rachel up the steps to a wide flagged terrace, slowly limping, the stick doing most of the work. There was a table set for two in the small dining area at the back of the house. Despite the urgency of her summons, Margaret didn't mention the reason for it until they sat with coffee and cigarettes on the shaded terrace. The cool air was crisp and pine-scented with a pungent overtone from the nearby laboratory. She seemed reluctant to broach the subject and Rachel's curiosity grew.

It wasn't like Margaret to hedge. One of the most striking facets of her strong character was her ability to ignore trivialities and trimmings and to concentrate on facts: she was a scientist by training and by temperament. The two women were so dissimilar: Rachel — slim, svelte, exuding an aura of sheer femininity an sexual allure; Margaret — angular and wiry, an almost asexual figure and personality. Their friendship stretched back over the years: Rachel's mother and Margaret had been distant cousins — that complicated structure of cousinship that prevails throughout the island, whatever the social category. Although the difference in age and outlook was so marked, there was still a singular affinity between them, each appreciative of the other's qualities, a complementing of minds.

At last Rachel asked, as the helper finished clearing the lunch table and had disappeared into the kitchen, from whence came a clatter of crockery. "How is Eleanore? Is she here?"

Margaret Cameron's lips tightened slightly. She drew deeply on her cigarette before she answered, "Eleanore…yes, she is here — but she has a migraine. That is why I had to ask…" She stopped, either unable or unwilling to go on.

Rachel decided that unless she precipitated the revelation of the reason for her summons she would be at the cottage until nightfall.

"Margaret, what is it? You ring me in what is for you great agitation, get me up here at the double and then talk about everything under the sun except why you wanted to see me. I must know now — I have to get home."

The older woman rose slowly to her feet, scrabbling for the stick, and limped to the edge of the terrace. She gazed out at the wild lushness of the garden, her back as straight as ever, yet her whole body was heavy, lacking its previous buoyancy.

"I'm sorry, Rachel. It was good of you to come up here at such short notice. You're right — I'm prevaricating, behaving like a fool, like a child who pretends that if she ignores an unpleasant fact it will go away." She was silent for a long moment, then said in a firm impersonal tone: "There is …a package…that has to be delivered *today* to — to an address which I will give you — later. I cannot go myself because of this wretched ankle and Eleanore is prostrate in a darkened room. I…the only person that I could trust to deliver the …" she stumbled over the word, "… package, and not ask questions — is you." She turned to Rachel with an imploring gaze that seemed out of all proportion to the simple request.

Rachel was silent. A feeling of unease pervaded her mind.

"Well?" Margaret asked, her face haggard. "Will you do it?"

Rachel had left her chair and had joined the other woman at the edge of the terrace. They looked at each other for a long moment, Rachel's wide grey eyes asking the questions she had been forbidden to put into words, Margaret's dark hooded ones holding an indefinable expression.

"The package — has a certain value, if — by any chance you cannot deliver it — then please bring it back here — as soon as possible."

Margaret avoided Rachel's enquiring gaze and in a voice roughened by — shame? — she gave the address. As she listened, Rachel's feeling of unease increased to a point that was akin to fear. "Let me write it down," she said, reaching into her handbag for a pen.

"*NO!*" The word came out explosively. "No don't write it down. Just memorise it — until the delivery is made, then — *forget it.*"

Chapter 3

It was nearly three o'clock. Outside, the full force of the mid-afternoon sun beat down on the dust-encrusted city. There had been no rain to speak of for months. Every scrap of vegetation was withering and dying, the water level in the dams that served the city was getting dangerously low, water lock-offs had become the norm and there was no sign of the drought breaking.

Inside the old building that housed Superintendent Rowan Rodgers' office, the high tray ceilings and wide jalousied windows afforded a little coolth, lazily helped by a ceiling fan that leisurely disturbed the warm air.

At the big, cluttered desk, Rodgers and Phillips worked carefully and methodically through the fat file, competently compiled by Goodbody and Pearson. Each had made copious notes and gradually a recognisable, definite pattern was emerging. A large ash tray was filled with the black acrid scrapings from Rodgers' well-seasoned pipe and a pile of stubs from Phillips' now depleted packet of Rothmans. Empty coffee cups indicated their having missed lunch.

Rodgers pushed his chair back and flipped his notes with a long finger. "Well, Phillips, what do you make of it?"

Phillips ran a finger round the inside of his loosened collar. "Not a pretty picture, sir. Over the past twelve months there have been fifteen cases of suicide in the middle to upper income bracket. Thirteen of these were women."

"Discount the men for the moment," Rodgers said. "Any proven reason in any of these cases for an act of suicide?"

"No, sir. Generally just a history of depression, moodiness, increasing tension. Then suicide — mostly by sleeping pills. Eleven out of the thirteen left notes."

"Eleven out of the fourteen left notes," Rodgers murmured. "If you add Mrs. Piers Smith-Watson to your list."

"Yes, sir." Phillips made the addition to his notes.

"Do you notice anything odd about the age group of these — victims?" Rodgers asked.

"That's a funny thing sir," Phillips had lost all trace of his local accent now and spoke with serious concentration. "Each of the ladies was between forty-five and fifty-five—in fact eight of the thirteen…fourteen—were between forty-seven and forty-nine."

"And all in affluent positions with wealthy or near-wealthy husbands?"

"No, sir." Phillips consulted his notes. "The ladies who were married, yes, but three of them were unmarried."

Rodgers whistled tunelessly. "Were they indeed," he murmured thoughtfully. "That makes the picture a little less easy to read." The telephone at his elbow, rang shrilly. "Rodgers here." He listened intently as the receiver crackled, then said, "Yes, sir. Thank you for letting us know. We'll be right up." He put the receiver down and looked across at Phillips. "That was Mr. Justice Piers Smith-Watson. He has something to show us that may be of interest. Let's go and see."

Phillips took one of the staff cars. He drove competently up the steady climb along Constant Spring Road to the residential district where the Smith-Watsons' comfortable home stood. The afternoon traffic was fairly light, only a trickle compared to what it would swell to an hour or so later.

Smith-Watson greeted them briefly. His face was haggard; the bitter realisation of his loss had passed from the first stage of shock to the second stage of unwilling acceptance. He led them through to his study. The small grandfather clock with its exquisitely painted face, ticked quietly in its corner. A big flat-topped mahogany desk, with its ordered clutter of papers, dominated the room. Flanking the desk on either side were book cases filled with thick heavy volumes. Rodgers gave a quick glance at them and then around the room. Unless the room was used entirely for work, the judge didn't read anything but law books. There was no sign of a novel anywhere — and the presence of a paperback would have seemed wildly frivolous in that atmosphere of judicial stuffiness.

Smith-Watson waved them to deep-curving, leather Spanish chairs, a type not seen in a house with any pretence to modernity, but their smooth, unbroken lines had a restful quality which allowed the body to relax. The judge seated himself behind the desk and swivelled around to pick up a pile of papers from a nearby table. As he swung back to face them, Rodgers noted that he held a sheaf of cancelled cheques in one hand and a number of bank statements in the other. He paused and looked down at the papers, reluctant to reveal their silent testimony. Then he began to speak in a voice that held no emotion other than that necessary for the examination of known facts.

"As I told you this morning, my wife had an ample personal allowance which she always protested was more than adequate, despite the many devaluations. This is confirmed by the bank statements, her cheque book and cancelled cheques, the latest of which I obtained from the bank today. This...affluence...has been seen to be so all these years — until the last six months. Since then, my...wife..." the hard carapace of self control cracked a little. He took a deep breath and continued in the same impersonal way, "My wife has spent all the accumulated savings of a number of years. Today there is not one cent left in her account. She withdrew the last five thousand dollars two weeks ago."

He was silent, the silence of suffering.

Rodgers said quietly, "It was good of you to let us know, sir. May I see the bank statements and the cancelled cheques?"

He glanced at the figures. Over the last six months there had been withdrawals of five thousand dollars at approximately two-weekly intervals. He made a rapid mental calculation. It came to around sixty-five thousand dollars. Small withdrawals of a hundred dollars or at the most five hundred dollars occurred two or three times. He examined the sheaf of cancelled cheques: all the large amounts were made payable to 'cash' and endorsed by Annabel Smith-Watson. Rodgers narrowed his nostrils, his aquiline nose taking on a sharper line. He began to pass the papers across to Phillips then drew back and checked a point. Yes, the smaller cheques were made payable to various stores or to Annabel herself, by name. He let Phillips take them and then looked with added compassion at the judge.

"What do you make of it sir?"

"Much the same as you, if I am to judge by your expression. My wife has been paying out large sums over the past months. Why? Either she had taken up gambling, which I doubt very much, or — she was being blackmailed — which I find impossible to believe." He looked wearily at Rodgers. "You too, I gather, have come to a similar conclusion?"

Rodgers nodded, "I'm afraid so, sir. Phillips?"

Phillips flicked the sheaf with a dark stubby forefinger. "No, sir," he said slowly. "Not gambling — the withdrawals are all for the same amount. She would *have* to have made a winning sometimes — yet nothing was deposited. If it was gambling then the withdrawals would vary. It's all too regular — every two weeks — almost to the day."

"So," Smith-Watson said after a long pause. "I'm inclined to agree with your reasoning, Sergeant, and that leaves us with — blackmail. I can't believe it."

His control broke and he thumped a clenched fist on the desk. "Why didn't she come to me?"

The other question: *Why was she being blackmailed?* hung unspoken in the air.

Rodgers stood up and assumed an easy air he didn't feel. "There could be another explanation, sir — an aged relative, a dependent who, perhaps for some reason, you were unaware exists." Even as he spoke he realised that it was outside the realm of probability.

Smith-Watson shook his head. "She would definitely come to me under those circumstances — and anyway, I know there's nobody; there's no member of her family that I do not know." He got up heavily. "Try and keep this from the press, Superintendent."

"We'll do all that we can, sir. But you know what the media boys are like. If you find anything — anything at all which might just have a bearing — let me know. Perhaps Phillips could have a word with...Clarice, is it? Good. Phillips?"

"Right, sir."

Phillips went in search of Clarice, whom he found in the kitchen. She was still tearful and was talking to herself in a dazed way and yet vicariously enjoying the drama of the situation. She abandoned her task of preparing vegetables for the evening meal with obvious relief and was only too ready to answer Phillips' questions, wallowing in the importance of her part in finding the dead woman.

"What a t'ing, ee, sah, Mr Phillips." She wiped her hands on her apron and leant her ample form against the counter top. "When me t'ink of poor Miss Annabel. Lawd, sir, it mek water come to me yeye. Eh-eh! It sad fe true." It seemed that Clarice was preparing to work herself up to a keening point over her late employer and Phillips forestalled this with a brisk, "You work here long, Miss Clarice?"

"Plenty, plenty year, sir. Miss Annabel..." sniff "...she a one nice lady, you 'ear?"

"And the judge?"

"Yes, sir. 'Im little fussy-like — but quiet an' a nice genkleman."

"They entertain much? Have plenty people in for drink and party?"

"Not so much. Little dinner, little party fe frien' dem. Not so much."

"Must have been lonely for the lady, here by herself all the time?"

She shot him a quick look from her small dark eyes. "Mebbe, me don' know nothin' 'bout dat," she said curtly.

"Did Miss Annabel — go out on her own much? Or have bridge party like I hear the St Andrew ladies do?"

Clarice shook her head. "She don' bodder wit' all that foolishness."

"But," persisted Phillips easily, "She quite young still. She don't have no family to care. She have a hobby?"

"Hobby?" The woman looked vague.

"Yes, man, something to take up her time — painting, needlework, golf?"

"She do little painting — long time. Not so much now."

"When she stop painting?"

"Me nuh remember, 'bout five, six month."

Five to six months — just when the payments began. Was that just coincidence or was there a tie-up there? He tried a new line.

"She have a boy-friend?"

Clarice's small eyes flared in their fleshy lids. "Lawd, Mr Phillips, what a way you go on so."

"You never know. She have plenty phone call?"

Clarice went suddenly still, then she twisted her hands in her damp apron and her face became withdrawn, mulish. "Me don' know an' me have plenty, plenty work. Is me alone 'ave to..."

"Right, Miss Clarice." Phillips stemmed the threatening wailing tirade. He was confident now that the woman suspected something had been amiss, even if she had no definite knowledge. OK, he could wait. A little sweetening up later, maybe she would be more expansive. He rose to his feet, his well-built stocky body impressive. He gave her the full benefit of flashing white teeth under the trim black moustache. "You remember anything — any little thing, m'dear — you let me know, nuh?"

She nodded, responding against her will to his virile charm. She said with a certain hesitation, "One t'ing — Miss Annabel on the phone — jus' before she...die. Me fin' the receiver hang down."

"You put it back?" Phillips tried to keep a sharp note from his voice.

She looked startled. "Yes, sir. Me tek it up to call the judge. Is wrong me do?"

It was done now, no cause for recrimination — and was it important anyway?

"No, Miss Clarice, no wrong."

* * *

Rachel drove thoughtfully down the twisting, turning road with the lush, wild beauty of the nearby hills, and the steep drop of precipices at every bend. On the seat beside her was the package she had to deliver: a fat manila envelope, unadorned by any inscription or address. She was uneasy about the assignment. It had an aura of intrigue and secrecy that she failed to reconcile with what she knew of Margaret Cameron. There had been none of the usual frankness and trust in their meeting. She gave a mental shrug, it was little enough to do for an old friend; just deliver the package and then forget the whole sordid business.

She checked her train of thought.

Why had she used the word: *Sordid?* It was an alien quality in relation to Margaret Cameron, yet the thought persisted. She reached Gordon Town without realising the passage of time or mileage. The traffic was increasing in volume as she neared the bottom of the hill and by the time she turned onto Old Hope Road and was approaching its lower end, she had to give all her attention to her driving. It was still too early for the afternoon press of up-town traffic, the returning shoppers and commuters from downtown Kingston's offices and shops. She drove through Cross

Roads and then made a left turn into a side street. The road was narrower here with no sidewalks, the houses old, long since outmoded as residences. Their trimness of fifty or sixty years before had a tawdry, tarnished neglect about them that brought a feeling of distaste to her fastidious nature. She turned left again, then right, trying to recall Margaret's instructions. How could Margaret ask her to come to such a rundown slum? Barefoot children scuffled in the gutters, lounging youths eyed her with a mixture of suspicion and leering lust. She felt very vulnerable in the little car.

And then she saw the place: a high encircling unpainted zinc fence with the number 25 daubed a foot high. There was no gate at the entrance. She drove through into a driveway that bounded a large concrete area where washing lines were strung across from metal posts. A few sheets were flapping in the afternoon breeze. A painted sign with a directional arrow pointed round to the back of the building: PARKING. The front of the building was old, a house of the traditional type fashionable in the late twenties when the locality was a genteel and modish residential area. Pointed shingle roof, sash windows, a multiplicity of French doors with fretwork transoms above them, wide verandahs with painted railings and a shallow, wide flight of steps leading up from the curving driveway.

Rachel slowly followed the sign to the back, a feeling of apprehension and bewilderment mounting, twisting like a knot in her stomach.

At the back of the original building was a large paved courtyard. One side was formed by the back of the old building, the opposite by a three-storey new building of steel and concrete, boxlike, its louvred windows like dead shuttered eyes. There was a car parked by a standpipe, an old V.W. , its faded duco showing signs of frequent retouching, the patches mismatching the original colour.

A dull-eyed, slatternly woman, blouse agape to disclose drooping breasts, hair sticking out in an uncombed frizz, was lethargically washing a sheet in a galvanised tub, her body resting on her heels, legs splayed wide each side of the tub. She paused briefly as Rachel parked the Metro and stepped uncertainly out of the car, her dull eyes vacant and holding no interest.

Rachel could hear Margaret's clipped instructions: Park at the back. Take no notice of anybody. Nobody will ask questions. Go up the steps of the old building, down a short corridor until you come to the door on your right. It's marked number 8. Don't knock. Go in, hand over the package to the occupant and *leave immediately.*

Rachel took a deep breath and walked quickly up the steps. The interior was dim and cool after the glare outside and she took off her dark glasses. It was absolutely quiet except for the faint sound of a radio playing music somewhere in the building. She noted that the place was full of doors, some wide open, some half-open and through them she saw dimly-lit rooms, in each a predominate bed. She faltered in her quick purposeful walk.

Good God, she thought, I've walked into a house of assignation! For a moment she was tempted to turn back, get in the car and drive as fast and as far as she could. Then she remembered the look of haunted agony in Margaret Cameron's eyes and the insistence that the package had to be delivered today.

Her heart was thumping so loudly that she feared that any of the presumed occupants behind the closed doors must surely hear it. She went along the corridor with growing reluctance and stopped irresolute outside the door marked 8. It was open a few inches. She lifted her hand to push it wider then, through some innate caution, pushed with the package that she held. It swung open slowly, silently, and no sound came from within the room. Again she felt fear rise and threaten to engulf her but she knew that now there was no point in turning back.

She entered the room.

It was about ten feet square. A big double bed took up most of the space. Apart from that it was unfurnished except for a wash basin with a shelf and mirror above it, a straight-backed chair and a hanging rail. The louvred shutters were tilted upwards, giving the room a shadowed, frightening quality.

But Rachel noticed none of this. She stood immobile, unable to move, unable to cry out.

Sprawled on the floor at her feet was a figure — alarmingly still. In her terror she couldn't tell whether it was a man or a woman — there was only the certainty that whoever it was, was very dead.

Chapter 4

Superintendent Rodgers and Sergeant Phillips were back at the station by four p.m. There was a message waiting for Rodgers to see the Assistant Commissioner.

"Ah, Rodgers," he said crisply as Rodgers entered the big room. He sat, short and broad, behind the flat-topped desk. He was in his mid-fifties, hair grey and cut close to his head, but the close curl was still evident. He'd risen to his position the hard way from the ranks in a country police station. The police training of his early days was vastly different from that of today. He rose to and held his position by sheer hard-headed common sense and devotion to duty that few could attain or surpass. The men respected him and not a few of the younger members of the force feared him, for he had no patience with slackness or inattention to detail.

He motioned Rodgers to a chair and tilted back his own. "What's all this about Smith-Watson's wife? Open and shut suicide?"

"It looks that way, sir," Rodgers agreed. "It's the reason behind it — the motivation — that I'm worried about. We've been checking the files covering the last twelve months. There have been far too many cases of suicide by women of that age and social category."

"Any ideas?"

"Well, sir," Rodgers was cautious, unwilling to commit himself at this stage. "If we can possibly manage it — and things seem fairly stable at the moment — I'd like your permission to look into it. There's a possibility that there's a blackmail racket going on. I'd like to have a shot at uncovering it."

The A.C. pursed his lips. "Tricky. The families involved won't talk."

"I know it'll be tricky, sir. But if there is a racket — organised — it needs smashing. It's filthy."

The A.C. made up his mind with characteristic abruptness. "All right, Rodgers, it's all yours. Try and wrap it up as quickly as you can, before we have any more suicides and the newspapers catch on that there's been a spate in the last few months and starts asking questions. Once that happens it'll drive them — whoever they are — underground. Remember that outbreak of rape cases about fifteen years ago?"

Rodgers nodded. There'd been a public outcry and the man was never caught. Some high-up heads rolled, a few St Andrew matrons had a brief moment of unwelcome publicity as speculation was made as to their morals and as to whether some cases *really* were rape, then the whole affair had sunk into obscurity.

"If I could have Sergeant Phillips and Constable Goodbody on permanent assignment until we break it, sir? With Constable Pearson on call if necessary."

The A.C. hesitated. Three men tied up and a possible fourth? But Rodgers never asked for what was — in his experienced opinion — unnecessary. He'd pulled off some difficult cases, had Rodgers — and, he had to admit, with Phillips' invaluable assistance.

"Phillips, yes. But why Goodbody?" As he asked the question the A.C. remembered that it was at Rodgers' request and recommendation that P.C. Goodbody had been transferred from St Ann's Bay.

"Young Goodbody's keen," Rodgers explained easily. "He's bright, always on the ball, wants to learn and works well with Phillips. He's got great potential."

"Right — he's all yours."

The A.C. tilted down his chair in dismissal and turned to his piled 'IN' tray.

"Now you're both in the picture," Rodgers said thirty minutes later to the stolidly attentive Phillips and to the suppressed excited attention of Police Constable Emmanuel Goodbody. "Good, find Pearson and brief him. I think that we'll need him on the team."

"Yes, sir."

"I'm taking this file home to study it overnight. Tomorrow I want you both to begin to question the families of these women." He flicked the 'suicide' file. "You've got a list?"

"Yes, sir. Goodbody make a copy," Phillips said.

"Good. It won't be easy. The ones who suspect nothing untoward bar illness will feel that you're prying into their most private lives, and the ones who do suspect that there is something hidden will close up like clams." The two men nodded. "I leave it to your knowledge of human nature, Phillips, as to how to tackle each case, but remember that you will be probing into people's most intimate lives. They could take exception and tell you to get the hell out."

"Yes, sir."

"Right," Rodgers reached for the telephone. "Eight o'clock tomorrow morning."

Left alone, Rodgers dialled Rachel's number. It rang unanswered, then just as he was about to replace the receiver, the ringing stopped and he heard a click as the receiver was lifted at the other end. Instead of the slightly breathless voice that he wanted to hear, he heard Ruel using his precise 'telephone' voice, "Mrs Groome resi*dence*," with an upward stress on the final syllable.

"Ruel? You took your time in answering. Mrs Groome there?"

"No, sir." Ruel answered the question before attempting to explain his tardiness. "She been h'out since marning an' it tek long time fe me water de flowers dem."

"Been out since this morning? Do you know where she went?" Rachel had told him that she had an appointment at the hair dresser's and after that she would be free for the rest of the day.

"No, sir, Miss Rachel get a call an' go off wit'out lunch. She say a mus' feed de cyat — but 'im won' tek nutten — 'im too fenky-fenky."

Rodgers laughed. "She'll come round. Ask Mrs Groome to give me a call as soon as she gets home. I'll be at home in about half an hour. It's Superintendent Rodgers," he added unnecessarily.

"Yes, sir. Me know, sir," Ruel said, a smirk in his voice.

Rodgers frowned as he put down the receiver. It wasn't like Rachel to go off without letting him know — he smiled to himself; here he was behaving like a possessive husband already. He picked up the bulky file and left the office. He'd go home and have a shower and wait for Rachel to ring him. He had planned to take her out to dinner later. There was a new restaurant just above Constant

Spring — The Black Crab — that was getting quite a name for itself. He'd take a chance and book a table.

* * *

Rachel stood unmoving for what seemed like an eternity, clutching the manila envelope tightly. As the situation penetrated her shock-filled mind her first instinct was to run, but as she took a step towards the door she heard a car drive round to the back. A door slammed, then came the staccato sound of quick footsteps up the concrete steps. The low murmur of voices followed, then the soft slap of bare feet ahead of a fairly light, but firm, tread that passed her door so closely that she was afraid that her shallow breathing and thudding heart would be heard. A man, she thought irrelevantly, lightly built. There was the sound of a door opening then closing quietly and the slap of bare feet passed again, this time in the opposite direction. Rachel leaned in weak relief against the half-closed door and it shut with a gentle click, nearly throwing her off balance.

She was beginning to gather her thoughts again after the first stunning shock of her discovery. She was obviously safe from interruption for the moment. Taking a tentative step towards the prone figure, she knelt down and with a shaking hand took hold of the hunched shoulder nearest to her and turned the body over.

She gazed down in renewed horror at the contorted face of the girl from the beauty parlour, The Looking Glass, the thin boyish girl, the one who had looked at her with such speculation. Her face was contorted in a grimace of pain, a trickle of dark blood ran out of the corner of her mouth and down her neck, soaking into the navy blue jacket of the pants suit that she wore. Rachel felt for a pulse at the girl's wrist; no sign at all. The girl's body was still warm, but in the climbing temperature of the afternoon that could mean sweet nothing: she may have been dead for minutes or for over an hour. There was no sign of how she had come by her death, no obvious wound, just he blood from her mouth.

Rachel stood up slowly, her mind beginning to register the danger she would be in if discovered. She heard the sound of another approaching car. It swung round to park with a squeal of tyres. A car door was opened and closed with a controlled click that made Rachel certain that the driver didn't want to further advertise his arrival — *her* arrival, she amended, as quick light footsteps passed her door hurriedly, then paused. A door opened and shut quickly.

Of course, Rachel thought, the arrival of the other party to an afternoon of illicit dalliance. She bent with sudden determination and opened the dead girl's handbag. Inside was the usual clutter: lipsticks, powder compact, tissues, the box that she had seen that morning when the girl took a capsule and offered one to Michel. She opened it gingerly. It contained half a dozen or more capsules; yes, they appeared to be tranquillisers. She put the box back and saw a small notebook. On an impulse she picked it up and opened it. As she glanced through the pages she realised that it contained a list of names in alphabetical order. Her eyes widened as the name of Eleanore Tarrant followed by — in brackets — Margaret Cameron, seemed to spring from its page.

She took a deep breath. God God, *what* have I got myself into?

She thrust the notebook into her handbag, put on her dark glasses, made sure that she had her car keys ready, then cautiously opened the door.

There was no one in sight — no sound.

She slipped through the half-open door, closed it gently with the tips of her fingers and went hastily down the corridor and out into the bright sunlight.

Her heart was still thudding as she walked down the steps and across to her car. She felt that a million eyes were noting her every movement. She was only half aware of the other cars: one was a big Japanese car, pale blue. Beyond that she could tell nothing. The other was a white Isuzu. And of course, the third car, the little beat-up VW. That must belong to the dead girl. Rachel closed her eyes for a moment in sudden nausea, then pulled herself together with an effort.

The slatternly woman was mercifully absent as Rachel got into the Metro. My God, she thought, with a car like this I'm screaming my presence if anyone wants to remember me. She reversed clumsily in her agitation and drove quickly — too quickly, she decided later — along the driveway past the paved courtyard where two women were hanging out sheets. Rachel felt rather than saw them stop and watch her go.

She felt dirty, degraded. How unspeakably sordid, she thought, then laughed bitterly at herself. Was it really any worse making illicit love in such a place than in the privacy of her own home or the anonymity of a resort hotel? Yes it was worse, much worse, she decided.

She drove more sedately now, out through the wide bumpy entrance, intent only on getting away and then returning the manila envelope to Margaret Cameron.

But first, she decided, she must go home and have a quick drink to steady her nerves. She could never face that winding hill road in her present condition. In her preoccupation, she didn't notice a grey Audi pull out from a side turning and fall in behind her. It kept about five car lengths behind her all the way until she turned into her own quiet driveway. It drove slowly past her gates then accelerated and disappeared.

It was not until about five-thirty that Rachel finally stopped shaking. Ruel had given her Rodgers' message and now she was in an agony of indecision. If she went up to Margaret now, Rowan would ask questions. This she *had* to conceal from him. If she told him, she would have to involve Margaret. If she kept silent, what would she do when the girl's body was discovered?

Would they remember her at *that* place?

What about the illicit pair of lovers? She consoled herself that even if one or the other had noticed her Metro, they had to keep quiet to protect themselves.

Surely the helpers were too moronic to have recognised a specific make of car, even one as outstanding as the metallic bronze Metro.

She lit a cigarette with fingers that wouldn't stop trembling. If she didn't go up to the cottage tonight, then she would go first thing tomorrow. Margaret Cameron would believe until then that the package had been safely delivered. What would her reactions be when she learnt of the girl's death?

Rachel stopped trembling as a new idea struck her forcibly — was the dead girl the person Rachel was supposed to meet or was she the victim of some lovers' quarrel? Had the real person to whom she was to hand over the package, also stumble over the body and left in fright? If that were so, then the intended recipient of the package would be getting in touch with Margaret — but no, that wouldn't do. Margaret had specifically said the room marked 8 — and the exact time to arrive. The body was still too warm and flaccid to have been dead any great length of time. If she had been there a long time and the room was booked for two forty-five, then surely one of the domestic staff would have made the discovery?

Rachel sighed deeply. She could find no answers to the questions that crowded her mind.

Then why a girl? Surely in a place like that it would cause gossip among the domestic staff to have a girl book the room and arrive first? Then Rachel recalled how the girl had been dressed: dark blue pants suit, short dark hair, and with her thin boyish figure. She could easily have been mistaken for a slim, rather effeminate young man.

The telephone rang, breaking her runaway, chaotic thoughts. She let it ring, unable to will herself to move. Ruel passed through the living room and answered the call. He returned shortly and said in a somewhat reproachful voice, "Is Mr Rodgers, Miss Rachel. He worried 'bout you. I tell 'im," he added, elaborately casual, "that is just this minute you reach."

"Thank you, Ruel."

She forced herself to get up, wondering what she was going to tell Rowan. How could she explain — convincingly — her long absence? She went to the telephone in a daze of bewilderment and with a steadily rising fear of the entanglement in which she found herself.

Chapter 5

It was nearing midnight when Rowan and Rachel left The Black Crab. The evening had not been an unqualified success. Rachel, with all her skill at masking her feelings had not managed to do so completely. More than once Rowan had given her a puzzled look and once he had asked gently, "Is there anything wrong, sweetheart?"

She had taken refuge in the age-old excuse of 'a headache'. She was still too bemused by the events of the afternoon to see that this was the weakest excuse that she could offer, for Rowan knew only too well that she very rarely suffered from such an affliction but he refrained from comment and outwardly accepted her explanation.

The Black Crab had lived up to its growing reputation. Deep piled seaweed-green carpets covered the floor, fishnet hangings masked the entrances and looped across the low ceiling. The lights were dim and diffused with an underwater phosphorescent glow. The tables were set discreetly far apart, each slightly recessed in an alcove. The food — mainly choice seafood — was superb. The bar was in a cave-like grotto at the far end, and in the centre was a small circular area for dancing.

Rachel had been vague as to her whereabouts since mid-morning and merely said that Margaret Cameron had a sprained ankle and she had spent some time with her.

"I have to run up in the morning to see how she is," she added, avoiding his eyes. It's a perfectly reasonable explanation, she told herself miserably, *almost* the whole truth, yet because of the circumstances and my feeling of guilt at my involvement — added to the deception I must practise because of my loyalty to Margaret — I'm behaving like a criminal.

She was grateful for the dim lighting that hid her expression and for the excellent combo that played traditional West Indian music and the reggae beat just loud enough to obviate the need for sustained conversation.

With the coffee and brandy, Rowan too fell silent. She was suddenly conscience-stricken at her preoccupation and evasions and asked, "You seem worried, Rowan. Difficult case?"

"Yes," he answered slowly. "You may be able to help. Rachel, what drives a woman — youngish — middle-aged, with all the worldly comforts — to suicide?"

She was silent for a moment, startled at his question then said, "Well, ill health, maybe, leading to an unbalanced mind, or..." she paused, unwilling to put her thought into words, "blackmail, perhaps."

"Right." He accepted that matter-of-factly. "And for what could a woman in that position be blackmailed?"

This was the question that Rachel had been asking herself ever since she had yielded to impulse and opened the manila envelope given her by Professor Margaret Cameron. It contained fifty thousand dollars in five-hundred dollar bills.

She was silent so long, gazing down into her empty coffee cup that at last Rowan asked, "Well?"

She answered by asking a question. "Is this a hypothetical query or does it have a bearing on your present case?"

"A definite bearing."

"Well, a woman would surely only be blackmailed — as indeed anyone — for something that she didn't want revealed. In the case of a married woman — adultery, I suppose."

"But, do you honestly think that in these days when every third adult you meet has been involved in some way in a divorce case, that adultery would be a cause for blackmail? Surely, adultery as such, is old hat. Go to any cocktail party or whatever and look around you. Hardly anyone is innocent either in thought or in deed. If they are caught, it causes a few days' scandal and comment, then the flurry settles down and society as a whole accepts the guilty and the innocent alike. If all the adulterous types were victims of blackmail it would defeat its own ends, for it would embrace such a large portion of the adult population that it wouldn't pay. Most people would shrug off the attempt and tell the blackmailers to get the hell out and do their worst."

Rachel looked at him, her wide grey eyes alert, her immediate problems submerged for the moment. "What a terrible indictment of the society in which we live. You're right, of course, so that means we must look for the type of person who would succumb to the threat of blackmail. Surely there are still some women — and some men — whose good reputation affects their very livelihood?"

"Such as?"

"Well, doctors and clergymen, judges and people like that. And then there's the middle-aged or young-elderly married women of comfortable means. If to lose her husband through disclosure of some indiscretion means to lose her creature comforts, if she has no means of supporting herself — no training, no aptitude – what then? She is going to pay and pay and pay. At the same time hoping that something will occur that will help her out of her morass. That sort of woman only sees as far as today. She is morally short-sighted and incapable of seeing that today's actions shape tomorrow's actions."

He looked at her with respect. "You seem to have my mythical blackmailer well summed up."

"Mythical? But you said…"

"I know, I was using you as a sounding board. There's much to be uncovered before we can be certain."

He went on to recount briefly the untoward spate of suicides over the past twelve months culminating in that of Annabel Smith-Watson.

"Annabel?" Rachel was shocked. "Oh, no! I saw her only a few days ago — she was on her way to the beauty parlour."

She heard her words repeated again and again in her mind. The beauty parlour. *The beauty parlour!*

The dead girl was from the beauty parlour. Surely, oh, surely, there was no connection? And yet…her eyes widened in renewed fear at the memory of the afternoon. She forced herself to say, "But what about the unmarried women on your list?"

And Margaret Cameron, she added silently. "You've got to search for another reason for blackmail in those cases."

"Yes," he agreed thoughtfully. "And it's interesting to note that the women on the list who were not married held positions of importance. Their reputations had to remain unblemished or their prestige and position — on which their livelihood depended — would have crashed."

They gazed at each other across the small table. "I don't like it," he announced. "The more I think about it the more sordid possibilities present themselves."

If only you knew how sordid, she thought. If only I could tell him — but I must speak to Margaret first.

Rowan got up abruptly. "Come, sweetheart, you're dead tired, I'm going to take you home."

As they passed through the main entrance, they almost bumped into a man who was entering. He bowed and apologised in a slightly Semitic way. "My dear Mr Rodgers, a thousand apologies. You have discovered my latest venture? I hope that you were well looked after?"

"Indeed yes, most enjoyable. Rachel, I want you to meet Khylos Mantanios. Mrs Groome."

Rachel smiled, trying to hide her overpowering weariness. "How do you do, Mr Mantanios. Do you own this delightful place as well?"

"As well?"

For a moment the urbanity dropped, then it was switched on again as Rachel continued, " I heard that you had acquired a controlling interest in the Peak Hotel?"

"Ah, yes. I have a finger in many pies."

They bowed goodnight. As he held the car door open for Rachel, Rowan murmured, "A finger, the man said. If you ask me, he's got the arms of an octopus and he's in many pies right up to the elbows."

As he walked round to get into the Mercedes, Rachel thought about the man they had just left. He had a face like an ageing fawn with smooth, taut, well-groomed skin the colour of light cedar wood. The nose jutted, parrot-like — she smiled at the unlikely combination of mammal and fowl — the head was balding, forehead high and unwrinkled. His plumpish body was encased — there was no other description possible — in a three-piece suit of dark grey silk, gleaming richly in the half-light of the foyer. Its impeccable tailoring proclaimed the highest craftsmanship. An aroma of expensive cologne enveloped him. He seemed urbanity itself — wealthy urbanity — until you studied his eyes: they were quite black, not the melting blackness of Rowan's but a cold, hard black. Rachel shivered slightly at the memory of their implacability.

"Cold?" Rowan queried as he slid behind the steering wheel.

"Not really, but I don't go for your Mantanios. Is he really a millionaire?"

"Could be many times over. Being a millionaire these days is no big thing since a Jamaican dollar is worth peanuts. Mantanios is the real thing. He owns property and real estate: hotels, apartments, night clubs — who knows what else."

The warm night air flowed past the swiftly moving car, warmer in comparison to the air-conditioned place that they had just left. The ribbon of road curved ahead, the headlights slashing the darkness, highlighting the wide green verges and the hedges that bounded private houses, heavy bunches of brilliant bougainvillaea or the more delicate hibiscus.

Rachel sat unmoving during the homeward drive, not even aware when the car stopped at her own verandah steps. Rowan helped her out and held her close in the warm darkness. "I know it's late and you're tired — but are you going to invite me in for a final drink?"

She nearly said 'no' unthinkingly but there was a note in his voice that checked her. After all, she hadn't been a very good companion all the evening. She relaxed in his arms, feeling the swell of the firm muscles. "Of course, she murmured. "But only for one drink."

He locked his car and held out his hand for her door key. Only after mounting the verandah steps did they see that the grille door was open. Beyond, the French door leading into the house was also open, and lying between them and the open door was the prone body of Ruel. Rachel made to dart forward but Rowan held her back. "Keep behind me. First we must see if anyone is still inside." He went silently back to the car and returned with a heavy service revolver.

They quietly entered the house. It was quite empty apart from Bamboo who was shivering in a frightened cream bundle in the kitchen. Nothing seemed to be disturbed except Rachel's bedroom which was a shambles: the contents of every drawer had been tossed out onto the floor, handbags had been turned inside out and her writing desk was a litter of jumbled papers.

Satisfied that the intruder had gone, they returned to Ruel. Rowan lifted him easily and carried him to his room. As he was lowered to his bed, he began to recover consciousness. He stirred, groaned then muttered something unintelligible. Rachel examined his head. Blood oozed stickily through the thick, tight-curled, black hair.

"Poor man. I'll get some hot water."

By the time she returned with a bowl of hot water, gauze and bandages, Ruel was sitting up and was explaining somewhat muzzily what had happened.

"Is like dis, Mr Rodgers. The phone ring an' a gentleman ask fe Mis Rachel. I tell him she gone fe dinner. Then 'im say she 'ave a package fe 'im an' if she lef' it fe call for? Me say me know nothin' 'bout h'it, an' then 'im say 'im will call roun'." He paused, remembering then went on. " 'Im drive up in one nice car, sir, me sure 'im a Miss Rachel frien'." He glanced in quick apology at Rachel, ashamed now of his gullibility.

"It's all right, Ruel" she smiled at him "It's not your fault. Then what happened?"

"Me h'open the door an' de grille dem an' the genkleman point down so an' h'ask if de key on de floor belong to the 'ouse. Me ben' fe look an'..." He felt the bump on his head gingerly.

"All right, Ruel. Not to worry tonight," Rowan said. "Miss Rachel will give you an aspirin. Try and sleep — I'll see you in the morning."

By this time Rachel had swabbed the wound with antiseptic and hot water and decided that it was not as serious as she had first thought. She left a pad of gauze on it in case it bled again. "All right, Ruel. Just keep still so the dressing won't fall off. The plaster won't stay stuck to your hair."

"Yes ma'am. Thank you ma'am."

A few minutes later in the living room Rowan asked, "Do you know if there's anything missing?"

"Rachel went over to the drinks trolley. "It's hard to say — all that mess . I just can't be sure until the morning."

"Here, let me do that." Rowan took the glass from her hand and asked, " What would you like?"

"I don't mind — whatever you're having." She was limp with tiredness as she bent and picked up the still-frightened kitten and cradled the quivering little body against her shoulder until the trembling stopped and a deep, contented purr took its place.

"We don't have to have policemen up and all over the place and finger prints, do we?" she asked.

"Not tonight — I'll get someone up in the morning. Don't

touch anything yet. Drink this. Things will seem better through an alcoholic glow — however small."

He led her to a wide, swinging settee on the grilled verandah. She dropped the now relaxed kitten in one corner and curled herself up in the other. Rowan sat down bedside her. "What did Ruel mean — a package? Does that mean anything to you or was it just a ruse to look for money and jewellery?"

Rachel made an involuntary movement towards her large shoulder strap handbag which was on the coffee table in front of them, then drew back, hoping that it had been so slight as to pass unnoticed. She answered the last part of the question and ignored the first. "It must have been a ruse, what else?"

"What else indeed?" he asked gravely, black eyes probing.

She felt that the package in her handbag together with the notebook were plainly visible to him through the leather and her hand trembled as she lifted her glass. She was mesmerised into immobility as he picked up the bag and weighed it carelessly. "What on earth do women keep in these things?" he asked lazily.

She forced herself to speak lightly, "Oh, most women have a number of possessions that they never actually use yet feel that they must carry at all times — just in case." She put down her drink carefully, trying to appear natural. She was quite convinced that the purpose of the attack on Ruel and the ransacking of her room wasn't a chance burglary but an attempt to get hold of the manila envelope or the notebook — or both. But how did anyone know that she had them? The realisation that she must have been kept under surveillance was unnerving in the extreme. Perhaps even now she was being watched — she impulsively clung to Rowan. "Don't leave me tonight — please, darling. I'm afraid of being here alone."

He bent his head and kissed her and despite her utter fatigue she felt herself spring alive with desire.

"I had no intention of leaving you alone," he murmured against her mouth. "But I didn't bank on being begged so brazenly."

Chapter 6
day 2, Tuesday

Professor Margaret Cameron spent a restless night. As the first signs of dawn touched the sky, she got up and went to the kitchen to brew coffee. She carried a steaming cup carefully onto the terrace and looked down at her lush garden. She never tired of its wild beauty. The mountain morning air had a crisp, invigorating quality that was unknown on the plains even when the temperature fell. She thought with sudden irrational annoyance that with all the peace and serenity of the remote cottage there were certain things that she still missed. For instance she missed the daily paper delivery with the early edition arriving by spitting motor cycle or beat-up car just after dawn: the delivery made with expertise by the vendor who didn't pause as he passed the gate. He would simply toss a folded copy to the foot of the verandah steps without disturbing the pile that rose so high in front of him that one could not believe that he could see where was going.

Oh well, she thought, there are other methods of obtaining the news. She drained her coffee cup, lit a cigarette and went into the house and turned on the radio. She glanced at her watch — almost six o'clock. She waited by the radio; the sound was turned down low so as not to wake Eleanore who was sleeping off the aftermath of her migraine.

The announcer, impossibly hearty at that early hour, first extolled the virtues of a well-known rum then a stomach antacid — she wondered if the juxtaposition was by chance or design. Then the heartiness gave way to the over-modulation suitable to the dissemination of the daily dose of battle, murder, treason natural disasters, police shootouts and so on, which seemed to be all that was considered newsworthy. Oh God, Margaret thought, unusually intolerant, why do we have to suffer from these drama school types — no happy medium between broad country patois, ersatz American or the over-refinement of suburbia?

She knew that she was being unfair and for the most part inaccurate, but her sleeplessness and anxiety were making her incapable of a reasoned approach to any problem — she was irritated by little things that she normally ignored. Then all such thoughts were blotted out as she heard the newscaster say: *"The Cross Roads police are investigating the death of a young woman found yesterday evening in an apartment building, usually reserved for bachelors. The exact cause of death has not yet been ascertained."*

The ambiguity of the phrasing 'usually reserved for bachelors' which would have amused her at any other time, passed unnoticed. She switched off the set and stood gazing at it, her heart thumping. It couldn't be — there must be dozens of apartment buildings of that nature. It wasn't possible that ...

She turned as Eleanore's door opened. The sound of a radio could be heard in the background. The two women stood facing each other, so opposite in every respect: the one so strong in mind, body and character, the other, soft in body and weak in character with a fluffy mind that was incapable of anything that required reasoned thought.

Eleanore, with her strangely shaped eyes. A line seemed to be drawn down at the outer corners giving her an expression of infinite pathos. Her face was small, pointed and childlike. She was given to making sharp little movements like a bird for no apparent reason. She was rarely in complete repose and the incessant movement became irritating — even a mild exposure to it. Her hair was still dark, the grey carefully rinsed away, the inherent crimp straightened and the style was more suited to the very young.

Now she stood for once immobile, the blood drained from her cheeks, her face waxen and blotchy.

"You heard?" Margaret Cameron broke the silence, her voice unintentionally harsh.

Eleanore nodded. "But it doesn't have to be..." The rest she left unsaid and the unspoken words hung between them.

"It doesn't have to be," Margaret said at last. "Come, don't look so stricken. I'll pour you some coffee."

* * *

Rachel was glad that Rowan had left her before the morning paper arrived. She was sitting on the front verandah sipping the first cup of coffee for the day, made as usual, surprisingly, by Ruel. Despite her protests that he should rest he had presented himself for duty with a cheerful, "Cho, Miss Rachel — is jus' one likkle coco me get pon me 'ead back."

Now the paper boy, his delivery bicycle angled by the pile of papers balanced precariously on the handle bars, tossed a paper at Rachel's feet as he rode by without a pause. She picked it up and spread it wide, unprepared for the shock of the headlines: *Girl Found Dead in Apartment. Lovers' Quarrel? Police Mystified.*

Rachel read on, her previous fears magnified. The coverage gave a veiled reference to the type of building that the apartment was in, without stating it to the point of libel. She scanned each line with bated breath and a sick feeling of helplessness, but to her relief, there was not the slightest mention of either herself or her car. *"The Police Continue with their Enquiries..."* gave her little comfort.

She carefully folded the paper, not knowing what she was doing, her fingers working independently of her whirling mind. There was a lot to be done in the house but she was in the grip of inertia, a lassitude that kept every limb heavy and inactive. She hadn't slept well, despite the comfort of Rowan's arms and the passion of their love-making. She had slept for an hour in dreamless bliss. Then the dreams began: over and over she walked into the darkened room to find the dead girl — she woke in terror then dozed, only to have the same dream with variations, each time more horrifying. Each time the squalor and sordidness of the apartment building was more pronounced.

She had woken eventually with a muffled scream to find Rowan holding her close. "Hey, hey," he admonished tenderly. "Nightmares. Hush, my love. This comes of mysterious doings in the day followed by Ruel being knocked out by the unknown."

After that she'd slept fitfully until daybreak. Now the memory of his words came back to her forcibly: "Mysterious doings..." God, he'd been too close to the truth for her liking. Was it just a chance remark or did he really suspect that she had been engaged in something that she didn't want him to know about? But — how could he? She'd got to the stage where she saw hidden motives and meanings in the most ordinary remark and action.

She pulled herself together sharply. She had promised Rowan that she would find out if anything was missing from her bedroom. She must do that now or he would think it odd that she showed no interest in the matter. Then she would go up and see Margaret Cameron. She remembered that Rowan was going to send up somebody to dust for prints. Well, she didn't have to be present for that. Ruel could take care of the matter — he'd have to give a statement anyway. She bent and picked up Bamboo who was making playful darts at her ankles.

"Sorry, sweet, mother's not in the mood — later." She nuzzled the soft cream fur in apology. She had no idea just how much 'later' it would be.

* * *

Rodgers swung the Mercedes into his parking lot at the station and strode into the building. Already, even at the early hour of seven-thirty, the coolness of the interior was in marked contrast to the heat outside. He had left Rachel just before six, driven to his own home, showered and dressed, then breakfasted under the reproachful eye of Maisie.

"Mr Phillips phone, sir. Las' night two time, and' me can't give nuh place fe reach you."

"Sorry about that, Maisie, I should have let you know where I was to be found. Not to worry."

Maisie nearly kissed her teeth. It's that Mrs Groome, she thought. Misser Rodgers no go on so 'til she come back. Iffen she move in wit' Misser Rodgers, same time me gone. Maisie knew that this was mental bravado; she knew that nothing or no one would ever make her leave Rodgers.

Rodgers was in a cloud of well-being, nothing could dampen his spirits. Even Rachel's rather odd behaviour the night before he put down to feminine vagaries. There was certainly nothing that he could complain of later in her response to his love-making; she had been, as always, completely uninhibited and satisfying. He was brought out of this pleasant introspection by the constable on duty in the main office coming sharply to attention then presenting a file. There was a memo attached which read: *Rodgers — would you postpone your suicide investigations and cover this? Phillips will fill you in. A.W. Assist. Com.*

Rodgers sighed. Old Willerton would come up with something like this: agreeing to one case one minute, then shoving in another. Surely — oh, well. He looked down at the waiting constable.

"Ask Sergeant Phillips to see me as soon as he comes on duty."

"Yes, sir."

Rodgers remembered after he was settled at his desk that Phillips and the two young constables were to report to him at eight a.m. anyway. He had barely begun to study the file when there was a knock and Phillips, followed by Pearson and Goodbody, entered.

"Good morning," Rodgers greeted them crisply. "Now, what's all this?" He flicked the file. "This why you wanted me last night?"

"Yes, sir."

"Well, what's the position?"

"Look like a jealous lover case, sir, a — what the French call, er..."

"A crime of passion?"

"Yes, sir. The girl — she work in a beauty parlour — The Looking Glass."

"Name?"

"She call herself Therese in the parlour but her real name was Icilda Clements. About twenty-five, thin, look more like a boy. She was found yesterday evening by a domestic at the..." Phillips consulted his notes, "...Mountain Glen Apartments. Strictly for men only," he added.

Rodgers jerked his head up. "Oh, one of those?"

Phillips nodded. "Seems so, sir. Well known in the district — which is no more like a mountain glen than I am. It below Cross Roads. From what I hear it have a brisk turnover, plenty fancy car there most of the time."

Phillips stopped and glanced at the two young constables. Pearson's expression showed that he was well aware of the nature of the place in question but Goodbody's fresh, young, country face bore only an expression of incomprehension. Give the boy time, Phillips thought, he'll learn all about the seamy side only too soon.

"The girl was alone?"

"Yes. She arrive jus' before three p.m. in a car, pay for the room and wait. So the helper said."

"*She* paid for the room?"

"A man phone and make arrangements first."

"So — and what about the man? Did they get a good look at him when he arrived?"

"No, sir." Phillips, true to his habit of using a good punch line, paused then said slowly, "Is not a man she meet there — is a woman."

Rodgers sat up straight. "A *woman*? Are you sure?"

Phillips smiled grimly, pleased at the effect of his words. "Yes, sir. The helper — she don't want to talk, you understand, sir. They're all employed on the condition that they keep their mouths shut — they see nothing, hear nothing — like the three monkey dem. They keep they mout' shut whoever go there. What a way it go, eeh, sir?"

Oh, Lord, Rodgers thought. Phillips is lapsing more and more into the vernacular and becoming more erudite in his similes at the same time — for similes read clichés, he corrected. Sergeant Phillips was as well known for his command of patois when needed as he was for his almost pedantic standard English when the occasion demanded it.

"So?" Rodgers prompted.

"Yes, sir. Well I talk nice-like to her, sweeten her up, you know. And she say that the lady come in a pretty little car. Then she go off fas'-fas' — the wheel scream on the driveway. Is not till late when them need the room that them find the girl dead."

"What was the cause of death?"

"No outward sign, sir. Plenty blood from her mouth. Waiting for the PM report now."

"How long was it between the arrival of the lady in the 'pretty car' and when she left in such a hurry?"

"She say it jus' a little time — but you know, Mr Rodgers, sir, little time can be seconds or minutes. Couldn't pin her down."

Rodgers got up and walked to the window. He took his pipe out of the breast pocket of his dark grey jacket. "This car — did the woman say what colour or make it was?"

"Not really, sir. She jus' say it sort of brown and shiny. She say is a pretty-pretty little car."

"A pretty little car — sort of brown." Rodgers rocked gently back and forty on his heels, his unlit pipe clenched between his teeth. " And the woman who drove it — what did she look like?"

"She can't say, sir. She say she have on dark glasses and her head tie up. She can't — won't — say any more."

"She'll have to be made to talk — if this is a case of murder. Your jealous lover idea — but then again you may be right. What about any other, ah, visitors?"

"She swear that no one else there at the time — but I sure she lie."

"Obviously. You said that they found the girl when they needed the room — so the others must have been occupied."

There was a knock on the door and a uniformed constable entered. He handed Rodgers an envelope. "Ah, the PM report." He scanned the sheet of paper then said, "Well, you can forget the mysterious lady in the pretty shiny car. The PM report is conclusive. The woman died of natural causes — a perforated stomach causing a massive internal haemorrhage. Case closed. What about the relatives, have they come forward?"

"Yes, sir, a brother. He identified the body."

"Right. Give him her personal effects and they can have the body as soon as they release it from the mortuary."

After Phillips and the two constables had left, Rodgers sat still, champing on his unlit pipe. He felt a vague sense of unease, coupled with an unexplained sense of relief at the outcome and quick conclusion of the case. He shrugged it off as imaginative nonsense as he tossed the file into his out-tray. Then he remembered that he'd promised to send somebody up to Rachel's house to dust for prints and to take a statement from Ruel. He picked up one of the many phones on his desk and gave the necessary instructions.

Phillips gave the gist of the post mortem report to the dead girl's brother who was as plump and effeminate as his sister had been thin and boyish. "Sorry, Mr Clements, but we had to treat your sister's death as a homicide until proven otherwise. We had to begin making enquiries."

"Yes, of course, I quite understand. You say that this was all that was on her?" He indicated the open handbag.

"Definitely, sir. Is everything in order?"

The man looked at Phillips. For a moment there was a spark of anger in the small, deep-set dark brown eyes, then it was gone as he said, "Why, yes, er, Sergeant. Everything is in order. I will make arrangements for the funeral. Good morning."

Funny sort of brother, Phillips thought as he watched the man go down the steps into the blaze of the morning sun and into a grey Audi. Seemed more anxious about the contents of her handbag than the girl herself. He dismissed the matter with a shrug and turned to Goodbody. "Come on, son, let's get going on those interviews. Where's Pearson?"

"Sergeant Green wanted him for a special assignment, sir. He say Mr Willerton say Pearson can only be with you when him not needed elsewhere."

"He did, did he? Remind me to have a word with Sergeant Green when we get back."

"Yes, sir. Here's the list of the lady them."

Phillips took the list that Goodbody held out to him: the list of the recent suicide victims. He gave it a flick with a dark stubby forefinger. "Look at these addresses, every one high up in St Andrew, Beverly Hills — one nice house up there, bwoy. Barbican Heights, Russell Heights, Millsborough, Stony Hill, Red Hills, Jacks Hill — Lord, it make you think."

The names meant very little to Constable Goodbody, up in Kingston from the country parts barely a month. He sat beside Sergeant Phillips in the passenger seat of the staff car, filled with anticipation at seeing at close hand those high sounding places.

Their first stop was at an ultra-fashionable house clinging to the hillside in Beverly Hills. The architect had let imagination run riot, presumably encouraged by the whims, and bank balance, of his client. The garden was landscaped in terraces, an ordered tangle of indigenous flowering shrubs, the flaunting purple of bougainvillaea beside the clear sharp alamander. Delicate pink oleander contrasted against deep red hibiscus. Obviously, the water restrictions in force were being ignored. P.C. Goodbody's eyes were wide in admiration. The view was magnificent, the sharp climb of just a few minutes from the main road revealing Kingston and the harbour at his feet. It was not too high to blur the identity of the larger buildings although the houses on the plains below looked like models displayed in a toy shop — the brown patina of shingled roofs, the pinks and blues and greens of extruded aluminium roofs and the white of concrete, the soft light colours of the walls of houses and the occasional deep blue of a swimming pool, vibrant against lawns that were becoming brown and brittle because of the protracted drought. Dotted throughout were the flaming red or gold of poinciana trees and the brilliant yellow of cassia fistulas.

"It pretty, eeh, Mr Phillips?" Goodbody observed as they waited on the porch for an answer to their ring.

The glass door was opened by a trim little helper. Her black hair was fashionably braided, the end of each braid covered with a white bead. Her full breasted, small-waisted figure was precariously encased in a blue dress with a white collar and cuffs sparkling against her near black skin. She looked at the two men, a provocative smile touching her mouth, her black eyes saucy and full of questions.

"Good morning, m'dear," Phillips began in a benign avuncular tone. "Sergeant Phillips from the C.I.B. and Constable Goodbody." Phillips showed her his I.D. and Goodbody quickly did the same.

The girl's eyes flared in alarm. "Police? Wha'ppen?"

"Nothing to be alarmed over. Just some routine questions. Is Mr Gale at home?"

Even as he asked the question he knew what the answer would be. What a fool he was. It was the man of the house — the surviving husband — whom he wished to see. All of those on his list would most probably be at work.

"No, sir. Mr Gale at him h'office."

"And where is that?"

She named a well-known firm on Duke Street.

"What time do you expect him home?"

" 'Bout five — unless him stop off fe play golf at him club." She reeled off the information like a parrot, at variance to her previous relaxed, natural speech. Then she said, "Miss Sandra at home, though."

"Miss Sandra?"

"Mr Gale daughter."

"How old is she?"

The girl looked blank at the question.

"I mean ," Phillips qualified patiently, "is she a little girl or old enough to answer a few questions?"

The girl dimpled suddenly and flashed a look from under her lashes at the silent Goodbody. "She not a little girl, sir. She old enough."

Now what, Phillips asked himself as he followed her trim figure, tight skirt outlining taut buttocks. Just what did she mean by that remark?

They were led through a wide cool hall that ran from the front to the back of the house. Off-white terrazzo tiles were scattered with bright Turkish mats, a few deep chairs, two brick-rose Spanish jars with high waving pampas grass, all combined to give an ambience of uncluttered restful opulence. A glass sliding door opened on to a wide patio which was furnished with white-painted wrought iron chairs, lounges and umbrella-shaded tables. Brilliantly coloured cushions were piled on the chairs and thick terry covered foam pads were scattered on the pool's deck. A flight of shallow steps led down into a star-shaped swimming pool. The only sounds were those of the hum of the filter plant and the gentle plash as the water was rippled by the pump.

Lying on her back by the edge of the pool was the bikini-clad figure of a girl. Her golden skin glistened with oil, her long blonde hair was spread out behind her.

"Miss Sandra?"

The helper's voice held a note not present in her conversation with Phillips: a hesitant, apologetic note.

Without opening her eyes the girl said, "Yes, what is it?"

The reason for the helper's hesitancy was now apparent. Sandra Gale had an autocratic voice, a voice that was used to command, a voice that promised a biting vituperative quality when commands — whether reasonable or otherwise — were not carried out immediately and to the letter.

"Two gentlemen, Miss Sandra, from the police."

The girl by the pool opened her eyes then got up with a swift sinuous grace that made Goodbody catch his breath audibly. She was slim and small-boned. Her full breasts, scarcely covered by the brief bikini bra, were dominant above her tiny waist and immature hips. Her hair fell below her shoulders, naturally blonde, bleached almost to silver by the sun. Her eyes, in contrast, were dark velvet brown. Her skin held a golden sheen, a satiny patina that told nothing of her mixed racial ancestry. As she stood there almost naked, quite unabashed by the fact, there was nothing in her looks to proclaim that she was Jamaican, but when she began to speak there could be no doubt. She had the annoying drawl of certain middle-class women, that lift at the end of each phrase turning each sentence into a question whatever the context of the remark. This trait coupled with her autocratic air produced instant dislike in Phillips' mind.

"All right, Sidonia, you may go."

She bent and picked up a towel then flopped onto one of the lounges. It was only then that she acknowledged Phillips and Goodbody's presence. "Do sit down, you make me nervous standing there," she ordered ungraciously.

Phillips tightened his lips. He was the most tolerant of men but he resented intensely the flaunting of wealth and the assumption that the accident of a fair complexion was a symbol of superiority. He glanced at Goodbody to see how he responded to the girl's arrogant attitude but saw nothing but admiration on the boy's face. They sat down and waited while she lit a cigarette, then for the first time she looked right at him.

"Well?" Her voice lost some of its careless insolence as she met Phillips' steady eyes. "What do you want to see me about? Did I park in the wrong place too long?"

"Nothing like that, Miss Gale. We really wanted to see your father but as you were here we felt that you might be able to help us."

"Help you? In what way?"

"Please understand, Miss Gale, you don't have to answer my questions. But we are pursuing an investigation and we would be grateful…"

She didn't let him finish. The stilted official phrasing made her lose her easily-lost temper. She threw the barely-lit cigarette in a high curving arc to fall hissing into the pool. "For God's sake, man, get to the bloody point. Yammering about questions and investigations. Just get to the point. *What* do you want?"

All right, girl, Phillips said silently. If you want it straight, you will get it straight. "I believe that your mother committed suicide a few months ago?" His voice was soft, cushioning the harshness of the question.

She went quite still, the spoilt petulance drained out of her face and she paled under her tan. "Why bring that up again? Didn't we go through enough hell for days and days?" The words were almost whispered.

"I'm sorry, Miss Gale. I realise that it must be a very painful subject for you. As I tried to say before, you do not *have* to answer these questions but there have been too many suicides similar to your mother's recently and we are trying to find out why — if there is any connecting link, any pattern emerging."

She stood up violently. The first shock of his question had worn off and she glared at him, her brown eyes almost black with anger. "You're damn right I don't have to answer your fool-fool questions. My mother's dead. I don't care what you're trying to find out about anyone else — but don't find out anything about my mother."

"So," Phillips said very quietly. "There *is* something to find out? Well, if you won't tell us, perhaps your father will be more cooperative."

She practically spat. "My father! You can ask him what you like — but you'll get nowhere — even if you're lucky enough to find him sober." She turned her back on them, dropped the towel and dived cleanly into the pool.

Phillips jerked his head at the bemused Goodbody. "Come on, son," he said heavily. "I hope that you like your insight into how the idle rich live. Anyway," he added more cheerfully as he slid behind the wheel, "unless I'm mistaken, that little blonde bitch knows something about her mother's reason for suicide. But to get it out of her — our hands are tied…" He sighed as they turned out of the driveway onto the main road.

Chapter 7

Rachel put down the receiver in its cradle thoughtfully. She had just called Rowan to tell him that as far as she could ascertain nothing was missing from her house. He had accepted the information coolly and made no comment other than, "Good — I'm not surprised."

She hadn't appreciated the ambiguity of the comment but went on, "I'm going up to see how Margaret is."

"Be careful on that road," he had said formally.

She wanted to ask him what was the matter but feared hearing the answer. She sat looking at the silent telephone. Surely he could have made no connection between her strange behaviour last night and the news item? Had he been put on the case? But he had said that he was on the blackmail case — her suspicions that the two seemed very probably connected weighed heavily. If Rowan had been put on this other case then he might have heard about her car — after all it was the only one of its kind and colour in the island. The thought made her go cold. He would have said something though, wouldn't he? He wouldn't have gone all withdrawn and formal without giving her a chance to explain?

Explain what?

It wasn't hers to explain. Margaret had bound her to secrecy. But surely, with the death of the girl — oh God, she thought for the umpteenth time, what have I let myself in for?

She drove up the winding hill road mechanically, and reached each landmark with faint surprise remembering nothing of the road between. The peace of the encircling hills, with the close-packed tree-tops making a solid velvet finish to the rugged rocks far below in the valley: the occasional grove of young pines, straight and elegant: the utter solitude, all gradually worked together to bring a sense of normality to her mind so that when she pulled the Metro to a smooth stop on the soft green turf at the foot of the cottage steps, she was able to greet Margaret naturally.

Margaret sat on a low rocker. Again there was no sign of Eleanore Tarrant.

"Don't get up," Rachel called as she ran lightly up the steps. "How's the ankle?"

"Better — I'll soon be able to get about again."

Rachel surveyed the older woman with a worried frown. She seemed to have aged overnight. Her hooded eyes were sunken and the lines of worry had deepened round her mouth and between her highly arched black brows.

"Did you ... did you deliver the package?" she asked at last.
In answer Rachel opened her large handbag and took out the manila envelope. Her fear over her discovery of the dead girl and the concealment of that discovery, enforced through loyalty, now turned to mounting anger.

"How could you send me to that place? Knowingly. You have jeopardised more than my good name — possibly my whole future."

"What do you mean?" Margaret asked, but her eyes dropped to the paper that she held in her lap.

"You have the answer before you. When I got to the ... room, the occupant was dead."

Margaret closed her eyes. "I'm sorry, Rachel. I know that's quite inadequate under the circumstances — but I am truly sorry. Believe me, if I thought that I was asking you to do more than to deliver the ... envelope — I'm sorry about the ... locality — but God, Rachel, there was no one else that I could turn to."

"Wasn't there?" Rachel's anger was still blazing. She walked across to the edge of the terrace and picked up a stick that was resting against a low wall. "Here's your stick — I'm sure that you will need it when you get up."

"Rachel," Margaret's eyes were blazing also, "I don't know what you're thinking — I don't want to know because when you calm down you'll see how wrong you are. I'm going to presume again on your friendship and ask you to take this envelope back with you. I'll telephone you when I get ... new instructions for delivery."

Rachel gazed at her in disbelief. "You want me to go back there? After what happened? After my description has probably been given to the police? Margaret, do you realise just what you're asking?"

"I think that I do. I know it's a lot to ask — but ... unless that envelope gets to its destination..."

"Why all the euphemisms? Why don't you say, 'Unless the money is paid' ?" Rachel stopped at the expression in the other woman's eyes.

"You looked inside? Rachel — I thought that I could trust you."

"For heaven's sake! *Trust!* You ask me to do your dirty work without even hinting at what I was walking into — then you have the gall to talk of trust."

She turned and walked quickly to her car.

"Rachel, please, I need your help."

Without a word or a backward glance Rachel slid into the driver's seat of the Metro and revved the engine hard to blot out Margaret Cameron's voice. She swung the car round viciously, going crisply through the gears, and sent the little car down the twisting road at a dangerous speed. Loose stones flew up and bounced off the chassis in bullet-like explosions. She took a double hairpin bend down a one-in-four grade at a pace that even the manoeuvrability of the Metro failed to stand up to, and she felt the car sliding out of control towards the opposite bank. She tried to remember all that she had been told about the counteractive measures to take with a skidding car but her mind was too much under the influence of her emotions. She wrenched on the wheel and the little car slewed crazily then came to a grudging standstill with its bonnet pointing uphill, its rear end tilted upon the slight rise of grass which grew close to the low, dry-pack stone wall— all that stood between her and the thousand foot drop to the valley below.

She just sat there, breathing deeply, all anger swamped by thankfulness at being alive. Then, with caution, she righted the Metro until its bonnet was again pointing downhill. She was still shaking and felt that she couldn't manage the rest of the downward drive for a few minutes. She lit a cigarette and switched on the car radio. She felt somewhat ashamed of her outburst towards Margaret. The circumstances and events leading up to Margaret's making such a request for help must have been overwhelming and Rachel felt that her loyalty had not stood the test — even given the extenuating fact of discovering the dead girl.

A programme of reggae music throbbed its way to a close then a disembodied voice enjoined: "Stand by for the eleven-thirty news." Rachel lit another cigarette from the stub of the first — she knew that she was smoking too much, but was unable to stop. The news began with the announcement of a minister of government's proposed visit to the States then a terse item made her heart skip: "The death of the girl found in an apartment building in the Cross Roads area was a result of natural causes. A stomach perforation was discovered by a post mortem examination."

Rachel sat very still.

By *natural* causes?

She thought back : there had been no obvious outward wound — just blood welling from the girl's mouth. She felt a flood of relief that invaded her whole body. Natural causes! It was just one of those unforeseeable coincidences of a thousand years — she *would* walk into it! And she had very nearly accused Margaret Cameron … of what? What exactly had been in her mind? Fantasy born of fear for her own safety — nothing more than that.

She stubbed out her cigarette, switched off the radio, made a three-point turn and started the upward drive back to Margaret Cameron's cottage.

* * *

Sergeant Phillips and Police Constable Goodbody were nearing the end of a tiring morning. Goodbody had learnt more of the art of eliciting information from unwilling informants in those hours spent in the experienced company of Phillips than he had learnt during the whole of his period at the Police Training School. It was once again the triumph of practice over theory. Phillips had the enviable knack of altering his approach to suit the occasion or the type of person whom he was questioning.

After the unfortunate interview with Sandra Gale they had concentrated on the homes of the three unmarried women who had committed suicide in the last twelve months. Their next stop had been at a small cottage just above Stony Hill. Phillips had carefully explained the object of their visit, but they had drawn a blank, more or less.

The late owner, a Miss Mann, had died six months before by taking an unspecified number of sleeping pills. They had been told this with vicarious sorrow not unmixed with a macabre enjoyment by the present occupant, a Miss Veronica McCawly, a middle-aged expatriate who had come to the island to teach Botany at a well-known girls' school fifteen years earlier. She had decided to stay on after her retirement. She was not unattractive with once-blonde hair now peppered with grey. Her short-sighted, pale blue eyes, slightly protuberant, were apt to fill with tears at any reference to romance or tragedy — possibly because both had so obviously passed her by. She was short and inclined to plumpness. What little figure she may have had was now obscured by a shapeless smock-like garment.

She had led them through the tiny sitting room to a large verandah with a magnificent view of the hills.

"Do sit down, Sergeant ... Phillips, is it? Yes. And you, of course, Constable," she had gushed, causing Phillips to sigh inwardly. He knew from experience how difficult this type of lady was to get away from. "May I get you something to drink? Tea? Coffee? Or perhaps..." she almost bridled at her daring "... beer?"

"Thank you, madam," Phillips was at his most correct. "But not while on duty, thank you. Perhaps just a glass of water if it's not too much trouble."

"No trouble at all," she had trilled then sat forward earnestly. "Why not fresh limeade? I do think it wonderful, even after all these years just to go out and pick the limes. Don't you agree?" She had waited for a moment for their rapturous response but had to be content with a polite smile from Phillips and a look of bewilderment from Goodbody. She had given a little laugh then fluttered away and was back in a surprisingly short time with three glasses of limeade on a tray with the inevitable lace doily. The glasses were tall with plenty of ice. Phillips had sipped his appreciatively; it was good and regret at having to say 'no' to a Red Stripe beer faded somewhat.

Miss McCawly had clasped her hands in an incongruously girlish attitude.

"Now tell me. What do you want to know about poor Miss Mann?"

"You knew her, madam?" Phillips had asked hopefully.

"Oh no — but I do think it so sad — I mean …" She had trailed off.

"Have you heard any reason given for the lady's suicide, madam?"

"No. The helper who was with her was so upset that she fled back to the country — somewhere in St Elizabeth, I think," she had added vaguely and to no useful purpose.

"Did you take this place furnished?"

"Why, yes. You see, the poor dear had no relations — nobody. Too sad."

She had pushed to the back of her mind that she too had nobody — neither in Jamaica nor in her native England — who would mourn at her funeral.

"In the course of your moving in and settling down, did you happen to come across any papers —notebooks — anything of that nature?"

Her eyes had flickered away, as a wary look replaced the wide innocence, and he had a conviction that even if she had found none she had certainly looked.

"Why, no," she had said brightly — too brightly? "There was a desk, but the solicitor who looked after the transaction — he went through everything…" She had trailed off again.

Phillips had sighed inwardly. "The name of the solicitor, madam?"

She had wrinkled her brow, "I can't remember — something like … no, it escapes me completely."

This was getting nowhere. "What was Miss Mann's work, do you know, madam?"

"Oh, she didn't *work* — she was quite wealthy. She was the last, the *very last* member of one of the *oldest* families in the island. The first Mann came out with Cromwell's army in 1655. She had a fine sense of tradition, that I have heard of and do so admire…" She had paused for breath.

Phillips pursed his lips — an idea, nebulous but nagging to be accepted, was being slowly formed: a fierce sense of family pride to be protected at all cost was a strong motive — but was it strong enough to induce suicide? He wished that he knew. He had tried a wild shot. "Since you have been here Miss McCawly, has anything odd happened? Anything out of the normal?"

A veil had dropped over the prominent blue eyes and the girlish look was replaced once more by a sudden calculating wariness. She had seemed about to say something but no words came. Then she had shaken her head and looked down at her clasped hands. He had waited but when at last she had raised her eyes they were as tranquil and naive as ever.

"Why, no, Sergeant Phillips. Nothing untoward at all." She had turned her short-sighted eyes towards the blue hills, the valleys and high ridges bright and clear in the morning sun. "It's very beautiful here isn't it? I paint, you know — oh, nothing special — I just dabble. But it's so relaxing and satisfying."

Phillips had risen ponderously to his feet and put his empty glass down on a low table. "Why yes, ma'am, it is peaceful." He had surveyed her thoughtfully and her pale blue eyes had dropped before his dark gaze. "If you remember anything, ma'am, which might be useful to us, would you let us know?"

"Why, of course, *of course*. But if there's nothing now. I don't see..." She had trailed off as seemed to be a habit with her. Phillips had wondered irrelevantly, how she had ever managed to teach with such an indefinite approach. As they were re-entering the staff car, he had sighed audibly. "Well, me son, what do you think?" he had asked Goodbody, not expecting much of a reply.

"I think , Mr Phillips," Goodbody had said slowly, "I think the lady do have something to tell. It seem like she — not quite afraid — but h'anxious."

Phillips had shot him a surprised look."Good for you, son. I get the same feeling myself."

Veronica McCawly had watched the car disappear down the hill road, an unusual mixture of feelings warring within her. She had wanted to tell the sergeant about the telephone calls but she *couldn't* — it would have sounded so silly. She had shuddered, hearing again that soft persuasive voice. It had a caressing quality that was almost obscene.

When she had remembered how very nearly she had succumbed to its charm — then she had found the cheque book stubs tucked behind a drawer in the desk. Her curiosity, fanned by loneliness, had spurred her to examine it. The cheque book had held fifty leaves, thirty of them had been made out to 'cash' for two thousand dollars each. They had been regular withdrawals at two-monthly intervals. At first she had not appreciated the significance of the withdrawals; she merely wondered how the unknown, deceased Miss Mann had managed to use so much cash in the quiet cottage. The remaining stubs were records of grocery payments, light bills, and the usual household expenses. Her unsophisticated mind had been slow to understand possible explanations, but as the weeks had passed, a growing uneasy conviction had made her connect the cheque stubs with her own disturbing telephone calls. What if Miss Mann had received similar calls? — and responded? Her mind had shied away from the possibility.

The telephone had begun to be the predominant factor in her life. She found herself waiting for it to ring, listening even when she was gardening down the hillside or half-absorbed in her painting. When it did, she would wait until the last minute before she answered it, willing herself to wait, hoping that it would stop ringing, knowing that she would make a last minute dash to answer it. When she did pick up the receiver and had gasped the number, it would seem an eternity before the caller spoke. More often than not, it had been a friend to talk trivialities, many times the usual wrong number.

After weeks of silence, when she had grown calm and convinced that the calls had ceased, he had called again. She had answered naturally, for once not obsessed with the idea that it was other than a normal call. The shock of hearing his voice again had left her bereft of speech and coherent thought for a long moment.

"Are you there ... Veronica? I know you are — why don't you listen to me and do what I want — and what you want, eh, Veronica? Come on admit it."

"And do what you want — like the late Miss Mann? Is that what you want?" The conviction that her fears had not been groundless and that this was an attempt to dupe and make a fool of her — and worse — was growing with each passing second. The voice had spoken again, now not so soft and caressing but with a chill undertone that was oddly frightening. "And just what do you know about Miss Mann?"

Anger made her reckless. "I know enough — more than you would like me to know."

The words were out before she realised their implication: she heard them repeated in her mind again and again, ringing and echoing all around her. She had waited, hardly daring to breathe, wanting to refute the statement, unable to do so.

"You do, do you, Miss McCawly? That is interesting. Let me warn you then not to use your knowledge. You hear me? Do not use your knowledge *in any way.*"

There had been a click and the line went dead and an uncanny silence filled the air. She had sat clutching the receiver until she stopped trembling. She had been half-proud, half-appalled at what she had said.

She had waited. She knew that she should report the calls to the police but cringed at the thought of possible questions.

Days had passed — weeks — months...

Gradually the fear had receded, there had been no more phone calls, no more insidious suggestions and invitations, until she was lulled into believing that the whole sordid episode was finished. She had been ashamed at her thoughts and longings at the time, at her slowly ebbing determination not to succumb. As the weeks had gone by, her turbulent feelings had subsided and she had been able to go about her household tasks, her painting and what little entertaining and visiting that she did, with the calm assurance that she had known for most of her uninteresting life. The fact that the calls had ceased had made her more convinced that her analysis of the situation was correct: she had mulled over the repugnant conclusion that her predecessor in the cottage had been driven to suicide by blackmail.

Over the weeks that grew into months, even this had receded into the back of her mind until now, when the two policemen had asked so many questions and had brought it all so sharply to the forefront of her thoughts again.

So she had been right.

Blackmail — she too had so nearly become embroiled. The reflection made her feel nauseated. The need to confide in that nice sergeant of police had been so strong — but it would have resulted in the exposure of her own silly reactions and the underlying fear that still remained of the voice that warned: do not use your knowledge. That had prevented any disclosures or confidences.

After all, she had argued with herself, what *did* she know? Nothing. She had bragged that she knew, when the reality was that she only suspected.

A new fear struck her: what if the visit by the police should be reported to 'them'? What if? — she gave a shaky little laugh — this was more than foolish. She had gone back into the cottage and shut the door.

As she had gone through to the back verandah to collect the empty glasses, the telephone had begun to ring.

Chapter 8

Rowan Rodgers looked up from the file that he was reading as Phillips and Goodbody entered his office to report on their findings. "Any luck?" he asked. He picked up his pipe and tamped down tobacco with strong brown fingers. "Smoke if you like." He glanced at his watch. "Good God, what happened to lunch?"

Phillips grinned. He knew his chief's predilection for letting the morning go by, so immersed in work that mealtimes came and went unnoticed. Only when insistent hunger demanded to be assuaged did he return to the world. It was now nearly three o'clock. Phillips and Goodbody had stopped off for a late lunch of a sandwich and a welcome glass of cold beer. They had returned to the station only to make their report, then had planned to go off duty until the evening at which time they would begin to question the working husbands.

"Not so much luck, sir," Phillips said heavily. The morning had strained his natural forbearance and sympathetic approach. The need for excessive tact, the rebuffs and receptions that he had received had not heightened his regard for his fellow men — or in this case, his fellow women. He recounted the interviews which they had conducted — the arrogance and hostility of the Gale girl, the conviction that she knew or suspected the reason for her mother's suicide, the fluttery spinster, Miss McCawly, and the equally strong conviction that *she* was withholding some item of information. Then there was their complete blank at the next call — house sold, no relatives, no one to give the slightest information — and finally their encounter with Miss Daphne Prestwick.

Daphne Prestwick was the niece of one of the suicide victims, Thelma Prestwick. In her looks she was the antithesis of Sandra Gale whose blonde, arrogant beauty was replaced by brunette, arrogant beauty. Her skin was like brown velvet, apparently untouched by make-up. Her naturally tight curls were clipped close to her perfectly shaped head. The resultant effect was of a meticulous sculpture, moulded and chiselled with infinite care. Her eyes were big, black and lustrous, fringed with thick curling lashes. Her figure was disappointing, slim to the point of thinness, but she exuded an aura of pure sex that engulfed Phillips who was immune, but had reduced the susceptible, inexperienced Goodbody to a tongue-tied partner. Phillips glanced sideways at him, suppressing a smile. The boy was certainly gaining a variety of experiences this morning.

Daphne Prestwick was in a vividly flowered dress, one shoulder bare, the skirt falling straight to an inch above her knees. She had the legs to wear short skirts successfully — slim, tapered, incredibly long. She received the men on a wide, cool verandah. The house was in sharp contrast to the Gale's near-mansion but just as luxurious in its way. It was old, about two hundred years, Phillips estimated. Its cool, high rooms with tray ceilings painted white, walls two feet thick with deep, shuttered windows, held a charm that steel and concrete fashioned in contemporary designs can never achieve.

Phillips studied Daphne Prestwick with interest. Her dead aunt had been a woman of note. She had held a position many years before on the old Legislative Council. She had sat on boards of hospitals, schools and voluntary organisations. She had written books on social welfare, prison reform and child guidance, and at the time of her death she was working on a political history of the Caribbean of the nineteenth century. This much Phillips had gleaned from the files; also that she was unmarried and had left her favourite niece as sole beneficiary of her considerable fortune.

Daphne waved a slim dark hand for them to be seated. The verandah was furnished with white-painted wicker-work. The chairs were beautifully antique, spreading fan-shaped backs above the sitter's head, arms wide enough to write on or to hold a tray, with pockets for books and other impedimenta, and leg rests to trans form the chairs to loungers.

Phillips settled back contentedly; this was the life, he thought, with no trace of envy. Then he remembered his mission and sat erect. The girl was waiting for him to speak, her innate good manners not allowing her to show impatience.

"Miss Prestwick, you must forgive my asking you some questions that may cause you to be upset," Phillips began, then went on to outline the reason for his visit. The girl listened quietly, her dark eyes watchful.

Goodbody listened too, to the easy flow of language from his sergeant. He was amazed at the facility with which Phillips switched from an easy patois to an equally easy cultured approach. That, he decided, was what he should learn to do. He listened intently, seizing mentally upon unfamiliar words, storing them up so that he could thumb through his well-worn dictionary and determine the meaning. He was paying more attention to Phillips than to Daphne Prestwick when suddenly he was startled back to the girl by her reaction to Phillips' questions.

"Sure, my aunt was being blackmailed and killed herself because of that. Why was she being blackmailed? Because of me. Does that surprise and shock you, sergeant? It shouldn't. In your line of work I should have thought that you would become unshockable."

If Phillips was shocked he concealed it admirably behind his usual stolid manner. "Is that so, Miss Prestwick? You knew why your aunt took her life and you have concealed the fact. Why?"

"Because I wasn't asked. Because I was the poor little bereaved niece I suppose. Oh, be your age, sergeant. My aunt was a fool for all her intelligence and learning. She lived in a world where ideals and moral concepts were rigid, where one did or didn't do certain things. Her world had no relation to the world that we live in. She was the perfect victim for a blackmailer and from what you've told me there are more of her type left than I imagined — surprise!"

"You say that you were the reason. Can you be more specific?"

"Sure — why not?" She got up lithely, took a cigarette from a box on a table then pushed the box across to them. "Help yourself, I'm not like my late, lamented aunt. She mothered and smothered me from the time I was two — when my parents died. We had plenty of money and she hired good nurses to look after me then sent me to the best schools and finally overseas to study. That was fine — I only had to endure her zealous care during the holidays and quite often I would wangle an invitation to a friend's house so that frequently I was out of her care for a year at a time. Then I graduated and came home for good. We were the complete opposite of each other — her tolerance and understanding were limitless

— whatever I did she accepted with a forbearance that drove me nearly mad. It had the effect of goading me on to devise new ways to shock her. I'd played around and slept around for years — from the time I was fifteen — and before long I'd got myself involved in a rather messy affair. Somehow — this group of yours, these blackmail types — got wind of it. God knows it couldn't have been all that difficult, and they threatened Aunt Thelma with exposure unless she paid up. They were crafty, you see. They went to her not to me. And she paid and she paid and she *paid*."

"And you let her?"

Phillips' voice had hardened. He was unable to keep a note of contempt from his words. The girl had given such an impression at first of quiet, good breeding that her uninhibited revelations were doubly disturbing.

"I didn't know at the beginning. When I did find out I told her to tell them to go to hell — print the story and publish the explicit photos — I couldn't care less. But oh, no. She believed that a good name was more important than a good time, that the traditional honour of the family was more important than *anything*. She was prepared to sacrifice all her worldly goods to preserve the honour of the family name. I tried to tell her that that was old fashioned, that people didn't care any more for honour and tradition. I tried to convince her that our reputation...," her voice was mocking, "... would survive the shock of the four-inch tabloid headlines. Other people have survived and have come out of the blaze of publicity — only to fall again. But she wouldn't listen and when the demands were increased she killed herself to save the blood money she would have to pay until she was drained. She didn't want that. She wanted to leave enough for me to live in comfort. So — she killed herself," Daphne Prestwick repeated with a shrug, in a matter-of-fact tone.

During the whole recital she had kept a cool, impersonal tone. Phillips gazed at her in bewilderment; even his stolidity was shaken by her callous calmness.

"So she killed herself," he repeated. "That's all that it means to you?"

She laughed, "I told you, sergeant, she was a fool. I have no use for fools — aunts or otherwise."

She stood up, dismissing them.

They rose, then Phillips asked, "And what about you, Miss

Prestwick? After your aunt's death, you had the money bags. Didn't they try to blackmail you?"

She laughed again, "Sure, they tried. I told them: Go ahead, print the story. It'll be a nine-days' gossip and good for a dirty giggle or two — but that won't hurt me. And that was that."

Phillips was silent as they drove down the hill. As they reached the station, he said to Goodbody, "Well, you've had your eyes opened a bit this morning, eh, son?"

"The lady hard, eeh suh? Me never know say people go on so," Goodbody said in awe. Then he grinned. "But that Miss Gale — the one in the likkle swim trunk dem – she sure one swinging chick, eeh, Mr Phillips?"

Phillips gave an unexpected guffaw of laughter. "Well, me son, so you learn the city language so soon, eh? What happen to the little country bwoy?"

Rodgers had listened to Phillips' report in silence. "So," he said at last. "It seems pretty definite that there is an organised ring. And it appears as if each one of the women whom you interviewed this morning knew something. Pity the other two weren't as frank as the last one. Even with just three interviews a pattern is emerging. But until we get a definite pointer as to who is behind it all, the knowledge that we have isn't going to be of any real help. There are probably a number of women right now who could tell us all we need to break the racket once and for all — but no one will have the courage to talk."

* * *

Rachel arrived back at the cottage, ashamed of her outburst. Eleanore Tarrant was sitting on the terrace, alone. There was no sign of Margaret Cameron. The newspaper and walking stick were on the floor by the chair where Margaret had been sitting.

"Why, Rachel, this is a surprise." Eleanore fluttered her hands and Rachel felt immediately the rising irritation that Eleanore always triggered in her.

"I'm sorry to disturb you, I wanted to see Margaret."

Margaret's deep voice called from within the house, "Eleanore? Did I hear a car?"

Eleanore's cow-like eyes flickered, "Why, yes, it's Rachel." She called back with unnecessary forcefulness, a faint emphasis on the name like a note of warning.

Rachel kept her eyes lowered, her expression carefully neutral as the pause lengthened. Then Margaret called back, "Be an angel and bring my stick."

Eleanore shot a nervous glance at Rachel as she clumsily rose and took up the stick. A few moments later, Margaret came heavily out of the house, alone. She stood in the doorway and looked questioningly at Rachel.

"I'm sorry I was so hasty," Rachel said. "On the way down, I heard on the radio ... that the girl died from ... a perforated stomach ulcer."

Margaret shut her eyes. The colour slowly drained from her face but her voice was steady as she said, "I'm not going to ask you what you thought Rachel. I'd hoped that you knew me better than that."

"I thought that I knew you better," Rachel said, but now without any bitterness. "I never imagined that you would get me involved in something like this."

Margaret came slowly down the steps and sat down. She took a cigarette from a box on a low table then pushed the box across to Rachel and murmured, "Sorry." She blew out a cloud of smoke and watched it disperse in curling, wraith-like swirls, then asked, "Did you come back just to tell me that?"

"No, I came back *because* of that, and to say that I'll take the package if you still want me to."

The older woman was silent, then she said softly, "Thank you, Rachel."

Rachel sat forward. "Listen to me, Margaret. I don't know why — and I don't care to know — but you're being blackmailed, aren't you?"

Margaret's dark eyes were expressionless as they met Rachel's wide grey ones, then she nodded.

"Don't you realise that once you start paying you never stop? Tell them to go to hell and do their worst."

Rachel took a deep breath and stood up. "You're not alone in this. Rowan's working on a suspected blackmail ring or racket or whatever it is, right now. Why don't you help him and tell him what you know?"

"No! You don't know what you're asking." Margaret got up

and faced Rachel. Her face was the colour of vellum. "How ... how did Rowan get onto it?"

"By deduction — there have been too many unexplained cases of suicide amongst women of the upper middle-class, and roughly the same age bracket. Why don't you do something before ... you are forced to join the number?"

It was only when she was half-way down the hill, that she remembered that Margaret had risen quite easily from her chair — without the aid of her stick.

* * *

Later that evening, Sergeant Phillips and Police Constable Goodbody, refreshed by an early meal of curried goat, rice and peas and fried plantain, washed down by ice-cold Red Stripe beer, once more set off into the reaches of fashionable upper St Andrew. The sun was beginning to lose some of its fierce intensity and dark rain clouds obscured the top of the Blue Mountains with the promise of heavy rain, the promise unfulfilled as a breeze swept them away and the people in the town and on the dry plains sighed as one more day went by and the drought was still unbroken. There had been a little rain higher up and the dry, crisp grass of the low-lying land gave way to a soft green turf, the eddying dust from the crumbling banks became dark, moist earth.

Every house that they passed had two or more cars parked in its driveway. The muted twang of a tennis racquet was heard as a ball was hit dead centre; the splash of swimmers in pools; the cries of children at play; the sound of music from gleaming stereo sets — all the sounds of an opulent suburbia reached them as they drove slowly, ever upward.

"This is the time when all the rich folk have cocktails," Phillips said, intent on enlarging Goodbody's education on all facets of life in the big city and its environs.

"Cocktails?"

Country bwoy, Phillips thought, but with affection. "Is a mixture of spirit, your rum, your gin or your whisky, you take one o' them and mix it with soda or bitter lemon — whatever. Shake it with ice. Give me Red Stripe though, me son, any time."

"Same here, Mr Phillips."

They managed three interviews in the Red Hills area, all

abortive. Their — or rather Phillips' — questions had been answered frankly, although with some degree of reluctance. They discovered that each of the three dead women had taken her life under the stress of illness: one had an inoperable cancer, one was a manic depressive, and the third an incurable alcoholic. Phillips sighed; the pattern hadn't been continued or expanded since the morning. He hoped that the chief wasn't wrong about the emergence of a pattern — if he was, then they were just wasting time. There was, though, a niggling feeling that the chief *wasn't* wrong.

"Right, son," he said crisply to Goodbody. "We'll call it a day — and try and finish off tomorrow."

Goodbody nodded. He was enjoying his new life in Kingston, bustling, wild and wicked after the sleepy seclusion of the country. The knowledge that he was on a case — he savoured the expression again, 'on a case' — with the well-known Superintendent Rowan Rodgers and his equally well-known aide, Sergeant Phillips, filled him with a sense of well-being and importance. What he had seen and heard today had imbued his unsophisticated mind with some misgiving. All the high-up house dem with the shiny floor an' swimmin' pool, an' the way people go on so. There was no envy in his thoughts, rather a shrewd pity for the type of people who occupied these palaces. They didn't seem happy or content despite their wealth and creature comforts.

He signed out in the duty book, bade a cheerful 'goodnight' to the sergeant on station duty and went whistling into the soft tropical night towards his lodgings in Jones Town.

Chapter 9
day 3, Wednesday

The rest of the day passed slowly. Every time the telephone rang Rachel hesitated before answering — dreading to hear the expected instructions. One call was from Rowan who rang to cancel their dinner date, for which she was thankful. She didn't want to fall under the scrutiny of his eyes until she had collected her thoughts and had achieved some degree of calm. The relief that the girl's death was due to natural causes and that she need fear no questions as to her presence at the apartments left her limp and unable to relax. She slept badly that night. Her dreams were peopled with faceless women about to commit suicide, and when she tried to prevent them and reason with them, she was unable to move and no voice would come; she just had to stand helplessly by and watch. She woke, drenched in sweat yet shivering with cold only to sleep again and to endure a similar enactment. There was some small comfort in the soft warmth of Bamboo's furry little body, curled in the curve of her hip and thigh.

At last she gave up the struggle for sleep and went to the kitchen to make coffee. She looked wearily at the coffee-maker then settled for instant and took it onto the back verandah. Dawn was just touching the tops of the Blue Mountains, cotton-wool clouds tipped with pink nestled in the hollows, wisps of grey vapour spiralled down to the pockets between the hills, to disappear as the sun rose higher. The sky turned from the pale green of dawn to a clear silver-blue, and the birds chorused in the cool of a new day. The beauty of the scene washed over her and filled her with peace to face the hours ahead.

The morning dragged until about midday when she could stand the silence of the lonely house no longer. She told Ruel that she would not be in for lunch, then drove out to the cheerfulness of a crowded shopping plaza. She window-shopped, bought a new cassette for her Portuguese collection — the price of which staggered her. Then she had a leisurely lunch, all the time forcing her mind away from the possibility that the telephone might be ringing at home. This type of aimless time-wasting was alien to her nature and at last became unendurable. It's a form of escapism, she told herself sharply. That phone call has got to be made sometime and I've got to take whatever instructions are given. She gathered up her purchases, paid her bill and hurried back to the car.

She had barely reached home when the telephone rang.

"It's all right, Ruel," she called. "I'll get it."

The voice that replied to her unusually crisp "Rachel Groome speaking," was soft, almost caressing. It could have belonged to either a man or a deep voiced woman. She decided on the former without quite knowing why. There was something faintly familiar in its timbre that disturbed her.

"Mrs Groome?"

"Yes, who is that speaking?"

"My name doesn't matter — my business does."

There was a pause and she felt a tightening of fear. She knew without the need for more words that the caller was one of the group that Rowan would so dearly love to put his hands on.

"Well, what is it?" Fear made her breathless.

"No need for alarm, dear lady. Just do as you're told — and nothing will happen to upset you."

He paused again and Rachel wanted to scream, 'Tell me your business, what I must do — get it over with.' But she remained silent, her heart thumping painfully. If only Rowan would come in now, she thought. What a fool I've been, why *didn't* I tell him?

"Are you there, Rachel? I *may* call you Rachel, can't I?"

"No, you damn well can't. Just say what you have to say and get off the line." A sudden spurt of anger replaced the irrational fear.

He answered her with a laugh. "How refreshing — a woman with spirit. In my ... work ... I meet so few. Well, yes, a little spirit perhaps at first, but too soon succeeded by tears and pleading — so dull. I hope that you will keep your spirits up."

"Will you state your business — or else I'll hang up."

"That wouldn't be very wise, would it? You don't want your dear friend Margaret to ... suffer, do you?" She didn't answer.

71

"So," the voice took on a new note. "You will be at the same place — where the unfortunate death took place — the *same* room. Drive in, park, speak to no one — in exactly half an hour from now. At three p.m. exactly. And ... Rachel, remember to bring the notebook with you."

"The ... *notebook?*"

"Don't play games, I know you've got it. If you don't bring it then Margaret Cameron will have to pay again — very soon. I don't think that she would care for that."

"All right — but could you possibly make it three-thirty? I ... I haven't had lunch yet."

There was a pause, then the soft indulgence was back. "Of course, little to ask under the circumstances. But no later, the ... er, apartments get a little crowded from four o'clock onwards."

I bet they do, Rachel thought viciously as she put down the receiver. She had asked for the extra time for one purpose only. She took a sheet of paper and a ball point pen and, working fast, she made a copy of the names and addresses in the notebook.

"Ruel," she called, "Whip me up a cup of coffee. I have to go out."

She didn't stop writing as she drank, aware of Ruel's disapproving gaze. He didn't care for his excellent brew to be treated in such an off-hand manner.

She was calm now, her mind made up. She finished the copy, put it in an envelope and addressed it to Rowan, then wrote a short note which she included.

"Ruel, if by any chance I'm held up and Mr Rodgers arrives before I get back, give him this. Say that I'll explain when I see him. It's very, very important. Keep it safe for me."

He took the envelope solemnly, pleased to be included in some measure in what was going on. He'd had a feeling of exclusion. Ever since he'd been hit over the head there had been tension in the air an' what a way Miss Rachel go h'out fe so long.

"Yes, Miss Rachel, ma'am. You leave every little t'ing to me."

Rachel went into her bedroom and opened a drawer in her vanity dresser. She rummaged under a pile of underwear; cold metal met her fingers and she drew out a small automatic pistol. It was only a .22m but was capable of doing enough damage for her purpose at close range. She checked that the magazine was full and that the safety catch worked smoothly, then locked the safety catch and put the gun in her handbag. She looked at her watch: three minutes past three. Just timed nicely, she thought, the traffic at this hour is fairly light. She went quickly from the house, the Metro roared into life and she reversed cleanly along the driveway and out through the gate.

As she drove through Half-Way-Tree, she felt as if her destination was emblazoned on the windscreen. Once again she had tied a dark scarf round her hair and large dark glasses obscured nearly a third of her face, but it seemed as if the driver of every car that she met looked at her in recognition.

She was thankful to turn off the main road; there was more anonymity in the lesser-used byways. She was now passing the houses that had long since ceased to be dwellings. The front yard of one was packed with the rusting bodies of old automobiles. A sign at the gate of another proclaimed that coffins could be made at short order, another announced that it was Pete's Eatery and Drinkery. She reached the quiet backwater and the high surrounding zinc fence. Her feeling of shame and revulsion grew, for this time she *knew* where she was going.

There were the inevitable sheets flapping in a light breeze like a trademark, but no person was in sight, for which she felt weak with relief. She drove round the side of the building to the parking area at the back. She switched off the engine and opened her handbag, gently released the safety catch on the gun, then got out of the Metro. There was one other car, a dark grey Audi. She glanced round, dare she risk a peep at the licence disk? As she took a step towards it, a domestic came out of the new building across the way and Rachel turned and went quickly into the house. She stopped just inside to allow her eyes to adjust to the change of light, then went slowly down the corridor to the room marked 8. Her heart was thudding as she remembered too vividly when last she had entered that room.

The scent of a cigar wafted to her through the partially opened door. Without further thought she pushed it fully open and walked in. It swung to behind her but she heard no click of its closing. She took two steps, then stopped. The louvres at the windows were tilted up and the light was dim, but she could make out a man sitting on the bed. He was slightly built, young — about twenty-five, she thought irrelevantly. He was very dark complexioned, like old mahogany, gleaming in the half light. His hair was sculpted to his head and his eyes were — as far as she could make out — dark brown; she had never seen him before.

He slid off the bed and without a word came towards her. "Well, I didn't hope for such an attractive messenger." His voice was low and cultured but it was not the one she had heard on the phone. He reached out suddenly and whipped off her glasses. "Better yet, why cover up?"

She backed away from him. There was a pulsing animal magnetism reaching her in waves.

He smiled. "You have the money?"

"Yes," she opened her cavernous handbag and gave him the bulky envelope. He tossed it carelessly on the bed.

"And the notebook?"

"Yes." She held it out to him.

He glanced away from her briefly as he riffled through the pages. "Why did you take it in the first place?" he demanded.

"Don't know — it had fallen on the floor and I just picked it up. I... I'd forgotten all about it until ... I was told to bring it with me." Don't let me elaborate on that, she thought, keep it simple. He's *got* to believe it — just let me get out of here. She turned to open the door, when she felt his hands slide round her waist.

He turned her to face him, his hands holding her hips. She was incapable of getting free through surprise and fear. She felt again the waves of animal magnetism engulf her and she smelt a mixture of cigar smoke, after shave and the sweet foetidity of stale rum. She kept perfectly still in his hold. He was only a little taller then she was, his eyes almost level with hers.

"There's no need to hurry — we've got the room, we might as well make use of it."

His hands moved up and down her sides, caressing her in a practised way. She put her hands behind her and felt cautiously in the still open handbag, an action which tilted her body back and made her full breasts strain at her close-fitting blouse.

He bent and kissed the base of her throat as he murmured, "That's it baby. You're doing fine."

She'd got the smooth butt of the little automatic in her hand now and slowly began to withdraw it from the bag.

He raised his head and pulled her closer to him. She shut her eyes to hide the expression of fear and revulsion as his lips touched hers, and kicked him sharply on the ankle. At the same time swung her hand round with the gun, jabbing him sharply in the midriff. He uttered a uniquely Jamaican "raas" as pain shot through his ankle and even more so through his solar plexus.

"You ought to be thankful that I didn't bring my knee up," she spat out. "You filthy little swine — get over against the wall and put your hands on your head."

He swore at her again but obeyed.

With her free hand she whipped the sheet off the bed and threw it over his head. As he started to struggle in its enveloping folds she backed towards the door. Suddenly she could not move. A strong hand was clamped over her mouth and the other knocked the gun from her grasp.

"Okay, Stillman, you can get from under the wrappings. I've got her."

It was the voice of the man on the telephone.

Stillman disentangled himself and came across the room, his dark eyes blazing at Rachel. "You little bitch — just let me have half an hour with you and you'd wish you'd never been born. You got the picture?" he asked the other man.

"No. Orders are changed. Seems that her boyfriend is wising up on the angle. The boss thinks that she'll help get him off it."

Oh God, thought Rachel, this can't be happening. She began to struggle, but Stillman held her while the other man tied her scarf over her eyes, then taped her mouth with adhesive tape. Her hands were pulled behind her and taped firmly. She heard them rummaging in her handbag and the rattle of car keys. Oh God, she thought again, what are they going to do with me? She was sorry now that she had kicked Stillman and sworn at him. She tried not to think of his threat and just what he meant. And Rowan, how did they know that he was on the case? There'd been an unspoken understanding that it was to be kept quiet. Surely Phillips or the young police constables wouldn't — the answer was suddenly obvious and she felt nauseated at the realisation.

She was roughly picked up — by Stillman? No, this man seemed taller, more heavily built. If only she could get a glimpse of his face. There was a tantalising familiarity about his voice but she couldn't pinpoint it. She heard quick footsteps going outside, the sound of a car door being opened, then Stillman called softly, "Okay, the coast is clear." She was hurriedly carried outside. She had time to feel the heat of the sun and to be aware of light in front of her eyes, then she was thrust into the back of a car onto the floor. She heard Stillman say, "She can't give any trouble like that. I'll take the Metro and join you later."

The driver's door was opened and softly closed, the engine caught with the minimum of revving and they moved away, quietly, sedately, no dash and flurry to cause comment or give reason for anyone to remember the vehicle.

Rachel, bound and sightless, helpless on the floor, couldn't tell by the sound of the engine what type of car it was. She was fairly certain that it wasn't the grey Audi that was parked when she arrived, but she hadn't heard the approach of another car — her struggle with Stillman had most likely masked it. Her sense of direction was befuddled by her position. She knew that they were on a busy main road by the frequent slowing down, as if they were caught in the beginning of the afternoon rush. There were stops, regular as if for traffic lights and the recurrence of the steadily approaching hum of vehicles, a crescendo of sound as they met, then diminishing as they receded.

She was certain that they were going up through the Half-Way-Tree area, but after that she had no idea. Then they were moving more quickly, climbing, twisting. She lost all sense of time. There was just a series of painful jolts; she was unable to brace her body for the turns and rolled back and forth like a sack. Suddenly, they were off the main road and the jolts and bumps were trebled. She reckoned that they had been climbing steadily for a mile or more after leaving the smooth highway. Then they made another sharp upward turn. The road surface became even rougher. She could feel the car waltzing to avoid the potholes, then it stopped with a squeal of tyres as they clung for purchase on loose stones.

The front door opened and stayed open. The now well-known voice said, "Here's the end of the road for you, my lovely."

She was pulled roughly from the car and picked up easily, no straining muscles. She didn't like that statement by her unseen captor. She hoped devoutly that the phrase was used only figuratively and that it wasn't truly the end for her.

Chapter ten

Rowan Rodgers glanced at his watch: four-thirty. He'd be away in another half-hour. He'd ring Rachel again and ask her if she would have dinner with him. He felt guilty that he had had to cancel the night before, but he had a strong impression that she was pleased that he'd broken their date. There had been a note of relief in her voice as she accepted his apology. He frowned at the memory. Don't say that she was slipping away from him again? Surely not; she'd been loving, passionate, pliant yet not placid in his arms. He thought that Rachel made love and responded to lovemaking with more abandon and lack of inhibition than any other woman that he'd known, with an added deep tenderness that left a lasting memory.

He got up from the desk, still piled high with files for his attention, and walked to the window. He stared out of the dusty panes, unaware of the busy station yard below.

He couldn't lose Rachel. That year when she had run off to Europe, after her husband had died, had been one of unendurable loneliness. All right, so he hadn't lived like a monk, but no one else set him on fire, brought him so alive, meant so much, as Rachel did, as she did by not even touching him — by just being there. He thought that she had really come back to him after her return from Europe, she'd even agreed to marry him. He frowned again. This change in her was very recent – he could practically pinpoint it. He swung away from the window and picked up the receiver of one of the many telephones on his desk. The ringing at the other end went on and on, then the receiver was lifted, but instead of Rachel's soft breathless voice, he heard: "Mistress Groome residence," with a rise on the final syllable.

"Ruel. Superintendent Rodgers. Is Mrs Groome there?'

"No, sir. She leave again 'bout two hour ago. She say fe me to gi' a letter to you that she leave, if she don' reach back firs'."

Rodgers extracted the sense from this and said, "Right. I'll be along as soon as I can."

He replaced the receiver, puzzled at this new angle. Leave a letter? When she was certain of seeing him later? Where in God's name had she gone that she didn't know when she'd be back? He scowled at the pile of files. To hell with them — he'd never be able to concentrate. He'd get in early the next morning and polish them off.

As he picked up his pipe an tobacco pouch, there was a tap on the door and Phillips entered. "Something come up, sir. I think you'd like to know." Phillips' manner was solemn, with a diffidence of speech, a hesitancy that was alien to his normal mien.

"What is it?" Rodgers tried to curb the sharpness of his voice. He knew that Phillips wouldn't bother him with trivialities. "Sorry, man. I'm a bit on edge. What's the problem?"

"Well, sir. About that girl found dead in the apartment. Before we get the autopsy report that she die from natural causes, I tell the helper that if she saw the little car there again — the brownish one — to let me know. And to take the licence number." Phillips paused, his expression one of dogged reluctance. He kept his eyes averted from his chief's probing black ones.

"Well?" Rodgers prompted.

"Well, sir. The helper phone about three-forty an' say that the car was there. I go down but by the time I reach, the car gone. I look in the room she say the lady go to, the same room where we find the dead girl. It look like there was a struggle — and I find *this* on the floor." He held out his hand. On it was a small .22 calibre automatic.

Rodgers' lip tightened. "And the number of the car and the driver's name, if you've traced it yet."

Phillips swallowed. "Number 177 JP. Driver's name turned out to be — Rachel Groome."

The silence hung between them, growing thicker and deeper, almost palpable as the seconds went by.

"You say that the girl phoned you at about three-forty. Why didn't you come to me sooner?"

"Mr Rodgers, when I found out who the owner was, I didn't know what to do. If it hadn't been for the gun — I wouldn't have said a thing, sir."

Phillips paused, then went on, "She must have know about the dead girl. The helper say that is the same room she go into the... first time..."

"How did the helper know that?"

"She say she inquisitive-like. She say Mrs Groome not... not the usual kind of person to ..." he trailed off. "Yet Mrs Groome say nothing 'bout the girl. Why she go back with a gun?"

"We don't know that it is her gun," Rodgers said, although he knew that Rachel possessed one identical to it.

"Sorry, sir, but we do. I checked the records."

"Look, Phillips, there must be a good explanation for all this. Mrs Groome isn't the sort of person to ..." He broke off.

Phillips looked at him with compassion. After all his years in the police force, the chief could still say "not that sort of person." Hadn't he learnt yet that no one ever really knows another person — that anyone is capable of behaving quite differently from the front which they present to the world? Lord, but he himself found it hard to believe of that Mrs Groome. One hell of a woman.

"Sorry, sir," he said aloud. "Sorry that it happen and sorry that I have to tell you."

"Well, I'm going to find out more. There must be a reasonable explanation. She doesn't normally carry a gun. So why take it with her this time?"

"She must have felt she needed protection, sir ."

"Protection from whom? That's the big question."

"Right, sir. And — Mr Rodgers?"

"Yes?"

"If there any little thing I can do, call me nuh, sir?"

"Thanks, Phillips. You're a good chap. I'll do just that."

Then he was gone, long legs striding through the crowded station room and into the waiting Mercedes. There was a deep-throated roar, a scream of tortured tyres, the revving of up-changing gears, a swift acceleration as the car gained the main road, then the sound was lost in the general sound of road traffic.

Rodgers was caught in the heavy press of uptown home-going traffic. The offices and shops of downtown Kingston had discharged their hordes of workers, and cars stretched bumper to bumper from Torrington Bridge to Cross Roads, where police constable Bowen was on point duty. Another power cut; Rodgers gave an inward groan. The traffic lights were dead. The young policeman who stood where a number of roads converged, white gauntlets flashing balletically, was discovering the hard way that to keep traffic moving smoothly in a number of directions, which had seemed so easy and logical in theory in the classroom at the Police Academy or in simulated conditions, was in practice at four forty-five on a hot afternoon, a waking nightmare; theory and logic went by the board. All that it needed to produce a God-awful snarl-up was for one damn-fool driver to do the wrong thing and then stall. PC Bowen's round, dark face under the peaked cap was streaming with perspiration, but outwardly he was unruffled and showed no sign of his inner feelings. He'd just got the streams moving when a grey Mercedes 230 SL swept round the traffic island too fast, tyres screeching. PC Bowen made a mental note of the number. He was about to commit it away for future reference when he realised that the driver was the redoubtable Superintendent Rowan Rodgers. His disapproval changed to admiration. The Super drive one nice car, man, and *bwoy*, 'im can *drive!* His directional movements became more balletic, achieving a precision and grace even more to be admired.

The bronze Metro was parked demurely in the driveway as Rodgers slid to a halt behind it. He slammed the door of the Mercedes and strode into the house, his worry spilling over into rising anger. The house was strangely silent.

"Rachel!" he called, his tone harsh, concealing his concern.

There was a scurry of movement from the kitchen and Ruel appeared, trim in short-sleeved, green khaki shirt and pants, peaked green cap and his identity card on his left breast, ready for his evening security stint. He had a whistle on a cord round his neck and a heavy truncheon swung from a thong round his wrist.

"Evenin', sir. Miss Rachel don't reach yet."

"Not back? But her car is there."

"Yes, sir. Me did 'ear it come in, sir. Me wait but me don' 'ear Miss Rachel, so me go an' look, sir. Me fin' this on the car seat."

He held out a square white envelope. It was a good quality paper, the kind used for official invitations. It was addressed to: Superintendent Rowan Rodgers. Across the bottom left-hand corner was written archaically, ironically: *By kind favour.* Rodgers examined it for a long moment. This was not Rachel's handwriting. His anger was fast twisting into a knot of apprehension, fear of the unknown.

He glanced up from the white envelope to the watching Ruel. "You say that Mrs Groome left a letter for me?"

"Yes, sir." Ruel scurried away, and Rodgers stood immobile, the square envelope unopened in his big, dark, well-shaped hand. He took the envelope that Ruel held out to him, meticulous as always, resting on a tray.

"Let's take these in order," he murmured. Rachel's letter first — she had left it at about two to two ten. This other came about two hours later — give or take a quarter hour on each and assuming that the Metro came here soon after the woman phoned Phillips.

He became aware of Ruel asking, "Would you like something to drink, Mr Rodgers?"

Rodgers hesitated. A Red Stripe would be fine, but he felt that he might need more of a short hard drink to cushion what he might find in the two letters. Finally he said, "Thanks. A double light rum — on the rocks."

He sat down and opened Rachel's letter. First there was a long list of names, about thirty-five to forty, in Rachel's unmistakable sprawling handwriting. Eight or so had crosses beside them. Then there was a note she had scrawled in seeming haste:

Darling, forgive me — I should have told you, but it's not mine to tell. This list is copied from a notebook that I found in the handbag of that dead girl, Therese. She worked at the Looking Glass — where I get my hair done. I know for certain that some of the names listed are, or were, clients at the Looking Glass. It may be a useful lead. Will explain later.

Love, Rachel.

Rodgers ran his eye swiftly down the list, excitement rising within him. Rachel's "it may be a useful lead" was the understatement of the year. The names of the women marked by a cross were the names of a number of the suicide victims — and up to the minute, he thought grimly; even Annabel Smith-Watson's had a cross against it. This could be the lead that they wanted. If only the other women listed could be made to talk. The excitement of the discovery had made him forget for a moment the other letter. He folded Rachel's note and placed it very carefully inside his wallet. Then he slit open the square white envelope, handling it delicately, as little as possible.

The shock of its contents left him at first incapable of movement or of reasoned thought. He read it again; shock turned to nausea then to anger. It read:

>Dear Mr Rodgers,
>Your interest in certain cases of suicides has come to my attention. It would be against my interests for you to probe any deeper. May I suggest that you persuade your superiors to withdraw you and your colleagues from the investigation? I am holding Rachel Groome as insurance that you do this. If you do not comply — well, one more 'suicide' won't be too remarkable, will it? This is not an idle threat. Unless I read in tomorrow's paper that Supt. Rodgers has gone on sick leave and all his cases are suspended, an unfortunate accident will have to take place. If I do read this, then Ms Groome will be returned. Do not think though, that once she is back with you, you can return to the case — you cannot guard her for twenty-four hours a day. Forgive me if I leave this unsigned.

After the first shock, his mind settled to a cold, clinical appraisal of the problem. He thrust all thought of Rachel to the back of his conscious mind. He knew that if he once began to dwell on her present situation and the possibility of harm to her, his judgement and his ability to plan quickly and correctly would be warped. He felt that she was safe until the notice appeared in the press. There was no point at this stage in dusting the Metro for prints — he might be under observation. He must go straight back to the station, get hold of the Assistant Commissioner and do what the kidnapper demanded — resign from the case and persuade the top brass to drop it. He took out Rachel's note again — yes, there was the lead all right. But they couldn't use it now.

Chapter 11

It took some time to persuade the Assistant Commissioner. Alston Willerton was not noted for a vivid imagination — but eventually he agreed.

"All right, Rodgers, do it your way — but God help you if you play it wrong." He reached for the telephone. "I'll get on to the editor of *The Daily Gleaner* and get that item in." He paused, his dark eyes hard, but the creases about his mouth had deepened. "And ... good luck, Rodgers, man."

"Thank you, sir, I feel I'm going to need it."

Rodgers returned quickly to his own room and summoned Phillips and Goodbody on the way. He briefed them briskly, unemotionally. Even Phillips' stoical calm left him at the news. "Lord, Mr Rodgers. If they hurt Mrs Groome..." He trailed off. What could they do? The enemy was faceless, formless and which of those left alive on the list of probable victims would furnish the pertinent details?

Goodbody's face, still round, youthful, lines unblotted, took on an expression of unbelief and bewilderment.

"We get nothing from the other interviews, sir," Phillips said. "Just a feeling that some of the husbands are suspicious, but won't say."

"Yes," Rodgers said heavily. "You can understand it. And now we've got this." He flipped Rachel's list. "These people might have been encouraged to talk — even a few lives might have been saved." He sat thinking, worrying at the problem. Then he looked up. "The two of you — and Pearson — are off the case as of now." There was a peculiar intensity in his voice that brought an understanding gleam to Phillips' eye, but Goodbody, forgetting the deference due to rank, exclaimed, "But, sir, you can't do that, sir. You goin' to let them get away with it?"

"Mrs Groome's life is at stake, remember?"

"And you not goin' to look for her, sir?"

"And where would we look? She may be anywhere in the island. We have to do what has to be done, not go dashing off on any misguided rescue mission."

The boy fell silent, except for a muttered, "Yes, sir. Sorry, sir.'

Phillips glanced at him. "Not to worry, son. Just let it be known — all around, as many people as possible — but casual, not to overdo it — that you're off the case, right?"

Goodbody's eyes suddenly sparkled in quick understanding at Phillips' tone and meaningful look. "Yes, *sir*. Yes, Mr Phillips." He saluted with a snap of military precision and left the office.

Phillips grinned. "That country bwoy, him have plenty brain."

"Now listen, Phillips, there's not much time. I want you to get hold of Police Constable Browning. Stat."

Phillips, startled out of his usual calm twice in an hour, repeated, "Police Constable *Browning*, sir?"

Rodgers grinned. "Exactly, Phillips. PC Browning."

Phillips suddenly laughed, an unexpected sound. "Of course, sir. Right away." He left the office, still with a broad grin creasing his rather heavy face, white teeth gleaming against dark skin.

While Rodgers waited he allowed himself to think of Rachel. He hoped to high heaven that he was doing the right thing. He pulled out his pipe and tamped down tobacco with strong brown fingers, viciously. There was a slight tap at the door, then it was thrown wide open and Phillips, using one of his dramatic gestures, announced, "Police Constable Browning reporting, sir."

Rodgers rose and smiled. "Good. Sit down, both of you." He began to speak rapidly.

* * *

Rachel had been put in a vast barn-like place, which seemed at first glance to be an unused garage. The scarf had been taken from her eyes and the adhesive tape stripped painfully from her mouth. It was too dark to see her captor's face, he was just a darker blur in the pervading darkness. Then he spoke. Was it, she asked herself, the same voice as the one on the telephone? She had thought so at first, at that moment of capture, but now she couldn't be sure: it was soft but without that repulsive caressing quality, although there was still a tantalising familiarity about it. "Don't bother to scream — no one will hear you. And don't try to get away — you won't succeed."

Soft footfalls receded, a door creaked heavily, she saw a wide opening as a broad garage door swung outwards to reveal a glimpse of the pale blue of the early evening sky close-packed trees and a rough road. Then darkness took over as the door was pushed shut. She heard the sound of a heavy bar dropping into place, the sound of metal on metal as a padlock was engaged, footsteps growing fainter, dislodging stones — then the silent gloom wrapped around her like a warm blanket.

Gradually her eyes became accustomed to the lack of light and she could make out the details of her prison. It was an old — very old – garage. Originally, she thought, a coach house. A rotting saddle hung on one wall, tarnished stirrups were in a heap below. The heavy rafters of the roof were steeply angled, rising in the middle to an even blacker density. She heard the slither and scrape of claws above her and shuddered at what that implied. The walls were solid red brick, laid by craftsmen a century or more ago. The floor was more recent, roughly poured concrete, with a deep pit in the centre overlaid by rotting planks — once used, she supposed, for home service to cars. Now its depths housed unseen horrors. Her mind shied away from the obscenity of drummer cockroaches — they would revel in the dark, moist filth that would have accumulated over the years. The place was now obviously used to store junk. There were sheets of zinc roofing, lengths of timber, a pile of chipped floor tiles. She looked around her in dismay. There was no way out, even if she could manage to free her hands. There were no windows and the doors were of solid mahogany — the width of the boards proclaimed their age.

She glanced around again. No windows — so where was that faint light coming from? It seemed to be filtering from behind a pile of splitting cement bags in the far corner. She walked carefully across the uneven surface knowing that if she tripped her bound hands would be of no use in breaking her fall. She peered behind the bags, the musty, dusty smell made her want to sneeze – she felt the back of her throat go dry and hoped that she wouldn't get an attack of hay fever. The faint light was coming from behind the sacks; it seemed as if some of the brickwork had collapsed.

If only she could get her hands free. She had passed through the gamut of emotions, from fear to despair, finally to anger and a cold determination. Now she was in command of her emotions and only allowed determination to have full rein. But first, she *had* to get her hands free — she looked around once more: the lengths of zinc roofing, would the edges be sharp enough? Or a jagged tile from the heap? Not firm enough, unless she could find one jammed tight.

She decided to try the zinc first.

It was slow and painful. She had to stand with her back close against the rough metal, rubbing at the tape that bound her wrists, up and down, up and down. The constriction of her hands behind her back and the repeated unnatural movements tortured the muscles in her upper arms. In her haste she lost caution and jabbed on the flesh above the tape. A fierce pain shot up her arm, then she felt the warm stickiness of blood. She seemed to be making no impression on the strapping and bitter tears of pain and frustration coursed down her face.

She had to rest — she had no idea how long she had been trying to free her hands, and no idea of how long she had been imprisoned. Night must have fallen, for the weak filter of light had gone. It was now quite dark, a thickening, engulfing darkness that pressed in on her. She felt claustrophobic fear — she tried to fight it, but it swept over her, swamping her reason and making it difficult to breathe. She heard again the scrape of claws above — the scampering of little feet. She looked up at the rafters and gasped aloud in horror — two red pinpoints of light glimmered at her for a long moment, then disappeared with an intensified scampering.

Rats!

She had always been terrified of rats and utter darkness, now here she was, helpless in the face of both.

She shut her eyes and thought of Rowan, trying to draw strength and reason from the memory — but it was small comfort, knowing how she had deceived him, the evasions to which she had resorted these last few days.

The ache in her arms was becoming less now and she concentrated all her willpower on trying to relax her muscles, in readiness for a second onslaught on the tape around her wrists. Then she heard a sound from outside the heavy doors the click of metal on metal. Then, a pause, a slight rattle, subdued voices. She moved from the piled zinc sheets, as quickly and as silently as possible edged to the opposite wall, and leant weakly against it.

The door swung creakingly open. The beam of a torch raked the darkness and found her. Light footsteps came towards her and she felt a stab of dismay as she recognised Stillman. He played the beam of the torch over her face then insolently down her body. He held a tray in his free hand, then bent and placed it on the floor.

"If I had my way, you'd starve. But — orders."

"How can I eat with my hands tied?" Her voice was barely a whisper.

He came right up to her and put his arm round her waist, then he dropped the torch and pulled her close. "Sweetheart, I've got news for you, I'm going to untie them, but don't get any fancy ideas about getting out of here — believe me, you can't."

She was silent, hope beginning to well, despite the pressure of his arms about her.

"But before I do…" He bent his head and kissed her, a savage brutal kiss, forcing his tongue hard into her mouth. She was quite helpless, hoping that her disgust and anger wouldn't tempt her to kick him again — she dreaded what he might do in retaliation.

He drew his mouth away. He was panting as he muttered, "You won't be so cold when I finish with you. That was just the beginning. When you eat you may be a bit more loving."

She made no response and he took one hand from holding her and slapped her.

"You feisty, high-colour bitch. Me not good enough for you, right? You don't want it with a black man?" He spat out a string of obscenities and she shut her eyes. I mustn't antagonise him any more, she thought desperately, I must find the right approach. She opened her eyes and said softly, "It's not that. You … you took me by surprise…"

He was silenced by her tone, then bent and picked up the torch and flashed it in her face. She half-smiled and dropped her eyes, then looked up from under her lashes and said, "There … there was no need to hit me." The slight emphasis brought him close again. He held her throat then ran his hand down over her breasts, lingering on their full tautness. She willed herself not to shudder or lose the half-smile on her face. Then he put the torch down again and pulled her tightly against his body. Oh God, she thought, I've overdone it.

There was a call from outside. "Come on, nuh, Stillman man. Me want my supper too, you know."

Stillman relaxed his hold a little.

"My hands?" Rachel breathed against his mouth.

He kissed her again, then with his mouth still on hers, he took a switchblade knife from his pocket, flicked it open and slashed through the tape and ripped it from her wrists. She was glad of the darkness; he couldn't se how she had been trying to get free, and the blood that must be on the bonds and on her arm. She winced as the jagged cut above the strapping was stretched. He tossed the sticky bundle into the darkness of the garage. His earlier anger had gone and he seemed reluctant to leave. His hands ran down over her buttocks, and lingered on her thighs, then slowly up the front of her body until they cupped her breasts again. Her shudder of revulsion he mistook for one of ecstasy. "You like it, eh? I'll be back in about an hour," he muttered. "And then — I show you what you been missing."

"Stillman," a dark silhouette appeared in the doorway. "Come on, man."

Stillman released his hold and crossed quickly to the doorway to be greeted with a hoarse, "What you ah fool with her for? You don't know she ah de woman o' one high-up police?"

"Police? Cho — she going to give me a piece before she go."

The door slammed shut, cutting off the rest of the conversation. Rachel took a deep breath of weak relief, then asked herself, before I go *where*? I've got to get out. She gently rubbed her sore wrists, then picked up the torch which Stillman had forgotten in his amorous overtures and went to investigate the gap in the wall.

The bags of cement must have been there for a long time. They were cracked and broken in many places; the cement had spilled out and had become caked in the humid atmosphere. The gap between the bags and the broken wall was not big enough for her to squeeze through. She thought that if she could manage to pull out a few of the bags she might be able to make it, but it was no good. The bags were dead weight, jammed together, immovable. She broke her nails and tore her hands in an unrewarding effort. Now her confidence that she could make good her escape was shaken. Her fear of not being able to get out before Stillman returned was increased by the man's avowed intentions.

Perhaps she could use one of the lengths of zinc roofing as a lever — but that too, was a short-lived hope — the sheets of zinc were too long and unwieldy for her to move. There was one last resort: she climbed carefully up the pile of bags and inched across the top of them. The gap was wider there. She flashed the beam of the torch downwards and realised with sick dismay and disappointment that the opening in the bricks was still far too small for her to squeeze through.

Against her will, tears filled her eyes. She flashed the light on her wristwatch: ten-fifteen. Stillman would be back soon; she felt sick at the thought.

She became aware of the sudden patter of rain on the roof, quickly increasing to a bullet-like staccato. She wondered dully whether the rain would act as a deterrent to the amorous Stillman or only serve to increase his ardour. She gazed once more at the inviting and useless gap in the wall, then slid down into the confined space. As she fell, she felt something give under the impact of her body; she couldn't believe it at first, then she managed to lift her foot and push hard against the wall.

With a clatter and a cloud of dust, a dozen more bricks fell out. She was thankful now for the heavy rain, for it deadened any sound that she might make. She slid still further, braced her back against the stacked cement bags and squeezed her body, feet first, through the opening.

Chapter 12

Having thoroughly briefed Police Constable Browning, Rowan Rodgers went to the Finger-print Department and collected a few necessary materials. Under the cover of darkness, he was going to do a rough check for prints on Rachel's car. It was a long shot; the man would probably have wiped the steering wheel and gear lever, but there was the chance that an odd print might have escaped his attention.

It was well after six p.m. when he got back to Rachel's silent house. He was met by a worried Ruel who informed him unnecessarily: "Miss Rachel don't reach yet," and a lonely and furious Siamese kitten. She hurled herself at Rodgers' ankles and wrapped her paws round one of them, back paws scrabbling, uttering little growls deep in her throat. He stooped, picked her up and tossed her onto his shoulder. Her mood changed immediately; she began to purr loudly, blue eyes slit in ecstasy, kneading his shoulder with needle-sharp claws.

Rodgers went into the kitchen. "Don't worry about Miss Rachel, Ruel. She'll be back — tomorrow morning." He spoke cheerfully, confidently, but hid feelings and convictions were far from confident.

"Yes, sir," Ruel said automatically, but his dark face wore an unusual expression of worry. The assault upon himself and Rachel's odd behaviour were much in his mind. Now this latest development, the return of her car by persons unknown.

"Got anything for Bamboo to eat?" Rodgers asked.

"She won't eat nothin', sir. Not while Miss Rachel not here," Ruel said gloomily, with a fine disregard for double negatives.

"Got any chicken?"

"Yes sir." Ruel opened the refrigerator and took out half of a roast chicken. Rodgers sliced off a piece of breast and cut it up under the cynical stare of Ruel and muttered, "She not goin' eat it. She too fenky-fenky."

Bamboo jumped down from Rodgers' shoulder and stretched full length up against the cupboard door, paws flexing. She gave a little exasperated yowl at his slowness, then darted away to where her bowl was to be placed. She kept up a running commentary as Rodgers tipped the cut-up chicken into the bowl. Then she shot a malevolent glare at Ruel, switched to limpid adoration for Rodgers, crouched down and began to eat as if she had been starved for weeks.

Rodgers shook his head, *"Women!"* He said emphatically.

"Yes, sir," Ruel responded in agreement. "True word."

The incident with the little cat had diverted Rodgers' mind momentarily from Rachel. It had also served to calm him down. He went to the driveway, where the Metro still stood and dusted it carefully for prints. The steering wheel had been wiped clean, as he had expected, and also the gear lever. The switch-key was too superimposed with prints to be of any use. There was a smudged one at the edge of the rear-view mirror, but it was on the window frame of the driver's door that he struck pay-dirt: four finger marks on the duco outside and a thumb mark on the inside, where someone had held the door to pull it shut. They could, of course, belong to Rachel, but he didn't think so, the prints were too widely spaced. He went back to the kitchen. "Ruel, when last you clean up the car?"

"This mornin', sir. Me clean it up an' polish it, sir."

"Right. You know how Miss Rachel shut the car door, when she inside the car?"

The young man looked puzzled for a moment, then he flashed a bright smile, the new white dentures prominent. "She don' slam it, she pull it sof'-like from inside."

"That's what I wanted to know."

Rodgers finished photographing the prints then called Ruel again. He gave him the roll of film, carefully wrapped in polythene. "Listen, Ruel. I want you to take this package to the corner of Hope and Trafalgar; wait at the traffic lights on the left, going down. A white Toyota will stop, with two plainclothes policemen. They will ask you your name and say 'Rodgers'. Give them this, if possible, without anyone seeing you do it. If you are seen and anybody asks questions, deny giving the men anything." He noted Ruel's look of incomprehension and rephrased the last sentence.

"Say you ask where is the bus stop. And don't call my name. Understand?"

Ruel's face had taken on an awed look during Rodgers' instructions. He nodded solemnly. Rodgers went through all that he had said again, then made the man repeat aloud his instructions. Finally, he said, "This is important, you hear, Ruel? Miss Rachel is in trouble — you're helping her by doing this."

Ruel nodded again, then went to change from his security clothes to his usual off-duty high fashion gear: tight pale blue jeans, purple T-shirt with a prominent designer logo, topped by a black and red cap featuring the name of his favourite American baseball team. Rodgers had telephoned instructions to the nearest station about the handing over of the film. He turned as Ruel presented himself and almost did a double-take at the metamorphosis but managed to preserve his gravity. "Right, man," he said. "Remember, it's up to you now to help Miss Rachel."

Ruel left the house feeling as if every crook and gunman in the Corporate Area was after him. The knowledge that the famous Superintendent Rodgers had enlisted his help made him swell with importance. It had been impressed on him that he must act naturally, not to draw attention to himself. He tried to remember what he did do when acting normally on an off-duty evening. He hooked his thumbs into the tight, low waistline of his jeans and swung along the quiet road, softly whistling his favourite dancehall tune through his teeth. He reached the main road and walked on until he came to a bus shelter. He waited, still whistling softly, wondering what the super meant when he said that Miss Rachel was in trouble. His uncomplicated mind worried over this. He was fond — in a way — of his employer. She was kind and considerate, paid good wages, allowed plenty of time off and the relationship between them was good. Not that the barrier of the haves and the have-nots was cancelled out completely, nor that of the employer and the employed. The long shadow of slavery still hung over the land, though fiercely repudiated by many, and that last shadow was taking a long time to disperse in the light of independence and nationhood. The country's woes and rising unemployment had a lot to do with that lingering shadow. Ruel, like most of his contemporaries, didn't understand this enough to be articulate on the matter: people like him plodded along, doing what work they knew — and could get — in the belief that the ambiguous promises made by the politicians would one day suddenly open up a new world of plenty.

The lights of an approaching bus came into view. It lumbered to a halt by the kerb, its brakes spitting, and the doors slid open with a hiss. Ruel climbed aboard and tendered his fare to the 'ductor. He took a seat at the rear — the bus was about half full — so far, so good. He swung off at the next stage and waited for another bus. This time it was a minibus, packed to capacity, but from experience Ruel knew that there was always room for just one more. He squeezed in and stood wedged between a fat lady and a thin Rasta with locks. He got off at the next stage and walked the rest of the way to the traffic lights. He leant carelessly against the wall of an apartment building and watched the passing cars. It was just before the dinner hour. Car after car passed, some opulent, others ancient and beat-up —taxis, vans, limos, some with a solitary driver, others packed with more than the licence allowed. Ruel watched them all, detached, as if it were the unreeling of a film. This was a different facet of the island, not his world. His world was in two distinct compartments: the cool, quiet, ordered life in Rachel Groome's household, and the off-duty life in teeming Passmore Town, out by Windward Road — the crowded yards overrun with near-naked children, the filth and squalor, the gaiety in the face of poverty. All this was more real than these unknown smooth faces that passed so quickly in automobiles.

The lights changed to red and a white Toyota drew up with two men in the front. Ruel stepped forward, the hand holding the concealed film resting on the edge of the door. The man nearest him asked briefly, "What's your name, son? Rodgers?"

"Ruel, sir."

"Right, give." A hand came up under the open window, Ruel dropped the film spool into it and drew back.

"Thank you, sir, jus' a chain you say," he said for the benefit of any eavesdroppers. The fact that the nearest person was a good twenty feet away was no deterrent to his playing out the drama. The lights changed to green, the Toyota shot forward, gathered speed and disappeared into the night.

Ruel stood there a moment, deflated at the tame ending to his adventure. He didn't have enough imagination to visualise all the possible actions that *might* have occurred, but had enough to be sorry that *nothing* had occurred. He made his way back to the house, his earlier feelings of high adventure swamped by anticlimax.

Rodgers was waiting for him. "All right?"

"Yes, sir."

"Good lad. Not a word of this to anyone, understand?"

"Yes, sir."

Rodgers drove slowly up to his small two-bedroom house. The lights of Newcastle were obscured by heavy clouds and there was the smell of rain in the air. If only it would rain, he thought. The drought had gone on month after month, the worst in living memory. Once carefully tended gardens were arid and one quickly knew those home owners who ignored the water restrictions. Rose plants had died, nothing remaining of their delicate glory but brown withered sticks. Even the hardy, sun-loving coconut palms were dying. Their curved feathered fronds first turned brown, then drooped and angled to ungainly shapes, then finally dropped with a rustling crash and a shower of dry nuts. Rodgers sighed; food prices would soar after this, he thought gloomily. They had spiralled already almost out of sight.

He was deliberately thinking of other matters to keep his thoughts from Rachel. Although he didn't really fear for her life, he feared for her safety. He now had a pretty good idea how she had got herself into this mess: the name of Eleanore Tarrant was included in the list that she had left for him, with Margaret Cameron's in brackets and it was Margaret Cameron who had asked Rachel to go up and see her. What fools these women are, he thought with a burst of anger as he swung the Mercedes into his driveway and brought it to a screaming stop.

He ate a solitary, unwanted supper, served by a silent Maisie, He tried to read later but Rachel's face kept floating between his eyes and the print. The fact that he was powerless to help her, that the long night and part of the next day must pass before he could be sure of her safety, was becoming unbearable.

The smell of rain was stronger now and suddenly it broke, lashing down out of the night. The drumming on the galvanized zinc roof was the most pleasant sound that he had heard for months. He went round the house and closed the windows and brought in the verandah furniture, glad of something to occupy even a few of the dragging minutes. He went to the kitchen and took a Red Stripe from the refrigerator, but before he could uncap the bottle he heard the sound of the telephone ringing over the pounding rain.

"Rodgers here."

"Mr Rodgers?" It was a man's voice, he thought, although it had a feminine quality that didn't preclude a deep-voiced woman, a quality which he immediately took exception to, by the two words spoken.

"Yes?" he prompted sharply.

"Mr Rodgers, you got my note? Did you do what I asked?"

Rodgers took a quick inward breath, his hand tightened on the receiver.

"You dirty swine, what have you done with Mrs Groome?"

"Losing your temper and using abusive language will not help the situation. Just answer my question. Have you given up the case?"

Rodgers thought swiftly, why was the man checking up now when he would read it in the papers tomorrow? What had he got to gain or lose by lying to the man?

"Yes," he said. "You will see an announcement to that effect in tomorrow's *Daily Gleaner*. Now tell me..."

He wasn't allowed to complete the sentence. The line had gone dead.

Chapter 13

The rain lashed Rachel as she staggered away from the broken wall. She was drenched to the skin instantly. Now that she was free of the prison she had no idea how she could use that freedom. She hadn't the slightest idea of where she was or in which direction she should go. She knew that the obvious course was to make her way steadily downhill; sooner or later she would come upon a road of sorts. On the upward journey they had climbed fairly steeply and then had turned off onto a rough, unpaved road. The hill roads out of St Andrew were well-defined and well-used. Once the car had reached the secondary road they hadn't gone all that deeply into the hinterland.

The driving rain and her sore wrists added immeasurably to her discomfort; she was incapable of clear, reasoned thought. One thing was dominant though, and that was that she had to get as far away from the garage as possible before they discovered her escape and came in pursuit. But if she made her way down the driveway she would, in all probability, be seen. In this kind of weather? she asked herself scornfully. The night was as black as pitch.

Was the main house up the hill or further down?

Was there in fact, a main house? The garage was very old and unused. The main house could have fallen into disrepair and she might have been put there only for the sake of convenience, temporarily. But Stillman and the other man must be in some sort of building — one of them had said that supper was waiting. She began to make her way round to the back of the garage and tried to peer through the blinding rain.

There *was* a building, higher up, a darker mass in the black night, with a flicker of light that was blurred by the rain. So that meant that she could go down the driveway. She wouldn't have to risk passing Stillman and company. The danger was if they discovered her escape before she got far enough ahead. It was imperative that she put enough distance between herself and them, and find some sign of human life — and help — as quickly as possible.

Underfoot, the driveway was covered with sharp marl chips, interspersed with unexpected potholes. Rachel contemplated taking off her high-heeled shoes, shoes which were not made with that terrain in mind. But the alternative was far worse. In no time, in the dark, and barefoot, she could easily cut her feet to shreds — she decided to hobble along in her unsuitable footwear. Wryly she cursed in her mind the dictates of fashion which demanded that the well-dressed woman should wear high heels.

She tried to ease the pain in her feet by walking along the grass, but immediately gave up the idea when she stumbled against a small shrub and fell headlong. In any case, she realised that on the grass she had no idea of which way she should be heading; at least the driveway was a path to follow. Reluctantly, she stuck to the rough stones, but kept to the side of the driveway. She repeatedly looked back towards the dark form of the building to see if there was any sign of activity which would signal that her escape had been discovered, but her luck held.

Suddenly, she realised that the driveway had come to its end. She took a few steps forward gingerly and tottered precariously onto a public road. It was obviously a secondary road, still unpaved and deeply rutted but happily, less trying to her feet. She turned to the right, which led downwards, and, still keeping close to the bank, she stumbled on.

Water was streaming from her hair and her plastered clothes in a series of rivulets, her shoes were sodden to pulp, squelching at each painful step. The night took on the quality of a waking nightmare: it seemed as if she had always been fighting through the wet darkness and that she was destined to continue to do so endlessly.

She passed through a little district: two or three small one-room houses, the inevitable shop that did double duty as a bar and meeting place for the men and youths. All were close shuttered against the blinding rain. A kerosene lamp glowed faintly, but she didn't stop; the delay might be fatal. There would be no chance of a telephone there and the lengthy explanations which she would be called upon to make in order to send for help might well result in her former wardens catching up with her.

She was moving automatically now, the pain in her lacerated

wrists, the throb of her feet, the heaviness of the lashing rain, all seemed outside reality: it was just an automatic continual forward movement, fast, faster: no matter that breath was coming in ragged gasps, that pain and rain enfolded her, just on and on and on...

She could see a street light ahead and realised with utter relief that she was approaching the main Red Hills Road. It must be; she had passed the spot hundreds of times. So, she had been held captive off the Swain Spring Road — not that the knowledge was of much use. She would never be able to identify the place — except the garage and even that would look different in daylight.

She hurried now, spirits lightening as she recognised a landmark: the street light stood at the entrance to a town house complex. It had a white cut-stone wall and cut-stone columns at the entrance to the roadway. She'd driven round it a few weeks earlier and had thought what attractive houses they were, in a glorious setting. And...there had been a phone box. Where? To the left? Yes, there it was to the left, by a bus stop.

She pushed open the folding door, and then bitter disappointment flooded through her — she realised that vandals had been at work; loose wires greeted her. She left the shelter of the box and shivered. It seemed as if she were near a ghost town; the houses, not yet occupied, were shuttered and dark. How different they had seemed in the warm light of day. She once more battled downhill, the water now swirling about her ankles. She had wasted precious minutes, all to no avail.

Headlights from behind threw her shadow far ahead, waving and weaving on the shining wet surface. A sob of fear choked her and she began to run. One of her shoes twisted under her and she was flung into the middle of the road. She heard the shriek of brakes above the sound of the rain and then nothing — nothing at all.

* * *

Rodgers put down the receiver slowly: he hoped to God that he'd done the right thing in admitting that he had severed all connection with the case. If only he could fathom the motive that lay behind the call, and, he thought ironically, if only we had the means to trace it. That was something that was accomplished so easily in detective fiction. "Just let anyone try doing it here," he said aloud. He glanced at his watch: eleven-ten p.m. *Why* had that joker phoned him at this hour?

He went heavily back to the kitchen; the beer had warmed up, but he drank it anyway, hardly aware of what he was doing. The rain was still cascading off the roof in a solid sheet of water. He peered out into the wet night and thought: if this keeps up we'll have roads blocked by landslips and the usual snarl-up of traffic.

He hoped that it wouldn't keep on at this rate. The earth was so dry and cracked, it needed a soft continuous soaking to do any good, not this torrent, which would not be absorbed in the solid crust. His mind drifted to the backlash of the hurricane a year before, when it had rained solidly for days. Great chunks of road, fifteen feet deep, and as many wide, were gouged out, leaving huge fissures, and there had been massive flooding throughout the island...

He dragged himself from the window, knowing that once again he was forcing his mind to other matters so that his thoughts wouldn't dwell on Rachel. He swore that when he got her back — he refused to even think 'if' — he wouldn't let her out of his sight, day or night.

He went round the house, snapping off lights, then went resolutely to bed. Surprisingly, he fell asleep.

The persistent ring of the phone woke him. He snapped on the light and automatically glanced at his watch as he lifted the receiver: two-thirty-three a. m.

"Rodgers here." His voice was slurred by sleep, but he was thinking, If it's that damn joker again...

"Superintendent Rowan Rodgers?" At least this unmistakably masculine voice was not the same as the other.

"Yes, speaking."

"Sorry to disturb you at this hour, but we have a lady here who asked us to telephone you..."

"A lady?" He was wide awake now, voice crisp.

"Yes, a Mrs Rachel Groome..."

"Thank God," he began, then suspicion flared — was this a hoax? Was this just another...? "Look here," his voice sounded too aggressive, even to his own ears, but the uncertainty was making him on edge. "Who are you and where are you?"

"Don't be alarmed, Mr Rodgers. We — my wife and I — found Mrs Groome on the Red Hills Road. We very nearly ran over her. She's very tired and soaked to the bone — but I think all right." The caller went on to give details of his name and address, then ended by saying, "Mrs Groome was most anxious that I should call you tonight, but..."

"I'll be right up," Rodgers interrupted.

The rain had stopped, but water was still dripping noisily off the roof. A few faint stars glimmered above and the night breeze from the mountains was cool and moist. The Mercedes' engine was cold from the heavy downpour, but started at the second attempt. The roads were deserted at that hour, but there was a lot of water on them, inches deep and often covering the entire width of the road. He drove quickly, despite the conditions, and passed the gas station at the foot of Red Hills, swung right and then left, climbing in a series of steeply banked curves. The surface was slippery with mud; loose crumbling earth had been washed down from the high banks. Rocks and large stones were frequent hazards and he had to curb his impatience and slow down.

He still wasn't convinced that this wasn't some sort of a trap — but why should 'they' want him? If he had refused to abandon the case, he could understand some adverse action being taken, but to stage at trap. Surely they would know that if anything happened to him — a senior superintendent of police — the whole of the force would be after them like a pack of wolves. Then he gave himself a mental shake — he should have contacted Phillips. But Rachel having been kidnapped, the early hour, the isolation of the night and the unexpected rain storm, all had combined to warp his judgement and fire his imagination.

He slowed down: turn sharp left, then keep left at the fork. We're the second house on the right, had been his instructions. A blaze of lights on the right announced the end of his journey and the Mercedes took the turn and the curving driveway with a scream of tyres. He was met at the foot of a flight of steps that led up to a wide verandah by a short, thickset man in his early fifties. His high, balding forehead gleamed darkly in the reflected light; his face was long, sensitive, at variance with his body. He wore a small, clipped moustache above a mouth which was thin to the point of non-existence. He was formally dressed in a dark grey, three-piece suit, a light grey shirt and a dark red bow tie. His voice was pleasant, deep and precise.

"Mr Rodgers? My name is Oxford — Merton Oxford."

"How do you do." Rodgers wondered briefly at the origin of the name. "It's very kind of you to go to all this trouble."

"Trouble? My dear sir, it was the least we could do. Come in, my wife is expecting you."

Well, Rodgers thought as he followed Merton Oxford up the steps, if this is a trap, from the suavity of mine host and the lush surroundings, they deserve to get away with it. All the same he felt some comfort from the hard pressure of the .48 in its snug shoulder holster.

Mrs Oxford met them in the big living room. She was plump, middle-aged. She had impossibly black hair, grossly over-styled. Her dress was too avant-garde for her figure. Her make-up had turned to orange streaks by over application in the first place, followed by too frequent repairs, but her small dark eyes were clouded by genuine concern, and her voice was charming despite her habit of over-enunciating every other word. She clasped Rodgers' big hand in both her small, plump, many beringed ones and exclaimed, "I'm so *glad* that you're here. We didn't know what to do — that poor child — well, hardly child, I suppose, but *so* sweet and so brave — *what* she has been *through*. I cannot bear to think..." She led him through an archway, up a short corridor to a partially closed door, still twittering, repeating herself, contradicting herself and over-emphasising profusely. He felt a sudden pity for Merton Oxford if he had to endure such a constant spate, then he thought it unlikely. It had probably been exacerbated by events — it wasn't every night that they almost ran over ladies in distress.

She opened the door fully. "He's here, dear," she said softly, then gave Rowan a look that could only be described as arch. "I'm *sure* that you'd like to see her *alone*," she said, then was gone.

Rachel was lying on the bed, wrapped in one of Mrs Oxford's fluffy housecoats. Her face had been washed, her hair dried, but nothing could hide the gash on her wrist, the red weals raised by the tight strapping on her face and arms, and her cut and bruised feet. He sat down on the bed and put his arms round her.

"Sweetheart, what happened? Do you feel well enough to tell me?" Then before she could reply, he went on, "No, not now. We can't keep these good people up any longer. I'll take you home and explanations can wait until tomorrow."

He picked her up and carried her out to the living room. The Oxfords protested that she could stay all night, that it was no bother, but Rowan said, gently insistent, "You've been more than kind. Perhaps tomorrow I could come back and thank you properly and collect Mrs Groome's clothes."

The Oxfords watched the Mercedes go slowly down the driveway, then Celia Oxford said in a voice from which all affectation had vanished, "It's all rather peculiar, Merton, isn't it? What do you think *really* happened?"

His eyes were neutral as he replied dryly, "I've no idea, my dear. But I am quite sure that you will find out."

Chapter 14
day 4, Thursday

The morning paper carried the story prominently that Superintendent Rowan Rodgers had relinquished his duties for a few weeks on medical advice.

Margaret Cameron read the item with a worried frown. What did this mean? Rachel hadn't mentioned that Rowan was sick. She said that he'd been put on the blackmail case — she drew in her breath sharply — that was it. Someone had got wind of it and...

"Eleanore," she said peremptorily.

Eleanore Tarrant came slowly onto the terrace. Her eyes had their usual pathetic droop, but she was singularly composed, the incessant movements stilled for once. "You wanted me, Margaret?"

Margaret handed her the paper without a word, her long index finger on the news item. She watched her friend's face as she read it, and noted the slight twitch of satisfaction about her mouth. She stood up, her habitual self-control at snapping point. "I was right. You had something to do with it. You plotted to get him taken off the case."

"You flatter me, Margaret. Do you believe that I have that amount of influence?"

"Influence, no. Information, yes. Somehow you let out the information that Rowan Rodgers was investigating..."

"What if I did? Do you want him to uncover — all the – the..." Eleanore paused, searching for the appropriate words, which Margaret supplied, curtly, coldly, anger under control again. "Slime and filth? Is that what you want to say?"

"Margaret, don't turn on your pious act. You've been instrumental in the concealment so far. The slime and filth as you call it, will spatter you as well — don't forget that."

"So I am to pay, am I, on and on and on? Have you ever

stopped to consider that my funds may be exhaustible? That one day I won't be able to pay — what then, what happens to us both then?" Eleanore kept silent, and Margaret went on passionately, "Haven't you begun to realise *yet* just *what* you've got us into?"

"And haven't you yet acknowledged the fact that if it wasn't for you and your outdated attitude to — inescapable truths — I would not have had to put myself — and you — in this position?"

She stood looking at Margaret calmly.

Margaret viewed her with sudden loathing. Her face went grey, the lines became more deeply etched. "You are more vile than I believed possible. And I tell you — I'm not going to be bled of all that I've worked for, for such useless *trash* like you."

* * *

Rachel Groome read the news item in bed, a breakfast tray across her lap. Her wrists and feet were bandaged. She'd been given a tetanus shot and ordered to rest. She looked up from the paper at Rowan, sitting opposite her in an armchair, blue smoke curling from his pipe.

"Rowan, I don't understand. Why are you giving up the case? You're not really sick are you?" Her eyes were wide and anxious.

He grinned. "The answer to our second question is: no. The answer to the first is: you."

"Me? But — I know they kidnapped me to force your hand — but now that I've got away... you mean, this was put in before I escaped?"

He nodded.

"Oh, darling, I'm so sorry. But you can't. I needn't have gone to all that trouble to get away," she said. Then remembering Stillman, she added, "Yes, I had to."

Rowan took the pipe out of his mouth, got up and crossed the room and sat down on the edge of the bed. "I think," he said slowly, "the time has come for you to tell me everything. This is not a time for loyalty. However admirable that quality might be, there are times when to give it unquestioningly can cause untold and often unnecessary trouble, as in this case in point."

"You seem to have guessed the reasons for my actions," she said.

He nodded. "After reading that list, I've got a pretty good

idea. Now, suppose you start at the beginning." He put his pipe down and put an arm round her.

It all came out: Margaret's telephoning her urgently; her request for Rachel to deliver a package; Rachel's dismay in learning the nature of the apartment and the grim discovery of the dead girl.

"Did you recognise her at once?'

"Yes, I'd seen her only that morning when I'd had my hair done."

He nodded.

"Oh, Rowan, it was awful. But how could I have reported the girl's death without revealing my own presence in such a ghastly place? My loyalty — displaced as you point out — to Margaret, seemed very important then. There was nothing that I could do to help the girl — she was quite dead."

"Why did you take the notebook?"

"I don't know — yes I do. I looked through her bag, wondering if she was indeed the person I was supposed to meet, for if she was, then she was connected with the blackmailers. The book had a list of names that convinced me that she was the person I was to meet, and not — not just the victim of a lover's quarrel."

"But you didn't know then about the blackmail racket? I told you that evening."

She was silent for a moment. "No," she admitted. "But I suppose that the suspicion of some such thing was gaining hold. For someone so level-headed as Margaret Cameron to act so out of character..."

"But," he interrupted. "The name actually listed is Eleanore Tarrant — Margaret Cameron's is in brackets."

"Obviously it's Margaret who is paying. Eleanore is a sort of — non-paying guest."

He looked at her levelly. "And hasn't that very fact given you cause to think?"

"You mean... a lesbian relationship? I think, at the back of my mind, I realised it but I didn't want to believe that of Margaret," she said firmly.

"But you could of Eleanore?"

"No... I... she's so fluffy and, oh, I don't know — odd."

"Exactly. Look, my love, it's not so easy for a woman to spot a lesbian as it is for her to spot a homo. If you stopped to think, your ideas about the sexual status of some of your — acquaintances — might change. Anyway, finish your story."

She continued how on the day after finding the dead girl, she'd gone back and accused Margaret of knowing what she was sending her into. "Without putting it into so many words, I practically accused her of causing the girl's death."

"And even now you suspect that the sprained ankle was a fake?"

"I may be mistaken, but when I got there the second time Margaret was in one place, the stick in another."

Then she told him of how she had gone down the hill in a rage, nearly driving over the precipice, and while waiting to regain her composure hearing on the radio that the girl's death was from natural causes. "So I went back up to Margaret's all contrite, and promised to deliver the package." She described the phone call the following day, and the caller's caressing silky voice.

"That must be the joker who called me," he said. She showed her surprise and he said, "Go on, I'll tell you when you've finished."

"That's when he said I should bring the notebook — I suppose that's what they were looking for, the other night, when they hit Ruel over the head. When I got there – the apartment place – he asked me why I had taken it in the first place. I mumbled something about it being on the floor and that I'd picked it up automatically — that I'd forgotten its existence until he phoned."

"Good for you — did he believe you?"

"I think so. Anyway, after he'd insisted on the phone that I bring it, I realised that it must be more important than I'd thought, so I scribbled off the list for you."

She paused, then shuddered as she recalled the next few hours. She reached the point where she had arrived at the call box in Red Hills then burst into tears and clung to him. "It was awful, darling, awful. I thought that at any moment that beast Stillman would catch up with me and..."

"It's all right, sweetheart, it's all over." He silently hoped so, and made a vow that if he ever caught up with the swine, that would be the end of his amorous excursions.

"And then," she went on, sniffing, "I started down the road. I know it fairly well, and there are a number of houses around — then...then I saw the headlights and I panicked. I tried to run, turned my ankle on some loose stones and went headlong. There was the most terrifying screech of brakes and the car spun across the road, missing me by inches. It was the Oxfords; they were so sweet and kind and *incredibly*, they didn't ask any questions. I don't know what they must have thought." She suddenly grinned wickedly, "Probably that I'd been out on a date with my boyfriend and he pulled the old one about running out of gas."

"So the Oxfords didn't want to offend your lady-like sensibilities by referring to the grim and sordid matter," Rowan teased.

She giggled and he bent and kissed her.

"Nobody thinks like that these days — I wonder why they didn't ask. What did you mean about the smarmy-voiced man phoning you?" she asked.

He told her about the note in her car and the follow-up phone call that night with the enquiry as to whether he had relinquished the case. "I wondered at the time what it was all about, but now I think that it must have been about the time that they discovered that you had escaped. If I had already complied with their demands then there was no need to go in search of you. I've a feeling that these jokers we're dealing with are out of their element in this sort of crime — kidnapping — they're too amateurish. Now tell me, could you recognise the place again?"

She shook her head. "I'd know the inside of the garage, but I only saw the outside through torrential rain. Not really saw — it was just a blacker shadow against the night."

He gave an inward sigh; that's what he had feared.

"What about the road? Could you possibly remember how far down to the street light it was from when you hit the Swain Spring Road from the side turning?"

Even as he asked the question he knew the answer — with the weather conditions and the emotional stress that she had been under, it was practically impossible to hope that distance and landmarks would register.

She shook her head, then said slowly, "There was a little district, just a few little houses — and a shop. I remember seeing a kerosene lamp."

He got up and walked to the window. She put aside the breakfast tray and slipped out of bed. Hobbling on her sore feet, she went to him. "I'm sorry, darling, if I hadn't got involved – you'd have solved the damned case."

He drew her close, feeling the warm, taut, yet yieldingly soft body beneath the terry robe. "I'm not so sure. You may have altered the sequence, but you've also brought to light a number of facts that might otherwise be hidden."

"But darling," she tilted back her head to look up at him. "You're off the case, aren't you? *Aren't you?*"

He grinned.

"There are many ways of being on a case – without shouting it to the world. It's all right, sweetheart, those jokers won't know. We've — gone underground, so to speak. And one very interesting point has come to light." He paused.

She looked at him expectantly.

"I don't suppose that it registered when you learnt your rescuers' name, but your kind, sweet Celia Oxford was included." He smiled broadly at her shocked face. "If that's not a gift from the gods, then I don't know what is."

Chapter 15
day 8, Monday

The Monday morning crowd at The Looking Glass was at its peak. Every dryer was hooding a St Andrew matron, suffering the torture necessary to achieve the hairstyle which fashion decreed was the ultimate. Each basin received a dripping head; each chair was occupied before each mirror, reflecting the client and her attendant. The dryers whirred, the water gushed, the clients and the operators chatted in the uninhibited way common the world over in such a setting. Secrets and confidences were exchanged with a frankness never achieved elsewhere, apart from the psychiatrist's couch.

A mingled assortment of perfumes and other odours pervaded the air, various shampoos, rinses, setting gels and final sprays, together with the customers' own perfumes, all producing a heavy atmosphere of femininity that was in no way challenged by the plump presence of Michel.

He surveyed the crowded salon with satisfaction, his small dark eyes gleaming from the surrounding folds of flesh. His gaze rested on the new assistant, Barbara Barton who, together with a number of other hopeful applicants, had arrived at the salon a day or so after the announcement of Therese's death. She had gotten the job with ease since her experience included a course in beauty culture in New York, followed by a year in Paris and another in London. Her references were almost eulogistic, added to which she had personality, poise and a face and figure guaranteed to turn every male head. To all these virtues could be added the obvious fact that the customers liked her. She was competently professional, exuding a confidence immediately apparent and appreciated.

The telephone rang on the receptionist's desk. "It's for you, Michel," she called. Michel took the call, his thoughts about Barbara Barton interrupted, and as he took the receiver his unctuous smile changed to a closed watchfulness. He listened intently, making no response to the rapid crackle that reached him.

Then he said, "Yes, sir, I understand. Yes, we are expecting her... quite, sir, the utmost caution."

He put down the receiver, picked up the appointment book and ran a plump mahogany-coloured finger down the page. "Ah, Madame Groome. Her appointment is for tomorrow at eleven." He shut the book with a snap. "This Madame Groome — I attended to her last week — what do you know of her?" he asked the bored receptionist.

She gave a shrug. "Not so much. She in the news last year when her husband kill himself."

"*That* Groome? The doctor who went crazy and killed someone, then killed himself?" In his interest in the matter, Michel let his Gallic accent — always rather precarious — slip completely, and the Jamaican original reasserted its dominance, "I t'ink the name familiar when she say it." He caught the girl's faintly mocking eye and slight smile. He snapped his fingers in what he considered to be a Continental manner and tried to recapture the image that he had created. "Ah, now I recall— there was a detective, a friend — quite high, *n'est-ce pas?* But of course, one Superintendent Rowan Rodgers." He brought out the name with a creditable attempt at French r's and the French syllabic stress, then ,feeling that honour and prestige were partially, if not fully, restored, he minced away to supervise the salon.

The girl watched him go and kissed her teeth sharply in contempt.

* * *

Barbara Barton watched the last customer of the busy Monday depart with a relief that she concealed admirably. She had been working at The Looking Glass for a few days now and had quickly appreciated that the type of customer changed each day. On Monday in the hours before noon the customers were all of a high social bracket, mostly middle-aged, unencumbered by children. They all chattered endlessly, about their husbands' preoccupation with golf, sailing or fishing, about the ever-increasing problem of getting and keeping domestic staff, and allied petty subjects that had no value nor merited a second thought.

Barbara was impatient with that type of woman; she had thought that the breed had disappeared years before, yet there they were, down from their expensive homes in the hills or from the luxury high-rise apartments. She felt that they were a parasitic breed which was taking an unconscionably long time to die. But nothing except interest showed on her smooth oval face as she listened attentively to their inconsequential chatter. This same group returned on Friday to be groomed for yet another useless weekend. Tuesdays and Wednesdays were slack in the mornings but crowded in the afternoons, the younger residents of St Andrew who couldn't spare the time in the mornings from their household chores and shopping, and teachers after school had ended in the mid-afternoon. Thursday and Friday followed the same pattern, with the whole of Saturday a rush of smart young office girls, older career women, and the occasional customer who regarded a beauty salon as a place to patronise only for special dates.

Barbara quickly cleared away the lotions she had been using and changed into a pale blue two-piece. There was no sign of Michel, and the other assistants had gone long before. The receptionist was still there, making up her face with elaborate care. She had lost her sullen, bored expression now that the day's work was over and she could get down to the important part of life — enjoying herself.

Barbara smiled as she passed. "Got a date?"

"Sure, man. Heavy, you see — him have one nice car."

She leant closer to the mirror and opened her eyes wide as she applied yet another layer of mascara. Barbara paused in her walk to the door, took out a compact and flicked a puff at her nose. "Serious? You going to marry him?"

The girl threw her a sideways glance. *Marry!* Cho, man — him married already — wid four children."

"Well, in that case," Barbara murmured, "You'd better be careful, hadn't you?"

The girl tossed her head. "Cho, can't worry 'bout that. Been on the family planning since me a twelve." She ran an assessing eye over Barbara's svelte figure and well-cut two-piece. "You have a boyfriend?"

"Sure," Barbara said. "Two or three. I'm not aiming to settle for one yet." She gave the girl a knowing grin, then took out a packet of Rothman's. "Smoke?" The girl nodded and took one. Barbara flipped a lighter, then asked casually, "You been here long?"

"Two — three months."

"Like it?"

"I get so bored y'hear, sitting all day at that damn desk but is good money." She shrugged her shoulders. "These days if you 'ave a job, you hang on to it."

"Michel own the place long? When I was here a couple of years back, one Mrs Keagan used to own it."

The girl gave a shout of laughter. "Michel? That fat slob don't own nothing – not even himself. No, man, Mrs Keagan force to sell, 'bout a year or so ago."

"Forced? But it used to do so well."

"So I hear. But she sell— then little later, she dead."

"Dead? How?"

"Cho, man, how I know that? Can't remember every little thing."

"So, if Michel doesn't own the place, whose is it?"

The girl's face lost its animation, she glanced round and lowered her voice. "They try to keep it quiet — tax or something — but I stay on one evening to give myself a facial an' I hear Michel on the phone — hear 'im say: 'Yes, Mr Mantanios. No, sir, no one else here.' So I keep quiet till 'im gone. Next day I ask Therese — she the girl whose place you take — an' she say that Mr Mantanios own the place but not to talk 'bout it."

"He own a lot of places. You been to The Black Crab?"

"Who? Me? I can't go to them kind a place." She looked curiously at Barbara. "You been there?"

"Sure — plenty times. I hear that Mr Mantanios owns that too."

Barbara left the cloying atmosphere of the beauty salon and went round behind the building where she had left her car parked. The heat of the late afternoon enveloped her like a blanket. She narrowed her eyes against the glare and put on a pair of dark glasses. The interior of the car was like an oven, the steering wheel searing hot to her hands, but she hardly noticed the discomfort. She swung the car onto the main road and joined the stream of uptown traffic, then made a left turn into a shopping plaza where she parked and crossed rapidly to a call box. She dialled crisply then waited, listening to the ringing at the other end.

A man's voice answered. Barbara said, "B.B. Listen, I think

that you'll find this interesting." She spoke briskly for a few moments, then waited as the man replied. "Right," she said. "I'll do that — if anything comes up at the time and I feel that you should know, I'll ring you as soon as I can.'

She rang off and went back to her car, a dreamy smile on her face, as if she had been having a satisfactory conversation with a lover.

* * *

The sun was sinking in a blaze of glory as Rowan drove Rachel up to say thank you to the Oxfords. The hills were sharply jagged against the pale blue of the north-eastern sky. For once, they were a uniform dark blue, except for the most distant, highest peak which was purple with a high pink cloud behind it. The heights caught the last rays of the swiftly dropping sun. A wisp of soft, transparent, grey cloud clung to a lower peak, then Rowan swung the Mercedes to the left and there was only the apricot glow of the sunset sky as the hills dropped away behind them. A turn to the right, and they were confronted by hills again, the foothills of the Red Hills area.

Rowan glanced across at Rachel. "How are you, sweet? Feet troubling you?"

"No, not really." She smiled at him. " I was just thinking of the last time that I travelled this way." She was silent for a moment, then said rather hesitantly, "Darling, don't think that I'm being stupid or a scaredy-cat, but — *we* know that I don't know the way to the house off Swain Spring Road but *they* don't know that I don't."

He grinned lazily. He'd hoped that she would not reach that conclusion — and knew that it was a vain hope. "Why do you think that I've stuck to you like a leech?" he asked.

"I thought it was love — or at least sex," she retorted. "Heaven only knows what my neighbours are thinking — and as for Ruel," she giggled as she remembered Ruel's disapproving look.

Rowan reached across and took her hand. "In this day of permissiveness, no one thinks anything if two people live together. It's the norm. But we can make it ultra-respectable — I could get a special licence. What do you say?"

"Well, I can't make the usual maidenly retort of its being so sudden..."

"You can't make a *maidenly* retort, period," he interrupted, black eyes sparkling. "Come on, sweetheart, don't go all coy on me."

"All right — as soon as possible," she said.

"It's a pity that we can't stop on this road and satisfactorily seal the bargain, but we'll make up for that at a later date."

The Oxfords were sitting on their front verandah as Rowan and Rachel drove up. There were glasses on low tables beside them. The formal attire that they had worn the night before had given way to casual clothes. Merton Oxford was in trim, dark-brown slacks and a cream silk, short-sleeved, open-neck shirt. The voluble Celia was in a brightly-coloured, wide-sleeved, loose dress, that did more for her figure than the over-elaborate formal gown which she had been wearing at their first meeting.

Oxford rose briskly and hurried down the steps to meet them. "Mr Rodgers, Mrs Groome. How good of you to call so promptly. No worse for your experience if appearances are any judge." He helped Rachel from the car with an old fashioned formality.

She smiled at him. "We just had to say thank you once again. And return Mrs Oxford's robe."

"Why, Mrs Groome, how nice." Celia Oxford had lost some of her intensity and there was a veil of preoccupation in her small, dark eyes.

Rachel examined her keenly for the first time, wondering anew why her name was on the list in the late Therese's notebook. She didn't seem in any way to be the type of person who would put herself in a position to be open to blackmail.

When they had been offered and had accepted drinks, Celia said with what Rachel felt was forced interest, "What a terrible experience for you, Mrs Groome. We were so distressed for you." She looked expectantly at Rachel as if she hoped for an explanation.

Rachel gave a little laugh and offered the one which Rowan had suggested. "It was all my fault, I'm afraid. I'd been to see a friend up in the hills, and when it began to rain, I was on my way home. As usual, I was driving too fast. I got into a skid on a corner that I'd misjudged; there must have been a lot of loose stones, as well. I don't know what actually happened; it was all so fast. Anyway, the next thing that I knew I'd hit the bank and been thrown out. I'd smashed both my headlights. I was miles from anywhere, so I decided to walk. I'd have done much better if I'd stayed in the car until the morning."

"You poor dear." Celia seemed to accept the story without question, and Oxford said easily, "It's always difficult to make the right decision under stress." He turned to Rowan. "But you, sir, you look quite fit, yet I read in the paper that you were on sick leave."

Rowan took a pull at his glass and said, "Well, Mr Oxford, we sometimes find it expedient to give an announcement to the press which is not always strictly in keeping with the facts."

Rachel suppressed a desire to give him a querying look. What was he doing, revealing the fact that there was a reason other than the one given? Almost admitting that he was still on the case?

Oxford leant forward. "I see. It must be an interesting life, that of a policeman. You must come across a lot of the seamy side of life not revealed to the ordinary man in the street."

"Too much, I'm afraid, though most of a policeman's work is unexciting routine — and the man in the street sees the seamy side."

"But, of course, the popular press always lays stress on the sensational and ignores the mundane. The former has more, ah, 'newsworthiness'; I believe that is the phrase. For myself, I hate publicity and sensationalism. I've always managed to avoid both, thank God."

Rachel glanced from under her lashes at Celia. She was looking fixedly into her glass, an expression of despair on her smudged features. The thick make-up seemed more prominent than ever, and Rachel felt that Celia had paled beneath it. Poor woman, she thought, why doesn't she tell her husband, whatever she's done? He seems kind and understanding, even if he is a bit pompous. Then Celia raised her eyes and said, "As you have gathered, my husband is a man of fixed views and high principles."

"Well, my dear, at least that's nothing to be ashamed of, and if all goes well, those — assets, may I call them that? — have taken me where I want to go."

"And where is that?" Rowan asked casually.

"Well, it's not official, you understand, so I would appreciate it if you…"

"Of course."

"... I've been short-listed for a post highly placed on the ambassadorial staff in Washington. I hope to hear the final decision very soon."

Rowan snapped a mental finger; of course, Merton Oxford, backroom boy in local diplomatic circles, shrank from the limelight, utter integrity. He didn't so much as glance at Rachel as he said, "Congratulations, wonderful news, sir. Of course we'll keep it absolutely quiet."

"A little premature for congratulations, I fear, Mr Rodgers. It's not certain yet, of course," Oxford tried to keep the pride from his voice. "But unless something unexpected and catastrophic occurs..." He gave a light laugh. "Hardly likely, eh, Celia?"

His wife forced a smile. Both hands gripped the glass as if clinging on for dear life. "No." Her voice was barely above a whisper. "What — what could go wrong?"

Chapter 16

Barbara Barton was dining at The Black Crab with her latest escort. He was a large young man, powerful shoulders straining under the dark jacket of his suit. Barbara glanced across at him and thought, he must be the prototype of the strong silent man. Aloud she said softly, "Tell me more about underwater fishing. It sounds quite fascinating."

He smiled at her, his dark eyes lighting with enthusiasm, and began to talk about his pet hobby, with great attention to detail. Barbara listened with only half of her attention, but kept an eager look of interest on her face. She gave an occasional glance around the rapidly filling room noticing a number of people present whom she knew by sight, vaguely discernible in the dim lighting. There was, surprisingly in view of his recent bereavement, Mr Justice Piers Smith-Watson. She couldn't make out his companion.

There was the well-known Daphne Prestwick with her newest escort, a flamboyant young man in naval uniform, and leaning against the bar, in his usual position at this hour, was Khylos Mantanios, viewing the crowded night spot with a smooth satisfaction.

Khylos Mantanios, despite his name, was fourth generation Jamaican. His great grandfather had arrived in Jamaica in the late eighteen twenties on a Greek trading vessel. He had gotten into a brawl in a tavern in Port Royal and had been unconscious for two days in a bawdy house, so that his ship had sailed without him. He quickly established himself as a coastal trader and by the time he was forty he had built up a fleet of trading vessels, making the difficult and often perilous journeys between the other islands of the Caribbean, east to Barbados, north to the Bahamas, as far out in the Atlantic as Bermuda, and venturing as far afield as South America. By the time he died, he had made a fortune — not always by scrupulous methods. Over the years, the Mantanios family had prospered by any means that came to hand, and Khylos Mantanios — the last of his line — was no exception. He still owned the fleet of inter-island vessels inherited from his father, although at one stage he had been forced to sell them, when fortune turned against him. Later he had regained them and had added to his empire by acquiring hotels, apartment buildings and restaurants. He was completely unscrupulous, without a moral qualm over whatever nefarious methods he had to use to gain his ends.

The waiter brought the *spécialité de maison* — black crabs prepared in an exclusive way, an old island recipe with an added twist devised by the restaurant's chef. Barbara ate in silence whilst her companion enlarged on the joys of underwater fishing. She repressed a sigh and glanced unobtrusively at her wrist watch. By the time that they had reached the Bombay Mango *flambé*, she was gritting her teeth to suppress rising yawns.

A waiter stopped by the table. "Mr Cole?" he asked.

"Yes?"

"Telephone call for you, sir. Over at the bar."

Peter Cole murmured an excuse to Barbara and left the table. She sensed rather than saw Khylos Mantanios swivel round on the bar stool and look in her direction. Then Peter came back, a worried look on his handsome, but rather blank face.

"I'm awfully sorry, Barbara, I have to go. That blasted 4300 is acting up again. Stay and finish your coffee. I'll settle with the waiter and I'll try to get back soon. If I find that it's going to take some time, I'll give you a ring. Right?"

Her mouth tightened in a slightly petulant pout. "All right, Peter, but good God, do you realise that it's the second time this week? It's one thing sharing a man with another woman, but with a machine!" Despite herself her voice had risen and she was conscious more than ever that Mantanios was watching her. Peter stood looking down at her like an unhappy Great Dane. "I'm sorry, Barbara," he said again. "I really am — but I have to go. It's my job and..."

"All right," she cut in impatiently. "Don't just stand there — Go." She softened her words by adding with a dazzling smile."Then the sooner you'll come back."

She watched him go, big, lumbering, utterly dependable and unutterably dull. He stood and paid the waiter at the bar, then looked back and waved.

Barbara lit a cigarette and accepted a second cup of coffee and the brandy that the waiter suggested. She smoked and sipped slowly, composed and relaxed, not at all embarrassed at being left unaccompanied in the restaurant, respectable and socially accepted as it was. She was completely confident of the picture she presented, her slim yet ripe body accentuated by the short, straight, white dress that she wore. Her shoulders gleamed darkly, like brown satin against the dull white crepe. Her black hair hung loose to her shoulders. She smoked slowly, contemplatively, without the haste of the unsure, idly watching her fellow diners. Added to the few she had already noticed were two others, both women. One, not over tall but with a wonderful upright carriage, strong aquiline nose, dark hooded eyes, dressed soberly in dark grey: the other, fluffy, bird-like in an unsuitable, out-of-date frilled nylon dress, who fluttered and moved her head and hands continuously. Barbara narrowed her nostrils in involuntary distaste. She looked more intently at the pair; oh yes, the strong one — masculine didn't fit the description — was Professor Margaret Cameron, a brilliant woman chemist, recently retired. The other woman Barbara dismissed as unimportant.

Distantly, through the subdued chatter of the diners, she heard the burr of a telephone. Her waiter approached her table. "Miss Barton? A Mr Peter Cole on the phone — the one at the end of the bar."

She thanked him, gathered up her bag and wrap, and made her way to the bar where she perched on the end stool. "Hullo?" Her voice was low but pitched to carry. "Peter?" There came a spate of explanatory crackles. "Oh no!... No, don't worry, I'll get a taxi... Oh, Peter, I said it's all right... Right, you do that." She put down the receiver and swivelled round on the stool, coming face to face with Khylos Mantanios. Her handbag brushed against his arm. "Oh, I'm so sorry," she said, slightly breathlessly.

He smiled. "Please don't apologise. I couldn't help but observe— first your escort leaves you, then apparently phones to say the party's ended." He raised his dark brows in the high smooth dome of his forehead. Barbara didn't attempt to move from her perch beside him.

"It's not as bad as it looks," she said. "Peter's sweet, really. He's an electronics engineer and the wretched machines always seem to break down at night. It's as bad as being a doctor in some ways, I should imagine. So you see, he didn't really stand me up." Mantanios smiled. " I should think that it's most unlikely that anyone would want to stand you up," he said.

She gave him the full force of her smile. "That's very nice of you. Now, I must get some change and phone for a taxi."

He put a plump, well-manicured hand on her arm. "Why? It's still very early, isn't it? I was about to order. May I invite you to have a drink with me?"

She looked doubtful. "But — I'm sorry to be prudish — but I don't even know you. It's very kind, but..." She slid determinedly off the stool and stood beside him.

His fingers tightened on her arm. "That's very easily remedied. I am Khylos Mantanios — I own this place."

Her embarrassed doubt gave way to relief. "Why, of course. I'm so sorry, I should have known. I've seen your picture in the paper many times. Do you forgive me?"

"Then you will join me?"

"I'd love to."

He signalled to a waiter and they were ushered across to a special table, set even further back than the others, in a deep alcove. "My own table. I observe the small world of The Black Crab from here."

Over their drinks he proved an admirable conversationalist and Barbara enjoyed the stimulation after the plodding, unimaginative Peter. She kept pace with him. She had a wide grasp of many subjects, a good mind and a more than average vocabulary. He ordered a second round of drinks and said, "You're a remarkable girl. I wonder now even more at your young man leaving you, work or no work."

She laughed. "He's not 'my young man' at all. I've just had a few dates and on most occasions... this." She gave a little grimace and picked up her glass.

"And what do you do?" he asked casually as he took from his pocket an old fashioned snuff box. She didn't answer his question. She was looking at the snuff box in faint surprise. He saw her expression and laughed as he lifted the lid. "Don't look so apprehensive , my dear. It's not snuff, just my asthma dope." He took out a capsule and swallowed it then took a sip of his drink. "Not," he added, "that many girls these days would recognise a snuff box when they see it."

"It's a very beautiful one."

"It's very old. It's been in my family for well over a hundred years."

She gave him her sudden, enchanting smile. "You asked me what I do. I'm a beautician - or a cosmetologist, as it's called now – you know, hair styling, nails, facials. It becomes deadly dull after a while, but it pays well."

He was suddenly quite still, his dark eyes watchful. "And where do you practise — this beautifying?" he asked softly.

"I'm quite sure that you won't have heard of it — I have yet to meet a man who knew the name of a woman's beauty parlour."

He smiled with his mouth only. "Try me."

"It's called The Looking Glass," she said, her eyes looking candidly into his.

His expression didn't alter as he said, "You were perfectly right, my dear. I have never heard of the place." He rose. "Shall we go?"

She seemed somewhat taken aback by his abrupt termination to the evening. "Of course. It's getting quite late. I must get a taxi."

"That isn't what I meant at all. Of course you must allow me to see you home. On the way, we can discuss — tomorrow evening."

Her heart gave a little lurch, then she smiled again. "That ... sounds great." She didn't try to evade the pressure of his fingers above her elbow as he guided her through the crowded room.

Margaret Cameron and Eleanore Tarrant at a table nearby, had watched the interlude with varying degrees of disapproval.

"Well," Eleanore said tartly, as Barbara and Mantanios disappeared through the main door. "If that wasn't a pick-up, then I don't know what is."

Margaret's eyes narrowed in contempt. "And, of course, you'd know all about such things, wouldn't you?'

Daphne Prestwick watched Barbara leave with Mantanios' hand possessively on her elbow. She switched her gaze back to her escort. "Did you see that, Larry? As neat as I could do myself."

Larry answered with the heavy facetiousness of incipient inebriation. "When I'm with you gorgeous, I see only you. What else was there I should have seen?"

"Just a very neat pick-up. I only hope she knows what she's letting herself in for," she added with a change of tone.

Larry reached across and took her hand. "How do you know

what she's letting herself in for? Been in the same position?"

She flicked his hand away. "I'm not sure that you are in a position to enquire about what I've let myself in for in the past."

"Aw, c'mon, baby, to hell with the past. It's the future that I want to know about — and not very far distant at that. I've only got a forty-eight hour pass. We've already wasted five hours — let's go."

She pushed back her coffee cup and stubbed out her half-smoked cigarette. When she answered, her voice was brittle again. "Sure, let's go. What have I got to lose?"

Piers Smith-Watson had also watched Barbara's meeting with Mantanios. In spite of his calling as a judge in which he came across the seamy side of life, he still held a chivalrous and trusting attitude towards attractive young women. He wasn't certain how to interpret what he had seen: whether Mantanios had taken advantage of the situation or whether the girl had cleverly engineered the meeting. He glanced across at his companion, who had also witnessed the incident. She had a disapproving look in her slightly protuberant, pale blue eyes.

"I do think that young girls these days just *ask* for trouble, don't you, Mr Smith-Watson?"

"I do indeed, Miss McCawly," he replied. He smiled across at her in a kindly manner, admitting that she had shown courage in contacting him and asking for advice. She had telephoned him that morning. "You must forgive my presuming on one meeting, but I need advice – which I feel you can give."

More than that she wouldn't say on the telephone so, welcoming a change after the loneliness of the empty house since Annabel's death, he had suggested dinner at The Black Crab. She had fluttered a little at the suggestion and he'd half-regretted the impulse, but now he was glad. She had been reluctant to broach the subject on which she needed advice, and had chattered in her inconsequential way, over-emphasising trivialities, gushing sentimentally over the most mundane subjects until at last, while they waited for dessert and coffee, he said firmly, "Now, Miss McCawly, I shall begin to think that you inveigled me out to dinner under false pretences."

"Why, Mr Smith-Watson," her blue eyes flared and colour flamed in her soft, flaccid cheeks, then she said, "I'm sorry, but it is very difficult to...to put into words."

She was silent for a moment longer, pushing a spoon across the white cloth, then she took a deep breath and began to speak quickly, in a low voice. She told him what she had heard of the late Miss Mann's death, the persistent telephone calls — she faltered at this point, colour staining her cheeks again, glad of the dim lighting — of her subsequent discovery of the cheque book stubs, and the deduction that she had made from those stubs. She told him of how she had answered the man when next he called, and of his threat. "It was very silly of me to tell him that I knew a lot about him — but I didn't stop to think."

Smith-Watson nodded, his eyes alert, seeing the close relationship of this story and the events that led up to Annabel's death. He didn't like the logical conclusion he had reached but he was a man of facts. "Go on," he said quietly.

"Well, after that I heard nothing for months and then the other day two policemen came to see me. They said that they were making enquiries into a number of cases of — of suicide. They thought that blackmail was probably the cause. They asked me for my help and I said I … I didn't know anything. I know that it was cowardly of me, but I kept hearing that man's voice, threatening me if I told what I knew."

She paused and he leant across the table. "But you don't really know anything —nothing to point to any one person — do you? The cheque book proves nothing."

"I know, but *they* don't know that. I felt that I should have told the police what little I did know — even my suspicions. It might have helped them somehow — knowing how the man — or men, I suppose — work."

He smiled, there was more common sense behind the fluffy exterior than he had given her credit for. "Why did you come to me?" he asked.

She swallowed. "Because – forgive me - your wife recently committed suicide." Her voice was little more than a whisper. "I wondered if you knew the reason, or…"

"Was she being blackmailed?" he finished for her. "Don't look so upset. I have a very strong reason to believe that she was. The familiar cheque book stubs. She'd gone through every penny of her allowance and she was frightened to come to me."

His voice was suddenly bitter. The fact that Annabel had been too frightened to confide in him was something that he would have to live with for the rest of his life.

Veronica McCawly touched his hand briefly, gently, amazed at her action, longing to comfort him. "I'm so sorry. I've reminded you, when all you want is to forget," she murmured.

He looked up and smiled, the bitterness dissolved by her sympathy. "Don't apologise. I've kept it bottled inside. I needed to talk. And at least it's a lead... in a way, I suppose. Two similar cases. What made you decide to come to me — what triggered it off? It's quite a few days since you were questioned by the police."

"Soon after the police left — the phone rang. It was that man again. He asked what the police had wanted. I said it was such routine questions, I hadn't been able to help." She shut her eyes at the memory. "Then he badgered me, trying to make me admit that I'd given information to the police. I swore that I hadn't. He said that if he had any proof in the future that I'd lied, he would *deal with me.*"

She was beginning to show signs of hysteria and Smith-Watson ordered double brandies for them both. She held the glass in both hands and sipped steadily.

"I've lived in terror ever since. Every time the phone rings, I want to run and hide. Since that call, each day at a different time he will ring and say, 'Don't tell the police — I'll know', and then ring off. It's driving me mad. Sometimes I think that I can only get away from it all by..." She stopped at the expression on his face.

He put a warm hand over her cold one. "You won't. You mustn't even think of it. He must be a mad man, certainly deranged in some way. He'll get tired of his little game — sooner or later."

She sighed, it was almost a sob. "I hope so. I can't take it anymore."

Smith-Watson drove home thoughtfully after dropping Veronica McCawly at her cottage. He had seen her safely inside and waited while she bolted the door. That Rodgers had been dropped from the case he had gathered from the news item, He wondered what lay behind the move and if it was authentic or just a bluff. All the same, he'd get in touch with Rodgers early in the morning — that poor little woman was being driven out of her fluffy wits.

Veronica McCawly listened to Smith-Watson drive away with a little thrill of pleasure. It had been so many years since she had been out like that with a man. Not, she admitted, that she had ever had many dates. She'd been pretty enough in her youth. She was still attractive in a soft dumpling way, but she'd always kept a barrier between herself and any male friends. She was too inclined to gush and over-enthuse on first acquaintance, then to dogmatise on any given subject. She was averse to caresses of even the mildest sort, and soon the invitations had become fewer and fewer, then none at all. She hadn't minded — not too much, she told herself, pushing back the fear that she had missed half of what life had to offer. She flung herself into work and it had filled the gap, but now that she was retired and lonely — yes, admit it, she was starved for companionship.

The sound of the car died away and she just stood there in the hallway thinking back over the evening, glad now of her impulse to confide in Piers —*Piers*, she blushed at her forwardness. He had been so kind so — she drifted into a state of inertia, induced by a surfeit of emotion, unaccustomed brandy and her new-found feelings.

She didn't hear the sound of the bedroom door opening behind her, nor the soft footfalls across the room. Suddenly, frighteningly, she was aware that she was not alone any more. She should have been alone, the cottage was locked and bolted — except for — oh, God, that window in the kitchen that she had meant to have fixed.

She began to turn, half hoping that this was just a fantasy, just imagination. She began to turn but hard hands about her neck prevented her...

There was no time to cry out...

... no time to think.

Just time to hear that hated voice say — so close this time, "You *shouldn't* have talked, Miss McCawly, you *really* shouldn't have."

He kept his hands about her plump neck until he felt the heavy sag of her body, then lowered her, almost gently, to the floor. Then he left quietly by the way he had entered.

Chapter 17

Sergeant Phillips was bored by the period of enforced inactivity. He realised only too well the need to have ostensibly abandoned all interest in the case and he was using the time to catch up on the mountain of paper work that always accrued.

He had Police Constable Goodbody to assist him, equally frustrated at the delay. "But Mr Phillips, sir, I know we have to look like we forget the case, but is nothing we can do?" he asked for the sixth time that morning.

"No, me son. One thing you got to learn is patience. *Think* all you want about it, though. If you get any ideas, trot them out."

Phillips himself was not feeling any too patient but he concealed his feelings behind his usual barrier of stolidity. He drew a file towards him as the telephone on Rodgers' desk rang.

"Sergeant Phillips speaking. Good morning."

"Good morning. May I speak to Superintendent Rodgers, please?"

"Sorry, sir. Mr Rodgers not in office. Can I help?"

"Sergeant Phillips, you say? This is Piers Smith-Watson. I believe that you were with Mr Rodgers at my house, just after my wife — died?"

"Yes, sir."

"Sergeant, I have a little information that may be of use. Possibly not of a tangible nature — but I feel that Mr Rodgers should have it."

"Is it in connection with your wife's death, sir?"

"Not directly, but it bears on... the whole picture, shall I say?"

Phillips hesitated. Any information was valuable, but did he dare follow it up? "Look sir, it difficult you see. Officially the case is closed..."

"I know all that," Smith-Watson said testily. "But good God, man, you're not going to sit down and do *nothing*?"

"No, sir. Look sir, I'll contact Mr Rodgers and ring you back."

"Right, I'm at home."

Phillips put down the receiver thoughtfully. It was a week now since they had been warned off. How close a watch was being kept on their activities? He dialed the chief's number.

"Rodgers here."

Phillips outlined the position, concluding with, "We don't want to ignore it, do we sir?"

"No," Rodgers said slowly. "Listen, Phillips, get a piece in the paper — you'll just catch *The Star*: attempted robbery at judge's home, etc. Get on all the radio stations and ask them to put the same information in their twelve and twelve-thirty newscasts. Use that as your front to get up there and see what's cooking. I think that his lordship'll play along those lines. I've taken Mrs Groome to the beauty parlour; I'm picking her up latter. So she's safe for a while."

"Right, sir."

There was relief in Phillips' voice, a new note at the prospect of some action, however nebulous the information might be. He rang the editor of the afternoon tabloid, got onto the newsrooms of the radio stations, then said briefly to Goodbody, "Come on, lad. Let's get moving."

***

Rachel sat in the waiting room of The Looking Glass, idly flipping through the pages of a magazine, waiting for her call. She had been relieved when the receptionist had said with her customary disinterest that Mr Michel could not after all attend to her, but that Miss Barbara was very efficient. This Rachel conceded later, as the firm capable fingers worked shampoo into a foaming lather. When she was turbanned by a soft warm towel, Rachel managed to inspect this new assistant. She was very impressed with what she saw reflected in the mirror. The girl had a quiet poise and an air of breeding, together with striking good looks. She liked the fact too, that she didn't waste time in the usual salon small talk."Have you been here long?" Rachel asked at last, wondering if the girl's voice would match her appearance.

"A little over a week." It did — low and cultured, without any annoying flatness or rising inflection at the end of each sentence.

"My predecessor was most unfortunate," she went on, eyes busy on her work.

Rachel gave her a sharp glance in the mirror. "Unfortunate?'

Barbara's eyes met hers briefly. "She, ahm, died."

"Yes — yes, of course, I read about it. Of natural causes."

Again the dark eyes met hers. The busy fingers didn't falter as she went on, "I knew this place a long time ago, before I went away to study. It is quite different — now that Mr Mantanios owns it." The last words were said softly in Rachel's ear, as Barbara bent forward to pick up a roller.

Mantanios? He was the present owner? Rachel's eyes asked questions that she dared not put into words, but Barbara gave the barest shake of her head. It might have been deliberate — Rachel couldn't be sure. If it was, what did this girl know? Whose side was she on? She relaxed as Barbara began to wind her hair deftly onto rollers. "Your hair is very fine, yet takes styling beautifully. Is this a routine set or for a special date?"

Again Rachel had a strong feeling that the question was not an idle one — or was she seeing too much into the most casual remarks? She gave a faint shrug. "More or less routine, I shall probably be going out tonight, though."

Barbara slipped a net over the rollers. "Have you ever been to The Black Crab? It's quite a place. I was there last night." Her eyes met Rachel's again in the mirror as she said evenly, "I'm going again tonight."

She held Rachel's gaze. This time Rachel was sure that this was no chance remark; it was deliberate. She raised her eyebrows and Barbara gave a slight nod, and said brightly at the same time, "There, I'll check if a dryer is free, and see about some coffee for you."

Rachel settled under the whirring dryer and thought back to the last time she had sat there. The girl, Therese, had been alive then. Who was this new girl? Barbara something or other? Had she imagined the significance of her remarks or was she being warned? Mantanios was a big man, his business empire stretched wide. Was he the man behind the blackmailing racket? She stirred uneasily, her thoughts still centred on Mantanios. Why had the girl mentioned his name? If she was one of 'them', surely she would conceal the fact that Mantanios owned The Looking Glass? If she wasn't one of them, then who was she?

She sighed and sipped her coffee. She was being fanciful and seeing something sinister in every innocent remark. This girl Barbara was after all no different from any other assistant: she just chatted to amuse the customers, and to show that she moved in a 'good' social circle, dropped names and made sure she was seen at places like The Black Crab. Which, thought Rachel wearily, brings us full circle to Mantanios again. She would tell Rowan and let him decide the significance or otherwise of the girl's remarks.

* * *

Sergeant Phillips, with the silent but watchful Goodbody, listened to Piers Smith-Watson's story attentively. "It's not really anything for you to work on, yet I felt that you should know about it," he ended.

Phillips pursed his lips. "You're quite right, sir," he said. "And it does add further to our theory that these suicides may be attributed to blackmail. We're not just surmising — well, not so much. And it also points to an organised racket, not just one man — although we knew that already by..." He stopped before he revealed Rachel's involvement.

"By...?" Smith-Watson prompted.

"Sorry, sir, I was about to speak out of turn."

The older man looked at him shrewdly. He hadn't been a High Court judge for nearly twenty years without acquiring good powers of deduction. "It wouldn't have any bearing on Superintendent Rodgers' withdrawal from the case — or on Mrs Groome, would it, Sergeant?"

Phillips' face was expressionless, although he was thinking: this old bwoy have more sense than I give him credit for. I wonder how he come up with that? Aloud, he said woodenly, "I'm sure I don't know, sir."

Smith-Watson gave a dry laugh. "And very commendable, Sergeant. I happen to know the Oxfords rather well and they mentioned Mrs Groome's little...mishap, the other night. Tell Mr Rodgers when you see him that I'm ready to help in any way that I can."

"I will, sir, and thank you. Perhaps you would keep a friendly eye on the lady — Miss McCawly? If we assign a 'Special' to her house, it's just broadcasting that she's talked."

"A good idea, Sergeant. I had that in mind. I'll phone her later."

Phillips let Goodbody take the wheel of the staff car, to the young constable's delight, and they returned to the station in companionable silence.

* * *

Rachel left The Looking Glass still worrying about the strange new assistant. As she stepped out of the air-conditioned salon the full heat of the day struck her. The air was humid, the drought had broken at last, and daily drenchings of rain were turning the parched grass green again. She felt her dress sticking between her shoulder blades and at her midriff, and moisture beading her face. She saw with relief the pale grey Mercedes turn in at the gateway. Rowan slid the car to a standstill at the steps. "You should have waited inside until I arrived," he said reproachfully.

"I'm not likely to be snatched in broad daylight in the middle of Constant Spring Road," she said lightly as she slipped into the passenger seat.

"Maybe not, but I don't want you to take chances, and I shall soon be able to enforce my wishes all 'legal and proper'." He reached into the glove compartment and took out a document. "Marriage Licence."

She looked at it wordlessly.

"Well?" he asked, keeping one hand on the wheel and taking one of hers in his free hand. "When's it to be? This afternoon?"

Suddenly she laughed. "As soon as you like — or else I'll keep running. But what about witnesses and so forth?"

"I'm not being selfish and rushing you into this — doing you out of a proper wedding with all the trimmings — but we don't want any publicity, and you need all the protection that I can give you."

She put his hand firmly back on the wheel. "I always thought that it was against the law to drive with one hand. You should set a better example to your men."

He grinned. "If you think that my men on the beat have x-ray eyes, you're welcome to do so – on any other occasion I'd welcome the thought."

He slid to a stop at the traffic lights.

"Rowan," she said, "what about Sergeant Phillips as a witness?"

"He'd be tickled pink — and let's have young Goodbody as a second witness."

She giggled. "I'm sure he'll be delighted at our legalising our relationship."

Rowan laughed as he remembered Goodbody's slight air of disapproval when they were all at the Santa Gloria Hotel the year before. "Right," he said. "That's settled then."

But it wasn't, for before he could ring Phillips, Phillips rang him.

"Sorry to worry you, Mr Rodgers, but it's one of the ladies who we interviewed — Miss Veronica McCawly."

"Oh, Lord," Rodgers groaned, "not another suicide?"

"No, sir. This time it's murder."

Chapter 18

The small cottage at Stony Hill was quiet an peaceful again after the scurry of activity caused by the arrival of the police ambulance; the finger print squad; the photographic unit; Rodgers, Phillips and Goodbody — not in that order, but more or less simultaneously.

Now, only the last three were left, together with a much shaken Mr Justice Smith-Watson. He was sitting huddled in a chair on the verandah, oblivious to the magnificence of the ever-changing hills. Rodgers joined him, tamping tobacco viciously into his pipe. "Now, sir, perhaps you could tell us what happened?" He gave a nod to Goodbody, unobtrusive in the background, notebook open, pencil poised.

Smith-Watson raised a haggard face. "Sorry to be so upset, Rodgers, but two weeks ago my wife, and now — she was a nice little woman." He paused and slowly opened a packet of cigarettes. He lit one with fingers that shook.

"Look, sir," Rodgers said. "I think that you could use a drink. Phillips," he called, "see if you can find some whisky — anything. I think that we could all do with a drink."

He glanced at his watch. "It's after five-thirty, so we're officially off duty — although some will argue that a policeman is never off duty."

"Right, sir."

They waited. Only the sound of Phillips' heavy tread, followed by the clink of bottles, the lighter clink of glasses and the crack of ice bursting from its tray, broke the difficult silence.

"Here we are, sir. Only brandy, I'm afraid."

"Well, we shan't quarrel with that. Here you are, sir, you need it."

Smith-Watson took a deep pull at the glass, remembering too vividly how he had ordered brandy for Veronica McCawly such a short while ago!

There was a sputter from Goodbody at the unaccustomed spirit, which brought a smile to Rodgers' worried face. "You should stick to Red Stripe, boy," he remarked.

"Sorry to be so tardy," the judge said after a long pause. "I'm all right now. Well, after Sergeant Phillips had left me this morning, I phoned Miss McCawly. There was no reply. We had dined together at The Black Crab — she... had confided in me. I felt some sort of responsibility for her. I waited an hour and tried again. I felt somewhat uneasy as she told me that she very rarely left the house after midday — she always shopped early. In the afternoon she worked – she dabbled in painting, you know. She said something about the light being right in the afternoon. So I drove up. The morning paper was still folded on the verandah. I knocked, waited, then knocked again. Then I peered through the glass of the front door and..." He paused, swallowed, then went on quickly. "I saw her on the floor. I couldn't determine whether she was dead or alive — so I smashed the glass and just managed to reach the bolts at the top and the bottom of the door. I'm sorry, I see now that I shouldn't have done so... but, well, training goes by the board when one is confronted with a situation like this. I realised at once when I bent over her that she was beyond help — so I telephoned the station." He took another deep pull at the brandy.

"You touched nothing else but the door and the telephone?"

"Nothing."

"And the front door was tightly bolted, before your entry?"

"I'm positive on that point.'

"Had you tried to enter by any other way? The back door?"

"No," Smith-Watson admitted. "I — I didn't think beyond getting to her — it seemed the best way at the time."

"Well, not to worry, sir, it was. The back door was also securely fastened and a tougher proposition to enter," Rodgers said briskly.

"Then how...?"

"How did the murderer get in and out? By a broken window – high up in the kitchen wall. One of the type that swivels horizontally — it was easy enough to remove and replace. Now, sir, what about last night?"

"Yes, as I told you, we went to dinner at The Black Crab." He went on to repeat what he had earlier told Phillips, that Veronica McCawly had telephoned him, her discovery of the cheque book stubs and the telephone calls, of how she had been warned not to talk.

"So — it is reasonable to assume that she was killed because they believed that she knew more than she did – and had talked to you."

His eyes met Smith-Watson's levelly.

"Which means that I had better be careful?"

"Not necessarily — now. If their surveillance is as good as it appears, they would know — or assume — that you have told us what she had told you."

"Then why kill her in that case?"

Rodgers' black eyes were hard. "So that if she hadn't told you much yet, then she would not be able to reveal any more to anyone."

"Mr Rodgers, the man behind this — ring, group, whatever it is – is utterly ruthless. You must find him. To hell with this so-called withdrawal — get back on the case, man." Smith-Watson spoke passionately, at variance with his usual measured delivery.

"I would like above all else to do just that," Rodgers said wearily. "But how? Not one of these women is going to talk — there's less chance now than there was before — and God knows it was slim enough before this. We're fighting in the dark with enemies that have no recognisable faces or forms. You say that you had dinner at The Black Crab? Did you go anywhere else?"

"No, I called here for Miss McCawly. We went straight to The Black Crab, and I brought her back here after dinner."

"Where presumably, the murderer was waiting. Somebody knew that she had talked, so somebody must have overheard part of your conversation."

"Not easy," Smith-Watson said. "The tables are quite far apart."

"Yes," Rodgers agreed thoughtfully. "Which leads us to either the waiter, or someone who can lip read."

"So there you have it," Rowan said gloomily to Rachel an hour later. "It looks as if there'll be no wedding for us today."

"We'll have to live in sin a bit longer," she said absently, then burst out, "Oh, God, darling, that poor woman — an absolutely senseless death. She wasn't even one of their blackmail victims."

"No, and by her death, they've drawn attention back to the case. It seems to me that her death was a mistake — not planned by the top man, but by one of the underlings."

"Stillman?" she asked with a shiver.

"You're guessing — as we all are. It could be. Could also be any one of their operators, and we don't know any one of them apart from Stillman."

"Rowan, there's something that I should have told you this morning — but what with your — *proposal*, if you can call it that — and then this, I forgot." She told him in detail of the conversation with the girl in The Looking Glass, and her seemingly pointed remarks. "I'm sure that The Looking Glass could give the answer to a lot of questions. Mantanios owns it and The Black Crab."

"Yes." Rowan felt a prickle of excitement. The coincidence couldn't be ignored. It was only from The Black Crab that the information about Veronica McCawly could have been passed on. The dead girl, Therese, had worked at The Looking Glass, and a number of women listed in the dead girl's notebook had been or were still, customers there.

And Mantanios was the connecting link.

He drew a deep breath. Was it possible that Mantanios was the brain behind the blackmail racket? He was ruthless enough for any type of business deal — was he ruthless enough for such a dirty game as blackmail?

Rachel sat forward eagerly, and interrupted his thoughts, "If you could keep a watch somehow on the people at The Looking Glass – Michel, the new girl, they might let something slip."

He bent down and kissed her, then gave a strange smile, "Sweetheart, you come up with the brightest notions sometimes."

"But, Rowan, I don't see…"

He laughed. "You will." Then he kissed her again: it started out lightly, but ended leaving them both breathless and shaken. He pushed her firmly away. "Woman, I've got a job to do. Would you mind not distracting me?"

"Well, I like that. Me, distracting you…"

But he wasn't listening. He walked to the windows and gazed out unseeingly at the smooth sweep of lawn. Then he turned and said quietly, "Rachel, darling, I'm going to ask you to do something. I hate to do it — after what you've been through in this case, but I want to set a sprat to catch a whale — I hope."

"And what am I to be? the sprat?"

"No. You're the bait to catch the sprat!"

* * *

Margaret Cameron's fine features had taken on an even more haggard expression Rachel noted as she ushered her into the living room, later that same day.

"Your ankle's quite better, then?"

"Yes, thank you, Rachel. Since you phoned and said that you had to see me urgently, I've been in hell, wondering what had gone wrong again. You hadn't let me know…"

"I'm sorry, I should have done, but after what happened…" Rachel told her of being kidnapped and held hostage and her subsequent escape. "And *someone*," she ended harshly, "must have revealed that Rowan was on the case."

"And you think it was me? I assure you it was not. Oh, my dear, I'm terribly sorry — when I think of what I asked you to do. Rachel, will you ever forgive me?"

There was utter sincerity in Margaret's face and voice. Rachel felt that she must have been mistaken in suspecting her of revealing the information, but she said stonily, "I don't know that my personal forgiveness enters into the matter. The fact remains that my confidence and trust in you have been destroyed and betrayed — and because of that, this swine of a blackmailer is still ruining the lives of countless women. Keeping them on the rack, making them live lives of deceit and intrigue. Now he has added murder to his crimes."

"Murder?" Margaret's face went grey. "But the paper said that death was due to natural causes?"

Rachel looked puzzled, then her face cleared. "Oh, no, not Therese or whatever her name was. No, I mean a nice little woman called Veronica McCawly, who wasn't even one of the blackmail victims. She just happened to live in a cottage once owned by one — who couldn't take it any more and committed suicide." She knew that she was causing pain by her words, but went on remorselessly, "The only crime Veronica McCawly committed was to find a cheque book — the stubs told a silent story. When she began to receive telephone calls, she was indiscreet enough to stand up to the man. She committed her final indiscretion by talking about it in a public place — she was, ah, eliminated. I think that is the word." She stopped. Margaret looked as if she was going to faint. Without another word, Rachel crossed to the drinks trolley and poured a double whisky. "Here, drink this," she ordered.

Margaret took the glass with a trance-like movement. She drank the whisky as if it were water, then turned her large hooded eyes on Rachel. "What do you expect me to do?" she asked.

"I want you to tell me all that you know about this racket, to give us some idea of where to look and whom to look for."

"You ask me to do that, when you've just told me of the death of that woman because she talked? Aren't you asking me to sign my own death warrant?"

"No. We're quite alone, nobody would know."

"Rachel, I can't — I don't know anything. I — I only pay..." She stopped, her eyes flaring wide in alarm.

"So it must be Eleanore who is the victim — we thought as much. And you pay the price for whatever she is guilty of. Margaret, don't you see — you must convince her that she must talk?"

Margaret shook her head. "My dear, when once you're enmeshed in a web like this, whatever little break you make, the spider quickly respins."

"Have you any idea who this particular spider might be?"

Margaret was silent, then she said, "Whoever I suspect, I have no way of proving guilt."

Rachel regarded her through narrowed eyes, then asked softly, "Does the fact that Khylos Mantanios owns both The Black Crab and The Looking Glass have any significance?"

The hooded eyes flashed with something like their former fire as Margaret said, "*And* The Looking Glass? No, I didn't know."

"It would be interesting to find out if he is by any chance the owner of that *apartment* that you sent me to."

Margaret winced, then said thoughtfully, "Perhaps it is possible to find out."

As soon as Margaret Cameron had left, the telephone rang.

"Rachel Groome speaking."

"Rowan here. Everything okay?"

"So far, yes. But Margaret refuses to help. She says that she knows nothing, beyond having to pay."

"She knew enough to know where to send you," he said shortly.

"Darling, I don't know — she could have got that information from Eleanore. I can't believe even now that Margaret *could* be a party to anything so — so utterly vile."

"H'm. As I've said before my love, your faith in human goodness is admirable — but one day you'll learn that no one's actions are predictable."

"Oh, Rowan, you make life sound so sordid."

"Only because it is. You know, in my job I see the worst of it. Anyway, I thought that you'd like to know that the afternoon edition of the *Star* carries a piece that I'm taking over the case again, with a broad hint at the blackmail angle."

She didn't answer for a moment, then said, "I hope we're doing the right thing. I'm a bit scared."

There was no sign in his voice that he was feeling not just "a bit scared" but downright terrified, as he said easily, "Not to worry, sweetheart. Everything's well under control."

I hope Rowan's right, Rachel thought, as she drove the Metro up Red Hills. She kept up a good speed, even on the deep climbing corners, a speed only possible with the road-holding Metro. She kept glancing in her rear-view mirror, and her heart gave a quick flip when she saw a car coming up fast behind her. It was gaining on her and she slammed her foot on the accelerator in a sudden panic, but the car behind stayed close. She noted automatically that it was a powerful BMW, then she had to concentrate all her wits and skill on keeping the Metro going at its utmost. As she eased round a deep left-hand corner, there was a burst on the horn behind her and the BMW overtook her as she came into a short straight, then disappeared round the next bend to the sound of a high revving engine. She eased off the accelerator with relief — just another commuter in a hurry and who knew his road well.

She forced herself back to some semblance of calm. She wasn't going to be of much use if she went to pieces at every passing car. She was being stupid. The news couldn't be out yet — but, yes, it could very well be.

It was with a sense of reprieve that she made the turn into the

Oxford's driveway; here for a while, at least, she could relax. With sharp disappointment she saw that the carport was empty. She switched off the engine and was wondering what she should do next when Celia Oxford appeared on the verandah.

"Why, hello," Rachel called, relief making her effusive. "I thought that you were all out."

"No, my car had to go in to be serviced. Do come in, Rachel."

Rachel followed her along the verandah to a cool corner away from the long rays of the setting sun. She was shocked at the change in the older woman; her firm plumpness had sagged, her face had sharpened. The makeup was still too thickly applied with a slapdash hand, with no apparent regard for enhancement. She looked vaguely at Rachel after they were seated. "I'm — I'm afraid that my husband is out…"

"That's all right. Better really, as it was you that I came to see."

"Me?" The vagueness was more pronounced now. The small dark eyes were dull and vacant, with a helplessness that made Rachel hate what she had to do.

"Yes, you. I think that you need someone to confide in, and you needn't be afraid to talk to me. You *are* in trouble, aren't you?"

Chapter 19

It was early evening when Rachel left the Oxfords'. Bands of gold flaunted across threatening black clouds that presaged further welcome rain. The drenching rains of the last few days had effectively broken the long drought and the banks were green again, grass encroached on the highway, clouds of yellow flowers had blossomed almost overnight and the dusty dryness of the past months had given way to a soft moist atmosphere.

A light wind from the mountains whipped through the open window of the Metro, as Rachel turned out of the Oxfords' driveway. She thought back over the conversation with Celia Oxford. What had it revealed? Only what they half knew already. At first Celia had hedged and maintained an attitude of bewilderment, until Rachel said bluntly, "Don't try to hide the facts from me. I *know* that you're being blackmailed. You've got to tell me what you know of these people, so that they can be stopped..."

Celia rose from her chair; she bore no likeness now to the plump, pampered St Andrew matron whom Rachel had first met.

"What do you know? Are you one of them? Have you come to make, to make even further demands?"

"I realise that you are getting near the limit of endurance, but try and be reasonable. You know of my association with Superintendent Rodgers — in fact, we're going to be married ..." She spared a moment and a piece of her mind to be slightly surprised at having put the possibility into words — so making it a fact? She pushed the thought away. "...So is it likely that I am one of *them*, as you put it?"

Celia closed her eyes and crumpled back into her chair. "I'm sorry, but I've been so overwrought — I don't know which way — to know that someone — *sympathetic*, knows, not just those *devils* — oh, God. Rachel, what am I to do?"

Rachel went and sat down beside her. Now that she had stared

Celia talking, she could drop the bullying approach. "Even to talk about it will help. If only you had talked to your husband earlier, you wouldn't be in this mess now."

"Talk to Merton? That's the last thing I could do."

"But you must," Rachel insisted, although she knew from experience what a difficult thing she was asking. "Tell me — from the beginning — how you became entangled and what the position is now."

Piece by piece the story came out. The husband, engrossed in work, socially secure and proud of that security, with fine high principles, principles which his wife with her lack of basic strong character, could not live up to, or even begin to appreciate. As affluence increased there had been less to occupy her butterfly mind, fewer household cares to worry about. Boredom took over:,boredom with her husband, with her house, and the uselessness of each day.

Then one day, a phone call: the caller male, with a low, cultured voice. A persuasive flattery, the insistence that they had met. Where? Oh, a cocktail party, a reception. She had impressed him so much, but he had hesitated so long to call.

She was sorry, but she couldn't remember... But of course, she must. He wanted so much to see her again... Impossible. Why? Because — impossible. Then: may I call you again?

Silence.

A soft goodbye.

No more calls.

She had waited, listening for the phone, wanting it to ring — but — what should she say? Of course she couldn't — impossible. It was all a joke, someone doing it for a wager — and yet, he'd sounded so...

Who would be so attracted to her? She was — middle-aged was a *kind* term. Face it, she was old. No, would soon be old. And life — what did she know? What did the future hold for her? Merton was self-sufficient — the thought of Merton in this context had made her grow cold with fear, as if he could read her thoughts.

If she did — what this man wanted — but after all, he had suggested nothing – she was letting her imagination run wild. It was a joke — a joke.

Then came the next call and there began the gradual breaking down of her fears and qualms. A persuasive invitation to a meeting. Celia shut her eyes at this point. "Just to put it into words makes it more unbelievable — I've never even allowed myself to *think* about it, consciously."

She had eventually agreed to meeting him. She could talk no further. Then she said bitterly, "*One* afternoon — and I've been paying ever since — until I've nothing left. I've used up what little money my father left me. I sold the property that came to me from my grandmother. I almost gave it away — I was so desperate for money. And now, I have no more. No more money, no more jewels, no more property. *Nothing.* No self respect, no future. And I have to meet the next payment."

Rachel felt sick. This was the confirmation of all that they had suspected, put into words by a frightened, foolish woman. This was the point that all the others had reached before the last desperate act of suicide. Rachel felt despair. This woman had reached the point when suicide was more than a possibility — it was a looming, menacing probability.

"Listen, Celia, I *know*, believe me, I know what you've been through. But don't you see you've got to tell your husband? Once you do the demands will stop. There will be no point any more."

Celia was haggard to the point of collapse. "You don't know my husband. He prizes prestige and social standing — his good name, his pride, his ambition, his conviction that he is always right. All of this will make him take the one course he will see possible — he will throw me out." Rachel started to protest, but Celia went on, "If he doesn't then he will be open to blackmail, for he will have to protect those qualities that he prizes above all else. No, Rachel, there's only one way out of it now."

The word was left unsaid and hung in the air between them.

"Celia, don't do anything foolish. Please wait. Tell me, you have your hair done at The Looking Glass, don't you?"

The abrupt change of subject and the apparent frivolity of the question made Celia frown in a puzzled, helpless way. "Yes, but..." she began, but Rachel interrupted, "Can you remember, was there anything — *any little thing* — that could have had any connection between The Looking Glass and that first approach by telephone?"

Celia clasped her hands, her eyes dazed. Rachel pushed away a temptation to shake her, but compassion kept the irritation from her voice as she said urgently, "Any slight reference to your husband? Any question about your private life? Any voice you recognised?" She stopped as Celia's eyes flared into life again "*Voice! Yes.* I knew that the man on the phone wasn't — didn't have the same voice as the man — I met. He laughed and said it was a trick of the phone, but I knew — and I've heard the voice before and since, however much he tried to change it — but I could never pin it down until..." She paused, the dazed look was less now, the faintest glimmer of hope lit her face.

Rachel waited. Why wouldn't the woman say the name? "Well, who was it?" she burst out at last.

"Who?" Celia opened her eyes in surprise, as if Rachel should know the answer. "Now I realise! It was Michel — the hairdresser from The Looking Glass."

So there we are back at the Looking Glass, Rachel thought, as she went down the hill road. Her thoughts had taken her mind from her own possible danger and her reaction was one of surprise when she was forced to pull up suddenly as a car shot out of a side turning right across her path. The light was practically gone now, but she recognised it with a sick certainty: the grey Audi that had been parked outside the apartment building on the day that she had been kidnapped.

She looked around wildly. The road was too steep to reverse and too narrow to make a U-turn. She fumbled with the door handle as a man got out of the Audi and loomed towards her. Even in the little light that was left she recognised Stillman. She flung open the door at last and stumbled out, although she knew that she had no chance of escape.

Then she screamed.

And she kept on screaming until the man reached her.

* * *

Police Constable Goodbody peered once again at the watch on his wrist: just on six. His long legs were cramped from sitting motionless in the dark parked car for so long. He felt a rising excitement at being on his own. At the same time there was a strong sense of comfort in the knowledge that Sergeant Phillips was parked a few chains away, and P.C. Pearson a hundred yards down the hill. Where the Super was he didn't know, but nearby, that was for sure.

He thrust his head out of the window and listened: no sound but the distant hum of traffic that drifted up from the plains, and close to, the gradual awakening of the nightly chorus of tree frogs, their voices in no way indicative of their diminutive size, the susurration of crickets' fast-moving legs and the occasional stridency of a croaking lizard in search of a mate. Faintly, from higher up, he heard the sound of an approaching car: then another from lower down, accelerating from starting point.

Then the screech of tortured brakes.

Then silence.

He felt a tingle of excited anticipation. Was this it?

He switched on the engine, eased the gear lever into position and waited, one hand on the handbrake.

Then it came — the sound that he'd been waiting for — one high-pitched powerful scream, repeated again. Then it was cut off in mid-scream.

Goodbody shot out from the concealment of the tall grasses and brought the car in a tight turn facing uphill.

* * *

Sergeant Phillips firmly grasped the familiar wheel of the staff car. He was worried: for once he had not agreed with the chief's plan. The element of risk and chance had seemed too great. They were dealing in the dark with unseen and unknown opponents. Phillips sighed; the chief had been adamant. He wished that he knew where Rodgers was at this moment. He'd given orders, then disappeared into the fast-approaching dusk. The lights of Kingston and lower St Andrew were winking on far below on the plains and lower foothills. The harbour was a placid silver within the long, protecting curve of the Palisadoes spit.

Phillips settled further down in his seat. I suppose those young bwoys, Goodbody and Pearson, enjoy this. Danger and excitement. He well remembered his own early days in the Force — no Police Training School; for him, just a few weeks training at Elletson Road Station. After that you learnt the hard way, and if you got an unsympathetic sergeant — then heaven help you. Phillips wondered briefly about his own sympathy or lack of it — the fact that he seemed to be able to get the last ounce of cooperation from young rookies seemed...

He sat up.

There it was, curling up the hillside, disturbing the birds just settled in their nests, startling a late lone higgler struggling up with her laden donkey, rending the sweet, jasmine-scented night with its shrillness, the rising crescendo of a woman's scream. Before the second scream had started, Phillips was on his way, down the hillside, no lights showing, the sound of his engine obscured at first, then startlingly loud at the abrupt termination of that third scream. He ripped through the gears as he went down towards that sudden silence.

* * *

Rowan Rodgers stepped into the main road from behind the grey Audi. He had placed himself high up on the hillside overlooking the road, armed with powerful binoculars. He'd watched cars come and go: Rachel roar up in her little Metro towards sunset, then one or two commuters, driving a bit raggedly after a day's work in the heat of the city below: a pair of lovers stopped to kiss, and Rodgers chafed at the delay, pushing back the memory of his own desire to do exactly the same at that spot so recently. They moved on at last...

Then a dark car — he couldn't be sure of the colour in the fading light — came up slowly, then disappeared from view. Minutes later it reappeared, stopped and reversed off the road into a clump of overhanging bushes that grew on a piece of fairly flat ground.

Rodgers smiled in satisfaction. He'd done a good 'recce' earlier on and had come to the conclusion that that would be the best place if one wanted to lie in wait and surprise someone.

The incident, inasmuch as it had confirmed his anticipation of events, cheered him. Earlier, he had briefed Ruel, "If a man ring for Miss Rachel and won't give his name, tell him that she gone up the Red Hills Road to visit a friend, and she'll be back for supper. Got that?"

"Yes, sir."

"If he does ring, let me know at this number."

Scarcely half-an-hour later Ruel had phoned. "The man phone, sir. I tell 'im like you say ."

"Good. What did he sound like?"

" 'Im voice sof' an' 'im soun' like a sweet talk man."

"That's the joker. Thanks, Ruel."

He knew that rachel would be at the Oxfords at least an hour — he could trust her to spin out the visit that long. He made his way silently down the hillside, passing far behind the parked car, mentally blessing his boyhood days spent in the country climbing over difficult scrub-covered terrain. He emerged on a partially overgrown track that led up to a now-deserted property. There was a dark shape ahead: he inched up close to it and whispered "Goodbody?"

The boy started, and Rodgers inwardly commended his quick recovery and his smartly whispered, "Sir?"

"Okay so far. Anticipation correct. Get through to Phillips on your radio. Keep your eyes and ears open. If you don't *hear* the signal, watch for mine."

"Right, sir."

Rodgers faded back into the bushes and made his way, sure-footed, back up the hillside to watch and wait. He knew that it wa a risky plan and he loathed putting Rachel in the slightest jeopardy, but it was their only chance — a gamble that might just come off. If it didn't — if the sprat didn't rise to the bait, then precious time would have been lost — and the whale's identity would still be unknown.

He shifted uneasily and wished that he could light his pipe. Then he heard the sound of the descending Metro about two curves above on the road. Immediately came the purr of the engine in front of him. He felt a rise of elation — he was right — if only there were no hitches at this final moment.

The car shot forward, lights blazing, cutting across the road ahead. He heard the wrenching screech of Rachel's tyres — God, he thought, let her stop in time.

Then silence descended as both engines were cut.

He waited breathlessly.

Not to rush it: wait — wait until there was no doubt.

As Rachel's first scream cut through the quiet night he was running forward, stumbling over the rough ground...

...he'd left it too late — just a few bare seconds of misjudgement. He was still about twenty yards away when Rachel stopped screaming — abruptly. The resultant silence too eloquent.

Chapter 20

Two hours later, Rachel had at last stopped trembling after a double whisky and Rowan's soothing arms. Now, she sat curled up in a corner of the long settee, wrapped in a terry robe.

"I was so frightened. I didn't know whether you'd spotted the car or not. Then at the last moment I felt that I wouldn't be *able* to scream — that no sound would come."

"You screamed, all right," Rowan grinned. "It echoed and re-echoed over the respectability of Red Hills. We've been getting call after call from worried citizens."

She looked at him doubtfully for a moment, and then laughed, "Don't be a clown, you've been here all the time."

He kissed her. "Anyway, sweetheart, thanks to your bravery, we've got that swine, Stillman. I'm pretty sure that he's responsible for Veronica McCawly's death. We found a print on the kitchen window — and if that checks, we've got him. Apart from which, he's the type of boyo to go off and do his own thing."

"He was horrible."

She relived that moment when she had felt his hand slam across her mouth, cutting off her scream for help. He'd grabbed her roughly round the waist with his other hand and said, "You little bitch — you run out on me before, eh? You trick me, but I swear, you won't get a chance to run when I finish with you — you'll be lucky if you can walk."

Oh, God, she'd thought, let Rowan get here. She was being forced backwards towards his waiting car. She'd given an ineffectual struggle and tried to bite his suffocating hand, then a dark shape had loomed, hurtling out of the darkness. There had been a sickening thud and the grip about her mouth and body had slackened. The man had fallen at her feet and she was sobbing in Rowan's arms.

Two cars had converged on the spot and Phillips and

Goodbody had sprung out as Pearson had appeared on the run.

"All right, sir?"

"Very much so. Take this swine away and lock him up. Book him when he wakes with assault and attempted abduction, extortion, blackmail — throw the book at him. We can add murder later if those prints add up. Goodbody, Pearson, leave your car, and take his. I want you to go and look for this old garage — here are Mrs Groome's directions as far as she can remember. If you can find it, try and discover the owner's name and report to me. I'm sorry to ask you to go up now, but if the rest of the bunch learn that Stillman has been arrested, they may destroy any evidence that might be there. I shall be at Mrs Groome's until about eight-thirty, after that at The Black Crab. Got it?"

"Got it, sir."

Goodbody and Pearson's dark heads had drawn together as they had scrutinised the instructions by the map-reading light in the Audi. Then they had given a smart salute and driven off up the hill.

Phillips had watched them go. "Them a good bwoy, Mr Rodgers, sir. Don't come no better. Glad that you all right, Mrs Groome, ma'm."

Rachel had given a shaky smile. " I knew you were all close."

"Right," Rodgers had said briskly. "You'll be all right with this joker? I couldn't send Goodbody up there alone."

"That's all right, sir. He's well cuffed. And out like a light from the blow you gave him."

"Good. I'll take Mrs Groome down. Send a man up for her car. Report to me at Mrs Groome's, then at The Black Crab, if you need me later."

Rachel gave a little sigh at the memory and asked, "May I have a cigarette?"

He lit two and handed her one.

"Thank you. Rowan, do we really have to go out?"

"Sweetheart, I know that you're tired, but it *is* important. I think that we should watch events at The Black Crab very closely indeed."

* * *

Police Constable Goodbody drove the grey Audi up the winding hill road. Yes, there on the corner of Swain Spring Road, was the housing development. So far so good. After the right-hand turn at that point the road became much steeper; the feeling of having plunged from modern civilisation into the hinterland of the past was very strong. The people of the little districts had an air of unsophistication and remoteness from the life of the city, just twenty minutes down the hill. To Goodbody, born and bred a country boy and in Kingston for only just over a month, it was an abrupt return to surroundings that he knew best.

The night air came crisply through the open windows, getting appreciably cooler with each foot they climbed. They passed the little shop that Rachel had mentioned. Tonight the shutters were thrown wide, a kerosene lamp glowed on the counter and cast soft shadows, spilling onto the road. A group of youths lounged on the steps, playing dominoes and listening to reggae music blaring from a radio beside them. An assortment of smells drifted to Goodbody and Pearson — the smoke from the lamp, the sickliness of wet sugar, coffee, the pungency of pimento, cheap rum and something that obviously was ganja smoke, but they had no time to investigate. The heavy beat of the reggae followed them for a while, then the silence of the night took command.

Pearson was also a country boy, but he had been in Kingston long enough to acquire a veneer of sophistication.

"Mrs Groome one brave lady, eh, Goods?"

"She too brave — me wonder how the Super ask her to do that — but it work."

"She goin' to married the Super?"

"It seem so, me son."

The road narrowed. The surface was still good, but the way turned and twisted, mostly upwards, although sometimes Goodbody came upon a surprising downward plunge, his headlights picking up, just in time, the bumpy peril of a cross drain.

He began to climb sharply again and slowed to look for a little used parochial road that led off from the left. He marvelled at the stamina that the fragile-looking Mrs Groome had shown in making the downward journey in the rain, on foot, with the added terror of possible recapture. Engrossed in these thoughts he overshot the road.

"Watch it, Goods, that could be it — 'bout two chain back."

Pearson warned. Goodbody reversed until Pearson exclaimed, "Here, man."

The side road was partially overgrown with lush, encroaching vegetation. The car made the turn; the surface was unbelievably rough and the Audi bumped and swayed crazily. He hoped that this *was* the right way. It was very narrow at first, then widened somewhat after a deep left-hand curve, which brought them round to another road — more like a track — that led off sharply uphill to the right.

"This look like it," Pearson said, as he examined the written instructions again in the light from the map-reading light.

"Yes, man, could be the driveway to the garage."

They went up slowly, in first gear, the engine labouring. The surface was rutted and full of potholes, slippery from the recent rains. Goodbody went into a skid on the last deep curve, but managed to correct it, then they came in sight of an old coach-house and they felt a thrill of recognition. This was it — this *had* to be it. This — even from the description given from Rachel's fear-filled memory, and the changes expected from seeing a building in the clear light of the rising moon, which had originally been seen through rain — was, nevertheless, recognisably the place.

Goodbody drew to a halt in the shadow of a large guango tree. Both young constables got out cautiously, glad of each other's company and thankful for the heavy comfort of their service revolvers, each snug in its shoulder holster. They approached the building on silent feet. Each was filled with an excited fear, an expectation of unknown perils which might confront them.

The big double mahogany doors were closed but not secured and Pearson swung one open; not surprisingly, it creaked loudly. They froze to immobility and listened for any sign of activity. There was no sound other than that of night insects and after a few moments they entered cautiously. The probing beam of Goodbody's flashlight roamed the emptiness — yes, this was the place, all right. The pile of rotting cement bags, a gleam of light from the moon outside, showed weakly through the space where Rachel had escaped.

"Is the place?"

"Yeah, man, mus' be."

They both felt a surge of satisfaction. Part one of their mission had been accomplished. They took a last look round and both shivered, then the scrabble of claws on the beams overhead made Goodbody flash the light upwards. Two points of glowing red and a vague grey shape moved quickly out of the light.

"Lawd," Goodbody spoke in a whisper. "How Mrs Groome stay in here so? The place have duppy fe sure."

"Cho, man, no such t'ing," Pearson said without much conviction.

They crossed quickly to the half-open door and, switching off the flashlight, slipped out into the fresh welcome of the night. They peered up the hillside to the dark shape of the main house. There was the faintest glimmer of light, coming from the first floor, Goodbody thought. The rest of the house was a black mass against the sky.

"Look like someone there," Pearson whispered.

"Seem so."

They kept close to the bank and followed the overgrown driveway up towards the building. They came upon it suddenly, big and sprawling, originally early Georgian, then new wings and an additional floor, repairs and alterations over the years, had reduced the architecture to a bastardy of styles. It looked utterly deserted and had an air of crumbling decay about it, that made Goodbody think once more of duppies. Luckily, his training and natural good sense had mostly eradicated the beliefs of childhood and heredity. Taking a deep breath, he removed his revolver from the holster and closely followed by Pearson, walked boldly up to the once elegant, but now sagging curve of the outside staircase.

The light that they had seen from below was coming from the entrance hall at the top of the double wooden stairway. They ran up lightly, feeling the tilt at the weight of their bodies. They heard a rustle from within, followed by the slow approach of dragging footsteps. The pool of light moved towards them as the sound of footsteps grew louder.

They waited, tensed, ready for action.

Into the opening where once a pair of double doors had proudly hung, appeared a little old man, storm lantern held high. His wrinkled face was like a shrivelled June plum, hair a contrasting white caracul above the blackness. An aura accompanied him, of an unwashed body, a mixture of stale and new-formed sweat, together with fumes from raw white rum, mixed with acrid smoke from the burning kerosene. It wafted towards the two young men and engulfed them. They narrowed their nostrils in distaste.

The old man raised the lantern higher and peered at them.

"Wha' you wan'?" he mumbled through the rotting stumps of a few blackened teeth.

"You get a message from Stillman?" Goodbody asked.

"Cho, man, me no get no message. Wha' 'im wan' now?"

"Him say 'im can't get up here tonight, again." Goodbody was ad libbing with a new-found professional touch.

The old man hawked and spat, a shining gobbet aimed unerringly over the railing. "Cho, me get the place ready, like 'im say me mus' do. When 'im gwine come?"

"I don't think that you going see him again — for a likkle while."

"Wha' dat you a-talk, bwoy?" Rum-laden breath, tinged with a foetid sweetness from the rotting teeth, came too close for Goodbody's comfort as the wizened face thrust up to his. "Who goin' pay me?"

Pearson took a chance, "Not to worry, man. Mr Mantanios wi' take care of you."

"Yeah, man. Mr Mantanios goin' take care of you. Don't 'im always pay well?" Goodbody added.

They waited. Were they going to strike pay-dirt or not?

There were further hawkings and guttural clearances, then the watchman kissed his teeth in contempt. "Since when Mr Mantanios see me, or the place, from the day 'im buy it?"

Goodbody and Pearson felt a surge of triumph — they *had* struck pay-dirt. Mantanios *did* own the place — one more nail hammered in.

"How long since 'im buy it?"

"Two, t'ree year."

"Who own it before?"

"Is de fam'ly house — long time — fe ol' Josh Cameron. Is one daughter 'im have, an' she say it too big for her — but wha' use it now? Is jus' me alone live 'ere. Keep out de goat dem. It goin' fall down, fe sure."

Goodbody silently agreed.

"So, what it use for?" Pearson asked.

The old man gave a lewd chuckle. "Dat Stillman, 'im 'ave one 'eap of lady frien'. Plenty-plenty, you see, son. It nice and quiet, don't it?" The lewd, obscene laughter welled up again, to be terminated in a fit of coughing, followed by more hawking and spitting.

"Yes, I see."

Neither Goodbody nor Pearson joined in the laughter. They gave a brief "goodnight" to the rheumy-eyed watchman, who shuffled back thankfully to his rum bottle, and went striding back down the driveway to the waiting car. They both felt a glow of satisfaction at a good night's work. That they had been lucky in finding the right place so easily didn't cross their minds. There were many disused tracks and parochial roads off the main road, mostly leading to dead ends, or joining each other further up the hillside. It was pure luck that they'd found the right one at the first attempt. Goodbody hadn't been in the force long enough to experience the discouragement of long depressing hours of painstaking enquiry that so often led nowhere, but Pearson had, and was more appreciative of the vital part that luck had played that evening.

It was only after Goodbody had made his triumphant report to Phillips, and the sergeant's rejoinder of, "So he own the place — that don't prove a thing," that his jubilation faded. All right, so he'd unearthed a fact — but where did it get them?

* * *

The Black Crab was crowded when Rachel and Rowan entered its dimness at about nine-thirty that night. They were ushered to the table that Rowan had reserved some hours earlier. From it there was a good view of the grotto-like bar and the entrance from the foyer. The air throbbed softly with a haunting Portuguese melody, played superbly by an unseen guitarist. The tiny dance area was packed. The level of conversation was a low hum, punctuated by an occasional high-pitched laugh, a strident variation.

There was a mixed aroma of expensive tobacco smoke, women's perfume, men's aftershave and cologne, alcohol and barbecued steaks — that assailed the nostrils and conflicted yet blended, to produce a scent that would, if caught again at any future date, bring that scene vividly to Rachel's mind.

She smiled at Rowan across the small table, with its centrepiece of a floating hibiscus in a brandy goblet. He moved the glass to one side, his large, well-shaped hands curving gently round its fragility.

"Nothing between us, not even something as ephemeral as that." He nodded towards the bloom, whose petals by the end of the evening would have spiralled inwards with approaching decay.

"I'm so glad that you persuaded me to come out, after all," she said.

The wine waiter hovered.

"You choose. Everything," Rachel said. "I still feel — drained, as if I could never make a decision again."

He ordered champagne. "This was to have been our wedding night, remember?"

He lit two cigarettes and handed her one. They smoked in silence, gazing around the crowded room.

"Look," Rachel said softly, her eyes flickering towards a table in an alcove.

He gave a barely perceptible nod. "The ubiquitous Mantanios and..."

"That's the girl — Barbara something or other — from the Looking Glass. Just a minute," she looked at him sharply, "just now you said 'Mantanios and...' as if you knew her. Do you?"

He gave her a bland look. "I was about to say 'and a very lovely little lady'." His black eyes met her grey ones with an innocence that she herself would have thought convincing, but she still regarded him doubtfully and said, "One minute you're reminding me that it was to have been our wedding night, and the next you're casting languishing glances at stray damsels?"

He laughed, "Sweetheart, I adore your jealousy act. It's a great booster for the male ego — but she doesn't look much like a stray."

They sipped the cold champagne and watched the diners and dancers. Then Rachel whispered, "I feel as if we were invisible, as if we were poised, waiting for the curtain to go up on the next scene."

"I wish that we were invisible — we could find out so much more. But the next scene hasn't been written yet — and it's going to be ad libbed all the way."

A waiter stopped by the table.

"Superintendent Rodgers? Telephone, sir. Will you take it by the bar or in the office?"

Rowan hesitated fractionally, then: " By the bar. Excuse me, sweet."

She watched him as he eased his big body between the crowded tables. He moved in the relaxed manner of a large cat. She half-smiled, then thought again of Bill — he hadn't been cat-like, he'd been taut, tense, nervous energy spilling over. Suddenly, she realised that she could think of Bill without that awful feeling of betrayal, she could remember him as he was, before he changed — before she stopped loving him.

Now, she thought, relief flooding through her like a heady wine, now I can marry Rowan.

He was sliding into the seat opposite. "You look radiant. Unutterable lovely. What happened when I took that call?"

She laughed. "I — I'll tell you sometime, not now. Was your call important?"

"Yes, and no. Young Goodbody." He lowered his voice and his lips barely moved. "Young Goodbody discovered that your erstwhile prison belongs to our friend here." His eyes flickered towards the alcove. "But, it had previously been owned by your very good friend — Dr Margaret Cameron."

Chapter 21

Barbara Barton sipped her drink and surveyed the crowded room. She saw Rachel Groome, exquisite in shocking pink and black, with that disturbingly handsome and attractive superintendent. She gave a little inward sigh — a man like that, and so obviously taken.

"You're very thoughtful tonight, my dear."

Barbara brought her eyes quickly back to her companion. "I'm sorry, I was thinking — it's a strange life — night life. All these people, one identity by day at their work, another by night."

He smiled, smooth face oddly Pan-like in the dim light. "Don't tell me that anyone as lovely as you has a philosophical bent?"

She laughed. "Not all the time. Only when I've had too many of these," she raised her glass.

Mantanios surveyed her through half-closed eyes. "And you, do you have one personality by day and another by night?"

Her eyes, large and limpid, didn't change expression as she said softly, "Indeed I do. These last couple of days, anyway. By day, just a plain working girl — and now by night, your guest at this fabulous place."

He put a smoothly plump hand over her slim dark one. "Is it a surprise to know that you work for me also? *I* own The Looking Glass."

Her surprise was perfect, not too quick, not too intense.

"But last night you said you'd never heard of it. Are you teasing me?"

"Perfectly serious."

"Well, how extraordinary."

"Why extraordinary?"

"Oh I don't know. You don't strike me as the type of man who — dabbles — in such, ahm, such a feminine type of business. I mean, well, a *beauty parlour*."

He smiled benignly as his fingers stroked the inside of her wrist. "I don't dabble, personally. But it makes money, and money is important."

She leaned closer, the table was very small. "Tell me more. What else makes money for you?"

He looked at her sharply, his parrot nose curving downwards. "Before I tell you that, I'll show you what money does for me; I'll show you my house up in the hills. Last night you said 'no', but tonight you'll say 'yes', won't you?

The hand he still held trembled slightly, her eyes flared for a moment, then she laughed and said gaily, "Why not? Yes, Mr Mantanios, I'd love to see your house."

He signalled to the barman and signed his bill. Barbara gathered up her bag and long white wrap, then Mantanios took her arm. They passed close to Rachel and Rowan's table as they went towards the foyer. Barbara stumbled causing the fringe of her wrap to catch on the edge of a chair and to drag across their table. A glass tipped over, spilling champagne. She stopped in confusion as Mantanios' grip on her arm steadied her.

"I'm so sorry." She looked quickly from Rachel to Rowan and back again to Rachel. "Why, it's Mrs Groome, isn't it? Do forgive my clumsiness."

"Of course." Rowan stood up and disentangled the wrap. "Please don't worry. Nothing broken." He smiled down at her, nodded to Mantanios, and they passed by on their way.

Rowan sat down, then glanced at his watch. He signalled the waiter. "Check, please, at the double."

Rachel regarded him levelly. "I think you might trust me," she said softly.

He grinned, white teeth gleaming against the dark skin. "I do, my sweet, but sometimes ignorance is safer. Come, let's go."

He reversed the Mercedes skilfully from the crowded car park and turned left up Constant Spring Road.

"This," Rachel said a few miles later after they had negotiated the deep curve at Red Gal Ring, "is not the way home."

He swerved to avoid a slow moving dray. "Maybe not to your

home, but somebody's," he answered cryptically. She could tell that he was smiling by his voice. She sighed, lit two cigarettes, handed him one, and settled back to wait.

"Well, if you want to go all cloak and dagger..." She left the sentence unfinished.

* * *

Barbara Barton experienced an unusual feeling of apprehension as she took her seat beside Mantanios in the big white Cadillac, which was rather ancient but still luxurious. She was a girl who knew her way around and could generally cope with any situation, but there was something unfathomable about the man beside her. That he must be ruthless to have got where he was, she knew too well. She thought briefly back to their meeting the evening before and wondered who had really engineered the encounter. She had been under the impression that she had been responsible, now she wondered if she hadn't been just a little bit too clever.

The road was climbing more steeply now, the cooler air from the foothills whipping through the open windows. The city lay sprawled beneath them, a mass of twinkling lights. Far out on the curving Palisadoes flashed the signal light of the airport control tower, and further still, the intermittent flash from the lighthouse at Plumb Point. To the west, the high stabbing flame at the oil refinery shot up and down.

"Well," Mantanios' voice broke the silence. "You're very quiet, my dear."

"I'm sorry. I was thinking how beautiful it all is."

He gave a brief downward, dismissing glance. "Yes, but like everything else, you get used to it."

"Like?" she queried softly.

"Perhaps not — money is an exception. Either the lack of it or a surfeit — one doesn't get used to either. I know, I've experienced both states." He caught her look of surprise. "Oh, yes, I lost everything that my father left, then built up again to what I have now, built it up the hard way. And of course," he glanced away from the road and she glimpsed his cold black eyes, "women — beautiful women. You note," he went on as she didn't respond, "I use the plural. I change my women as I change my clothes — to suit my mood or the occasion."

"And what happens," her voice was carefully casual, almost bored, "what happens if one particular woman doesn't want to be changed?"

He laughed. It wasn't a pleasant sound. "What a woman wants — any woman – and what I want, are two very different things. It's what I want that matters."

"Do you always make the position so clear when you invite a girl... to have a drink after hours?"

Her mocking tone matched his, and unexpectedly he laughed with real warmth.

"No, but this is not a usual occasion, is it?"

Once more he turned his head, and the black eyes were added points of darkness. He took one hand off the steering wheel and reached into the glove compartment. He fumbled for a moment then put something into his mouth. "Asthma," he said shortly. "Just a precaution, after the rain — and in anticipation, perhaps, of an exciting evening."

The gesture and the reason for it, made him seem more human, more vulnerable, and some of her apprehension faded.

* * *

Peter Cole watched the white Cadillac pull away from the kerb with that undulation peculiar to American suspension. He sat behind the wheel of his aged Austin and sighed with relief. He was getting cramped and was glad that at last there was to be some action. He slipped into gear and followed at a safe distance. Not that he was afraid of being recognised. Little battered old Austins were ubiquitous and not worth a second glance from a man like Mantanios. That little fool, Barbara — he hung far behind; he had a pretty good idea of where the Cadillac was heading. He'd done a bit of 'recce' early on. He could catch up the Cadillac easily enough if necessary, for underneath his bonnet was an engine that was capable of out-performing nearly any car on the road — not by any means a standard engine, not for that model or vintage anyway. He lit a cigarette with one hand and thought bitter thoughts about women in general and Barbara Barton in particular. Surprisingly, the rather vacant look that he had worn at dinner at The Black Crab had disappeared, and his dark brown eyes were shrewd and determined.

* * *

The Mantanios' mansion deserved no other description. It hung from the side of the hill as if held by an invisible support. White walls gleamed into he moonlight, a perfect example of Spanish Colonial reproduction. A high white wall, with a series of inverted horseshoe arches, surrounded the grounds. The drive swept in an upward curve, bordered on either side by fragrant frangipani, spaced closely. The delicate cream blossoms shone waxily in the brilliance of the moonlight, with an occasional splash of colour from the crimson variety.

Inside, the Spanish influence was carried throughout. Mantanios led Barbara across a wide entrance hall to a walled patio courtyard. Archways on all four sides led to the living quarters. The patio was tiled in a pattern of Moorish mosaic. In the centre was a round ornamental pool; a fountain sparkled and the gleam and flash of tropical fish added to the exotic quality. Apart from the underwater lighting in the pool, the place was lit only from the moonlight, which poured in from above, making sharp dark shadows in the Moorish arches.

She surveyed the place in amazement. "This is like something straight from the *Arabian Nights*. Do you live in this huge place all alone?"

He shrugged. "Mostly. The servants have their own quarters far removed, and know better than to be obtrusive — when I entertain."

She experienced a return of her earlier apprehension, magnified and pressing, but he went on in an impersonal voice, "Now, what can I get you to drink?"

He swung open the lid of a liquor cabinet.

"A very small whisky and water, please. I have to work tomorrow, remember?"

He poured the drink deftly and brought it across to where she sat on a low, white-painted, wrought iron chair. Then he went back and poured straight whisky on the rocks for himself. He took a deep swallow before he said, "You don't have to work tomorrow, if you don't want to. I'm your boss, remember?"

She smiled. Despite his words, his manner was still pleasantly impersonal. She was lulled for a moment into almost liking him, so that it came as a shock when he went on, still in the same tone, "After we have drunk a toast to your, ahm, continued good health, perhaps you will tell me who you are and what you want?"

The last words had a steely quality that made her shiver inwardly, but the hand that raised the glass was steady and her eyes held nothing but limpid innocence and puzzlement as she looked across at him.

"Why, Mr Mantanios, you know who I am."

"I know what you choose to tell me. That gambit of yours in the bar last night — very clever and would probably have fooled most men — but not clever enough to fool Mantanios."

Still, her face showed nothing of the thoughts that raced through her mind. "I'm sorry, but I still don't know what you're talking about. Our meeting last night was the purest chance – accident, call it what you will. If you were suspicious of my motives in agreeing to have a drink with you, then why did you ask me up here?"

He got up and moved close to her. He took hold of her wrist:;he had a surprisingly hard grip for such a plump and pampered person. "I asked you up here to find out what you're up to. *Now talk.*"

"I tell you, I don't know what you're talking about, and I think that I'd better go. I want to call a taxi."

She stood up, despite his hold on her, tall and regal. In grudging admiration, he said, "My God, you've got courage. I could use a woman like you." He still held her wrist and he drew her close to him as he said quietly, "You will not ring for a taxi, you will stay here until I am satisfied that I can trust you, then perhaps we can work out some..."

He stopped, a spasm of pain crossing his face. The grip on her arm slackened, and his glass fell to the ground, to be shattered on the tiled floor. His hands flew to his stomach as his colour changed to a waxen beige.

Barbara was startled into immobility for what seemed like minutes, by the unexpected turn the evening had taken. She gazed at the stricken man, then touched his arm. "What is it? Can I get you something?"

He tried to speak but made no intelligible sounds, then

crouched over in agony, until his knees were touching the ground, his hands clawing at his stomach. He looked up at her, his black eyes filled with pain and terror. Then blood, dark and mixed with a revolting brown slime, welled from his mouth and dripped down his impeccable suit onto the tiles. Barbara knelt down beside him, her eyes bewildered at the unexpectedness of his collapse.

"Try and tell me the name of your doctor," she began urgently, then stopped as he keeled over sideways from the crouching position, his knees drawn up to his chest. His eyes rolled up, showing the whites, and a long shudder went through his body.

Then he became quite still.

She felt for a pulse at his wrist. There was a final flicker – then nothing. She stood up, suddenly overcome with nausea. She took a deep breath to try and gain control.

She looked around wildly. Where in heaven's name was the telephone?

She crossed the tiles, high heels tapping with an unnatural loudness in the utter silence, and went through an archway into the square entrance hall. A slight sound from the grilled doorway made her freeze into immobility... then she flattened herself against the wall and inched back to the patio. She'd left her bag on the chair. Inside it was the small .22 automatic which she always carried.

The silence of the big house was almost palpable, broken only by the splash of the fountain and the plop of fish as they leapt out of the water for insects. She'd got her bag now and felt the comfort of the familiar cold metal in her fingers. she began to inch back again along the wall towards the ornamental grille-work of the big door. As she neared it, the grille swung slowly open and a dark shape slipped into the hall. Her finger was tightening round the trigger, when she recognised the intruder in the dim light. She gave a little sob of relief and ran towards him.

"Oh, Peter. Thank God you're here."

Peter Cole's large hands tightened on her shoulders. "What in hell's going on her? I came in because..." He glimpsed the gleam of metal in her hand. "Did that rat try anything? If he touched you, I'll..."

"No, Peter, he didn't. I mean — he's dead, I *think*..."

"Jeez! Did you...?" His eyes went back to the gun.

"No, I took this out afterwards. I heard a noise — you, I suppose. I was... he just clutched his middle and then, blood and... ugh! Horrible!" She looked down in sudden horror at her hands and the front of her dress. "Have I...?"

"No," Peter cut in, "You're not spattered or anything. What an awful experience. But, shouldn't we call a doctor?"

"I was about to look for a phone when I heard you." She stiffened. "Listen," she whispered. They heard a faint footfall outside. They stood, hardly breathing, as the door swung slowly open.

Again Barbara saw a man silhouetted in the open doorway, too far back in the shadow of the porch to be identified. Peter touched her hand lightly. She nodded and slowly raised her hand, the gun pointing steadily at the open door. A beam of light from a powerful torch cut through the too-dim lighting of the hall. As it swept over them, Barbara's finger again began to tighten, then slackened with relief as Rowan Rodgers said quietly, "Well, that's a nice reception."

"Oh," Barbara stepped forward. "I'm so glad that you are here."

"Good evening sir." Peter Cole moved from the wall to Barbara's side and Rowan grinned at the expression on Rachel's face as she followed him into the hall.

"Ah, Cole, I thought you were around. I saw your Dover Raceway special, parked further down the hill. May we join the party? Where's our host?"

"He's rather — dead, I believe. We... we were just going to ring for a doctor."

Rodgers' eyes snapped. "Dead? That changes things quite a lot. Rachel, allow me to introduce to you, Miss Barbara Barton, a.k.a. Police Constable Browning, and Mr Peter Cole, a.k.a. Corporal Peter Cole, both of the C.I.B."

Chapter 22

It was some two hours later. Rowan and Rachel were on their way home in the cool stillness of the night.

P.C. Barbara Browning had been driven home by an attentive Corporal Cole and the police surgeon had pronounced Mantanios' death to be due, after a preliminary examination, and subject to laboratory confirmation, to natural causes: to wit, a perforated peptic ulcer.

Rodgers had had the house sealed and had left a uniformed constable on duty. He planned to give the whole premises a thorough examination the next day, or he amended, later that same day.

"I can't believe that that gorgeous creature is policewoman," Rachel said. "I didn't know that you had glamour girls in the force."

Rowan laughed. "That young woman is a gem. She's easy on the eye..."

"That's an understatement."

"She's brainy, she's travelled, she's an expert on beauty culture, flower arrangement, she's been a receptionist, secretary. She's deadly at judo..."

"Stop, for heaven's sake. She can't be all that — she only looks about twenty-two."

"Twenty-eight, I believe," he said.

Rachel snorted, "You seem to know all about her. I suppose she dances divinely and cooks like a French chef?"

"Probably. I must put it to the test some time."

He glanced briefly at Rachel's set profile, then drew into the side of the road, stopped the car and kissed her. "This should have been our wedding night, remember?" he whispered against her mouth. "And don't ask me if P.C. Browning is as expert at this game as you are, because I wouldn't know."

"And you'd better not find out," she murmured. "Not even in the cause or course of duty."

"Agreed, neither in the cause or course."

He reluctantly restarted the car and moved off at a more sedate pace.

"Does Mantanios' death alter things very much?" she asked sleepily.

"You mean blackmail-wise? Probably simplifies things — if he is at the head of the racket. At least we can now probe through his affairs — we can get permission from his executors. If he was the brain behind the blackmailing group, with friend Stillman in our hands, we can rake in the smaller fry – we hope. Then I suppose the whole thing will just fizzle out through lack of evidence and cooperation from the victims."

She tucked her legs under her and Rowan put an arm round her. She snuggled against him — as much as the intervening gearbox allowed. "Hope none of your eager-beaver traffic cops stops us. Think of the headlines: 'Senior Superintendent Apprehended for Smooching in Car at Two a.m.' " Suddenly she straightened and was wide awake as she asked, "Rowan, don't you think that it's rather strange — *two* deaths in this case, *both* caused by stomach perforation?"

The car slewed to a stop with a squeal of brakes. "My God! I knew that something was niggling at the back of my mind. You're right, it *is* too much of a coincidence."

"But, darling," her sleepiness was completely gone. "Your police surgeon said that there was no doubt in the case of Therese. It must be a coincidence."

He looked at her in the dim light from the dashboard. "Nothing has to be a coincidence in police work, my love. When something seems impossible, that's when you start probing even deeper. Let's get home and get some sleep. I've a feeling that today is going to be a very busy one."

Rodgers' fears were fully justified. He was at his desk by eight a.m. in spite of the fact that he and Rachel had not gone to bed before four a.m. When he'd kissed her 'goodbye' she was still half asleep. She looked very young and innocent against the tumbled sheets, her dark hair ruffled out of its cap-like smoothness, her lashes a dark fringe against the coffee-cream complexion. He kissed her bare shoulder. "I don't know when, now, that I'll be able to make an honest woman of you."

Without opening her eyes, she murmured, "Not to hurry, honesty couldn't be better."

He lightly slapped her bottom. "I always knew it — you're a slut at heart."

She opened one eye, then winked it. "And you love it!"

Now he pressed a buzzer on his desk: it was answered immediately by a trim and energetic Goodbody. " 'Morning, Mr Rodgers, sir."

Rodgers smiled to himself: young Goodbody was modelling himself so closely on Phillips, that he was even picking up some of his verbal foibles.

" 'Morning." Rodgers flipped the open file in front of him. "You and Pearson did a good job in finding the house off the Swain Spring Road. As soon as Mr Phillips gets in, I want a word with you all."

"Yes, sir." Goodbody saluted and withdrew — there was no other word to describe it — it was a military manoeuvre.

Rodgers picked up the receiver. "Rodgers here. Would you get me the Forensic Lab... What?... only five past eight?... I know it's only five past eight, but I'm ... Oh, all right. But keep ringing until you get them. This is urgent." He replaced the receiver and picked up the intercom. "Is P.C. Browning here yet?... Good, send her in.'

Police constable Browning was efficient and remote in a well-cut black skirt and a white blouse, with three-quarter length sleeves and a small black velvet bow at the collar. She managed to impart glamour even to such severe clothing, although she obviously tried to conceal her charms and play down her attractive quality when on duty. She returned Rodgers' greeting with a cool, polite, "Good morning, Sir."

There was no sign of the exotic beauty whom he had seen dining with the late, but not lamented, Mantanios, or of the slightly dishevelled and rather tremulous beauty who had driven off with the protective Corporal Cole.

"Sit down, Miss Browning. Get home all right?" There was a flicker of wickedness in his black eyes, and her own lost their veiled businesslike expression for a moment. Her mouth quirked slightly as she said demurely, "Yes thank you, sir. Corporal Cole was — most attentive."

I bet he was, Rodgers thought; wedding bells and an arch of batons held overhead soon, or else I'm misreading the signs. "I'm waiting on the lab report," he said aloud. "Meanwhile, perhaps you will give me your verbal report and your findings, if any, from the time that you went to The Looking Glass, until last night. You can give in your written report at your leisure."

He felt a twinge of concern as he heard himself say the last sentence. He knew — and could do nothing about it — that he was treating this girl differently from any other constable, male or female. Was it just because she was an exceptionally attractive girl? He honestly thought not. Rather, it was because of her natural ability and proficiency which placed her high above her contemporaries in whatever assignment she was given. And, he argued, she wasn't likely to take advantage of being treated with some indulgence. He came out of his thoughts at the sound of her voice, low and musical, as she began to give an account of her investigations at The Looking Glass and The Black Crab.

He sat forward, intent, all personal thoughts sponged from his mind. "Tell me every little detail – however unimportant it may seem."

She nodded. "At The Looking Glass, there is nothing there that one can pinpoint, but there's an air of — of conspiracy about the place – an undercurrent — maybe I was looking for something like that, knowing the background. But quite definitely, all the customers are subjected to a careful questionnaire — very cleverly done. Is madam married? What does madam's husband do? Any children? Surprise at the age of the children — whatever. Madam's hobbies. After about two appointments a woman's life, her dislikes, thoughts and aspirations have been stripped from her so skilfully, that she was probably not aware of half the information that she was giving out. I might add that only older women were questioned; the younger ones were not included."

Rodgers looked thoughtful. "That figures. And who was responsible for this — gleaning of essential facts?"

"That slimy creature, Michel. I gather that the late Therese was also well-versed in the art. Michel told me that Therese always chatted a lot, that I must do that too, the customers liked to relax and talk when having their hair done, and I must encourage them. I think that he was leading up to the moment when they felt that they could be sure of me, then I would have been briefed and inveigled into the group. Just a matter of time."

"So the woman — the prospective victim – was encouraged to talk about her private affairs. Her character and her emotional state were summed up, and when they were convinced that they had found someone who *might play* — with a husband, or sufficient personal funds — who could pay, they prepared for the kill. Very pretty."

Barbara suddenly lost her quiet professional calm and burst out, "It's the most disgusting racket I hope I ever have to deal with. What these poor women must go through..."

"Don't forget that those poor women have all placed themselves, by *their* own weak foolish actions, into those positions."

"But they must deserve some sympathy. If their lives are so bare that they seize upon any chance of romance..."

"For God's sake, you're letting your feminine illogicality run away with you. Do you call *that* romance? Secret meetings in that squalid apartment house, or some such place — with someone you don't even *know*? My dear girl, it's nothing less than prostitution."

She winced as if he had struck her, then said sharply, "Don't. Don't say that."

He looked at her very keenly. She had gone very sombre and had spoken to him as a woman to a man, no sign, no remembrance of a junior member of the force addressing a high ranking officer. He let it go, as he sensed that there was a personal reason behind the outburst which had blurred her normally correct attitude and reasoned judgement.

She looked up, her eyes misted with tears. "I'm sorry, sir. I was very rude, but I should have told you when you assigned me to this case that my... my mother committed suicide about a year ago. I strongly suspected at the time, and I am certain now, that she was one of the victims of some such racket."

Rodgers said nothing for a moment; he blamed himself for not going more deeply into the girl's record and personal history. "I'm sorry," he said at last. "I don't recall seeing the name."

"No, you wouldn't. She divorced my father years ago and married again."

She was silent for a moment, back in the past. Rodgers pressed a buzzer and said to the constable who answered the summons, "Bring us some coffee, would you, Bennett? And ask Sergeants

Phillips, Goodbody and Pearson to come in, even though I am still engaged." He smiled at Barbara. "Let's take a coffee break, and I'll brief the rest of the team. Cigarette?"

"Thank you, sir."

She had regained her composure and was strictly formal again. The coffee arrived, simultaneously with Phillips and the two young constables. If any one of them thought that there was anything out of order in their chief drinking coffee and companionably smoking at eight-thirty in the morning with the most attractive member of the force, the fact was not registered on their faces. Phillips wore his usual, deceptively stolid expression, Goodbody his customary waiting-to-be-let-off-the-leash look, while Pearson gazed in open admiration at his glamorous colleague.

" 'Morning, Mr Rodgers, sir. ' Morning, er, Constable.'

Phillips had hesitated fractionally over the mode of address, and Rodgers' eyes twinkled. Old Phillips succumbing to the charm, eh, he thought. I swear that he almost addressed her as 'madam' or at least 'miss'. Aloud, he said, "Ah, Phillips. I want you, Goodbody and Pearson to go to this address. Owned by the late Mantanios. I've cleared all formalities with the authorities. Comb the place. Look for names, records, you know. Keep an eye open for a wall safe, either in the open or hidden, you know the sort of thing. If anything startling comes up contact me. I'll be here for the next half hour, then I'm going over to the lab. Okay?"

"Yes, sir."

They went out smartly, Goodbody and Pearson very conscious of Barbara's long, slim, brown legs. They both shot her a quick look, which she caught and gave them a smile. They practically stumbled through the door.

Rodgers laughed as the door closed behind them. "Have a heart, girl, they're only boys, and not used to such strong stuff."

She echoed his laugh. "Sorry, sir. One gets used to using all weapons."

"Not on my vulnerable young constables on duty. Save it for special assignments — and Corporal Cole," he added maliciously.

She blushed, but kept her composure. Rodgers, content that she had recovered from her outburst and emotional involvement with the case, said crisply, "Right. That takes care of The Looking Glass. What about The Black Crab?"

"Well," she said, thinking back, "I didn't get the impression that it's anything more or less than it pretends to be, although I know that one of the waiters — Ramsita Singh, a slim small Indian — definitely made reports to Mantanios. Each night that I went there, twice with Peter — Corporal Cole..." she avoided Rodgers' mocking eye, "... and then of course, with Mantanios himself — each night on a number of occasions, Singh made what seemed to be a report on a customer's movements or conversation. All that I managed to pick up was a snatch — something about two people leaving and going on somewhere — it was impossible to overhear what was said."

"But you feel that Singh acted as a look-out man and kept tabs on some of the customers?"

She nodded.

"What about the people who frequent the place? Were they the same people both nights?"

She recited a few names, well-known playboys and their swiftly changing girlfriends. The rather surprising combination of Smith-Watson and Veronica McCawly.

"And it was probably the vigilant Singh who reported that, with tragic results," Rodgers murmured.

"And twice, Professor Cameron and her fluffy friend. I thought it was odd; she seemed so out of place, somehow."

"She?"

"Professor Cameron."

"Oh." Rodgers realised with surprise that Barbara was referring to Margaret Cameron. "Of course. My — Mrs Groome knows her quite well. Nothing odd in dining out, the place has acquired a reputation for good food and service."

She nodded, rebuked somehow, she couldn't quite see why. For jumping to conclusions? But had she? She had merely recorded her impressions. She gave a faint shrug and continued with her account of her meeting with Mantanios, of his urging her to stay on and have a drink with him. His insistence that he see her home and that she should have dinner with him the next night, which she did. His repeated invitation to his home, which she had accepted. She paused at this point and Rodgers asked, "Was there anything in his manner to lead you to believe that he suspected you in any way?"

She shook her head. "No, he seemed to be behaving normally, although I haven't much experience with the tactics of — of an older man. And he was much older than my escorts usually are."

Rodgers nodded. "Fair enough. So you were reasonably confident that he supposed you to be nothing more than a good time girl on the make?"

She hesitated for a long time. "I don't know. Come to think of it, he did show some suspicion — he asked me what I was up to," she said honestly at last. "It's so easy to see things more clearly — looking back. I wonder where I went wrong and made him suspect me. I just can't put a finger on it. You ask if I was confident about the situation — I can see now that I wasn't, but because the set-up was —somewhat out of my line — I put my feeling of unease down to — to unfamiliarity with that type of man."

Rodgers smiled. "Don't dig too deeply. I'm not asking you to give psychological reasons for your actions and thoughts. So, you went to his house and he confronted you with not being all that you had represented yourself to be?"

She nodded. "I can't decide exactly what he did suspect. I'm quite sure that he didn't suspect me of being a policewoman. He seemed to be at the point of making me an offer of some sort when he went into those horrible convulsions. He was obviously in great pain – and then he died."

"On the point of making you an offer? You definitely got that impression?"

"Yes, he said that he wanted to be satisfied that I could be trusted and that we could work out — that was when he was overcome with pain. He could have been about to say 'work out some arrangement' — I don't know."

Rodgers got up abruptly and walked moodily to the window. "Blast it all — if that assumption is correct, he might have been on the point of getting you into the racket and we'd have been sitting pretty. Now we'll never know. It's all speculation now so it's just a waste of time."

There was a knock at the door. A constable entered, saluted and handed Rodgers a large brown envelope. "Report from the lab, sir."

Rodgers scanned the typewritten report: death had been caused by a massive internal haemorrhage, due to a perforation of the stomach. The extent of the perforation was such as to cause death within a very short time. There was a handwritten note attached to the form:

> *Dear Rodgers,*
> *In view of the extent of the perforation and in view of the fact that this case is similar to one recently examined under post mortem conditions, I am a little worried. I would have presumed that the cadavers would have had a history of stomach ulcers, but in the case of the first cadaver, Icilda Clements, this was not so. I state this after careful enquiry into her past medical history. I am in the process of pursuing enquiries along those lines with regard to this cadaver, and I should have the report later this morning. Perhaps you could drop by and see me at around 9:30 or so?*
> *Yours,*
> *E.B. Ericson, M.B., B.S., D.C.P.*

* * *

Rodgers glanced up at the waiting girl with a gleam of triumph. The first cadaver, Icilda Clements, alias Therese — he was thinking, there was now the first seeds of doubt as to the cause of death — perhaps not the cause *per se*, but how natural was now very much open to reconsideration. Rachel was right — somebody else thought it odd that two such deaths should occur so similar in character and connected by circumstances.

He glanced at his watch: nine a.m. Half an hour before he could find out anything more concrete.

"Right, Miss Browning, go off duty now. You went through enough last night to warrant some time off. If that conflicts with the duty roster, have the roster officer contact me. Report back to me at, say, fourteen hundred hours. Right?"

"Right, sir." She got up fluidly, a fact that Rodgers was too preoccupied to appreciate. The door closed softly behind her and he studied the report again.

The police surgeon had doubts — but doubts were not enough. What he wanted were hard facts. He tilted back his chair, lit his pipe and when the blue smoke was curling about his head, the bowl glowing satisfactorily, he shut his eyes and tried to think back to his days of swatting in the chemistry lab at school, and to a crash course in the Forensic Department overseas.

There was a tantalising feeling at the back of his mind that the answer to the problem was really very simple.

Chapter 23

The extensive search carried out by Phillips and the two young constables had yielded nothing. "Just sweet nothing," he reported in disgust to Rodgers some two hours later. "We went over the whole place carefully. Absolutely nothing."

"Did you find a safe?"

"Yes, sir. In the study. Just insurance papers and title deeds of property."

"Property?" Rodgers queried. "Did you examine them?"

"Yes, sir. This is a list of them."

He passed his notebook across the desk: Rodgers ran a quick eye over the names — The Black Crab, The Looking Glass, two hotels on the north coast, a number of department stores in the various shopping plazas, two apartment buildings in the respectable atmosphere of upper St. Andrew, and three bachelor apartment buildings in the more doubtful locality of the borderline between lower St Andrew and Kingston.

Rodgers flipped his finger at the list. "And you call all this 'sweet nothing'?" he asked.

Phillips grinned. "Is not for me to raise you hope dem, Mr Rodgers, sir." He lapsed by design into a broad local accent and idiom.

Rodgers grinned back. That meant that Phillips was not too dissatisfied with the morning's work. Phillips' grin broadened even further as he reached a large hand into his trouser pocket and brought out a key with a flat disc attached to it by a short chain. "And, sir," he said with infuriating slowness, "I find this — a key to a safety deposit box."

Rodgers took the key and studied the tab. "This, I hope, is worth its weight. I'll have the contents checked at once. You old fraud, Phillips, coming in here exuding gloom and despondency, when all the time you struck it rich."

"Not rich, but it mek a little loose change, sir," Phillips said complacently.

"And the loose change is adding up," Rodgers stated. "But what the final figure will be, I doubt if even a computer would be able to fathom."

He tossed the lab report across to Phillips. "The sting is in the tail."

Phillips read it, then asked, "You seen Dr Ericson yet, sir?"

"I have."

Rodgers recounted his earlier interview at the Forensic Laboratory.

Dr Ericson had met him with a worried frown. "I don't like this, Rodgers," he had stated flatly. "There's something here that doesn't correlate. I passed the first cadaver, Icilda Clements, with reservations in my own mind. So much so that I made exhaustive enquiries as to whether she had had a history of any gastric trouble whatever. I managed to track down her private doctor, and he was adamant on the point, absolutely nothing in that line."

"When last did he see her?" Rodgers had asked.

"About a month before she died — some gynaecological trouble, he said." Ericson had pursed his lips and added dryly, "I have my own ideas about that, but let it pass. The point that I am trying to make is that I was not happy that an apparently healthy stomach should perforate so extensively without any previous signs or symptoms. But as I said, I passed it as due to natural causes because there was nothing, absolutely nothing to warrant my withholding a certificate." He spread his hands. "And now you send me this one. The same — no, not the same. In this stomach there were *two* perforations — difficult to ascertain at first — again in an apparently healthy stomach."

He had paused, and Rodgers had asked, "Had Mantanios any medical history of stomach trouble?"

"No. I got hold of his medical practitioner." He had mentioned a well-known society colleague. "Mantanios was a bit of a hypochondriac and paid visits for regular check-ups very frequently. Apart from asthmatic tendencies — which he was apt to exaggerate — he was in pretty good physical condition."

Rodgers had sat stock-still.

Asthma.

"Was there any mention made of the treatment he took for this asthma?" he had asked at last.

Ericson had pursed his lips. "No, but I would imagine that it would be routine — some form of tablet, or more likely capsules." He had looked at Rodgers sharply. "You look as if I'd given you some good news. I don't get it."

"You may have given me a lead. Capsules! There was a box of capsules in the handbag of the late Icilda Clements — otherwise known as Therese. Not that time for asthma — just the everyday misused tranquillisers."

"And you think that's important?"

"It's a connecting link. Now we have *three* connections: two deaths by suspicious haemorrhages, capsules, and the two dead people linked to The Looking Glass."

Now Rodgers looked expectantly across at Phillips. "Well, what do you make of it? Think, man, think."

"I don't rightly know, sir. Is a connection all right, but Lawd, Mr Rodgers, every other person take tranquilliser these days. If is not pill to mek them sleep, is pill to wake them up."

Rodgers shrugged, deflated, and got up impatiently. "You're right, of course," he said wearily. "I'm seeing too much in too little. But, Dr Ericson is not happy about the medical findings. There's something unexplained. And you know Dr Ericson; he won't rest until he can be quite sure that those two little words 'natural causes' are the only two that he could possible use. So — we've got to follow it up."

"Where and how, sir?"

"Back to Mantanios' house. Wait, though, get me P.C. Browning on the phone."

A few moments later Rodgers was saying, "Sorry to disturb your off-duty hours, Miss Browning, but while you were with Mantanios, did he at any time take a capsule?"

"A capsule?" Her voice came faintly over a humming wire. "Yes, sir, he did. He took one on the first night that I met him — and one again last night."

"At what time last night?"

"I'm not sure as to the exact time, but it was while we were in his car on the way up to his house."

"So that would be about half an hour before he died?"

"About that, sir, give or take five minutes."

"You say that he took the capsule in the car? What were the capsules kept in?'

"In? Oh, he kept them in a little box — a jewelled snuff box. I think that he left the box on the dash board of his car."

"Right, thank you."

Rodgers rang off and turned to Phillips. "Did you search the car when you went over the house?"

Phillips looked annoyed with himself. "No, sir. Sorry, sir. I just glance inside for papers."

"Not to worry. You weren't expecting jewelled snuff boxes to figure. Come on man, let's go."

* * *

Rachel was finally woken at about nine-thirty, by the vigorous kneading of small, darkening paws in the vicinity of her waist. She rolled over and opened sleepy eyes. Two blazing blue eyes glared back at her, as Bamboo kneaded even more fiercely, at the same time slitting her eyes, laying back her ears and uttering a low, complaining wail.

"You little feline tyrant," Rachel murmured. She stretched out her hand to stroke the little cat, then immediately uttered a sharp cry. Bamboo had, with lightning speed, wrapped her front paws around Rachel's wrist, digging in her claws for tighter purchase and at the same time pedalling furiously with her back paws, trying to sink her teeth into the palm of Rachel's hand. Rachel managed to get her hand free only by giving Bamboo a little slap. She now sat gazing at Rachel malevolently and growling softly, deep in her throat.

Rachel massaged her sore hand. "Little beast. Oh, all right, I'll get you some breakfast — you poor starved creature. You're as bad as Li Po ever was."

She slipped on a terry robe and scooped Bamboo to her shoulder. She reflected that at last she could think of Li Po without a twist of pain. One more milestone passed, she thought with satisfaction. Ruel was in the kitchen preparing lunch when Rachel appeared in the doorway.

"Morning, Ruel," she said crisply.

"Morning, Miss Rachel. Coffee, ma'am?"

"When I've fed this creature."

She dropped Bamboo on a high stool at the counter top and opened the refrigerator door.

"But, Miss Rachel, me put down de food fe her, an' same time she jus' look at me so an' walk off." Ruel looked pained, his dark face without its usual cheerful grin.

Rachel laughed. "Don't worry, she likes me to feed her and as long as I'm here, she'll be stubborn. Don't forget, she's that formidable combination — female, feline and Siamese.

"Ma'am?" He looked bewildered.

"Not to worry, she'll get used to you."

"She let Mr Rodgers feed her. She won' tek nothin' from me, but when Mr Rodgers here, she nyam it up fas', fas'."

Rachel laughed again. "Ruel, I believe you're jealous. You'll just have to woo her," then interrupted hastily, "give her plenty sweet talk, nuh?"

He flashed his teeth in a sudden smile. "Yes, ma'am, she certainly need sweetenin'. She too fenky-fenky."

He clattered the cups as he brewed Rachel's coffee and she wandered out to the back verandah. She smoked a cigarette and looked towards the ever-changing hills, but she looked unseeingly, her thoughts occupied with the events of the night before. She couldn't get the two deaths out of her head —Therese (she refused to think of her as Icilda Clements) and Mantanios. It was definitely odd. She knew enough about medicine, superficially, to know that when a lab report came back with an answer like that, it must be right, but the niggling thought persisted that something was wrong — somewhere, somehow.

She drank the steaming fragrant coffee that Ruel placed beside her, and wondered if she dare ring Rowan and ask for the latest news. She rang the station and was told that Superintendent Rodgers was out of office.

She put down the receiver and suddenly felt useless, drifting.

Then she remembered Celia Oxford.

Oh God — she had said that she had to make a payment today. But if they were right and Mantanios was behind it all…

She flung off her robe and dressed as fast as she could, hardly bothering to make up her face and merely flicking the brush lightly through her hair. She went quickly through to the garage, calling to Ruel, "If Mr Rodgers phones, tell him I've gone to see a friend. I'll soon be back."

"But Miss Rachel, Mr Rodgers say you not to go out alone."

"Oh, cho, it's all right now."

"Ma'am?"

"No time to explain. Have to hurry." She reversed the Metro out into the driveway, while Ruel almost danced with frustration. He was thinking: Don' Mr Rodgers say she no fe go h'out? But 'ow me fe stop 'er? Oh, me Lawd, Mr Rodgers goin' kill me.

He desperately hoped that no harm would come to Miss Rachel, not entirely due to any affection that he felt towards her, but rather because of the hearty respect he felt towards the large frame and biting tongue of Rowan Rodgers.

Rachel's fear that she would be too late grew as the little car wove through the morning traffic on Constant Spring Road, then she was on Dunrobin and quickly under the bridge. A group of schoolboys straggled across the road. She put her hand on the horn, changed down fast, then slammed hard on the accelerator. The Metro shot through the lounging boys and scattered them in a cloud of khaki uniforms, startled faces and a choice of expletives that should not have been known to those of such tender years. One or two wolf whistles followed her and a few admiring comments at the little car's performance. Then she was away and had soon left the plains, climbing fast.

The Oxford residence was bathed in the brilliance of the mid-morning sun, its shuttered windows giving an air of somnolence. There was no sound from within the house or without, although the door leading from the verandah was open.

Rachel listened intently, almost afraid to break the still silence by knocking. It was unnatural, this lack of sound at this time of day. One would expect the clatter of crockery from the kitchen, the hum of a vacuum cleaner, the whirr of a food processor, the slap of slippers on tiles, *some* sign of domesticity.

There was nothing: not a whistle from a yard boy, not a mutter from a helper.

And yet Celia's car was parked once more in the double garage, back from being serviced.

Rachel stepped into the house. Its coolness wrapped around her in a distant welcome, a house perfect in furnishing and decor, flowers arranged as if by a florist — but a house dead and remote, like an arrangement of furniture in a store window.

The unease which had been with her on the drive up, increased to a point of fear. She walked to the centre of the living room, then stopped — the silence had been broken by a rasping sound. Her eyes widened in alarm as she understood the significance of that sound — it was someone breathing stertorously. She ran across to the archway that led to the bedroom, the silence broken now by the click of heels on tiles. The bedroom door was half open and she flung it wide. Celia Oxford lay on a bed, still fully dressed, as heavily and as badly made up as ever, her breath coming in the deep rasping gasps that Rachel had heard.

Rachel rolled up an eyelid then felt the barely conscious woman's wrist — her pulse was too rapid to count. As Rachel stood there, the rasping stopped, the breathing becoming deeper and deeper.

Rachel dropped Celia's wrist and gazed around the room – what had she taken? No sign of a bottle or — she hurried to the adjoining bathroom. On the wide ledge of the deep golden yellow basin was a small brown bottle — quite empty. She picked it up and examined the label: ONE TABLET TO BE TAKEN AT BEDTIME, WHEN NECESSARY. So, a fair assumption: sleeping pills. Oh, my stars, she thought, if I phone for a doctor, it'll have to be reported — and time will be lost.

She ran through the silent house to the kitchen, its shining whiteness was clinically impersonal. She opened one of a battery of cupboards. No — no — the third try was successful: a large canister of salt. She found a glass and ran warm water from the tap into it, then poured in salt lavishly. The water turned opaque, then settled to a slight cloudiness. She took a plastic bowl from one of the sinks and hurried back to the bedroom. She put an arm under Celia's head and forced the glass between her clenched teeth.

It was no good — the liquid just rolled down the slack face. Rachel dropped Celia's head back on the pillow and raced back to the kitchen. She had seen there a small, plastic, pot-plant watering jug with a long spout. She emptied the salt water into it. It was easier to force the spout into the woman's mouth and she poured the liquid down, holding up Celia's dead weight as well as she could, and hoped that the saline was going into her stomach and not into her lungs.

Suddenly Celia gave a convulsive start and vomited the salt

water. Most of it went all over the bed and not into the bowl. Rachel held the woman up and forced more liquid down. She herself was panting now with the exertion, sweat plastering her clothes to her body and running down her legs and arms, trickling into her eyes.

She kept on relentlessly.

She went back to the kitchen for more salt and water. Now Celia was beginning to fight; her eyes were wild and open, unfocused. She tried to speak in a voice that was hoarse and unintelligible. She was wracked with vomiting, but Rachel would give her no rest and kept pouring the saline down her throat.

Celia was struggling now. "Let... sleep. No... no!" She batted Rachel's hand away.

Rachel slapped her on the face, hard stinging slaps, first on one side and then on the other. "Wake up, Celia," she commanded. "You've got to stay awake."

"No... let me sleep. I... can't." She was wracked again by vomiting and at last Rachel felt that she must have rejected most of the tablets that she had taken.

She cleared up the mess as well as she could, then half pulled, half carried Celia to the other bed in the room and undressed her. The continuous movement effectively stopped the older woman from falling asleep again. There was recognition in her eyes now, as she tried to focus on Rachel's face.

"Why?" she whispered. "You should... have let... me... die."

"No, not now. It's all right, there's nothing more to worry about. Do you understand? There's nothing to worry about now."

Celia muttered, "I can't pay... can't pay..."

"You don't have to, not any more," Rachel insisted, hoping that it really was so. "I'm going to make you some strong coffee. You'll be all right until I get back."

Luckily Rachel found some instant coffee. She held it to Celia's lips. Her head was nodding again, but she managed to sip it. She didn't protest when Rachel insisted that she take a second cup and had almost finished it when the phone rang. Her eyes filled with terror as Rachel picked up the receiver.

"It's, it's... I can't pay. Oh, God, why didn't you let me die?" She turned her head into the pillow, tears of despair and weakness ran silently down her cheeks, runneling what little makeup was left.

Rachel held the receiver to her ear.

"Yes?" she said in a fairly good imitation of Celia's voice.

The soft voice that answered her made her catch her breath.

"Celia? I'm just reminding you — this afternoon at two. And, by the way, it's double the usual amount. Understand — double."

Rachel didn't answer; her mind was working fast. Had they been wrong about Mantanios? Was this...

"Are you there, Celia?" The caressing note was less now.

"Yes — at two, you say? Where?"

There was a click and the line went dead. Rachel returned the receiver to its cradle and turned to Celia. Her eyes were closed and her head was nodding. Rachel glanced at her watch: nearly twelve-thirty — God, she'd been working on Celia for over two hours.

The usual place? The same apartment — or somewhere else?

She shook the almost sleeping woman, then slapped her again, hating to do so, yet she knew that it was vital.

"Celia — listen to me. Where is it that you go to pay that man? You must tell me."

Celia's head lolled and she fell back on the pillow.

Rachel shook her and slapped her harder in desperation, but it was against all the odds. It was impossible to waken her to get the information that she so dearly needed.

* * *

The snuff box was still undisturbed on the dashboard of the Cadillac. Rodgers picked it up carefully in his handkerchief. "Not," he said, "that there's any likelihood of prints other than those of Mantanios."

He opened the lid; inside there were six capsules, the plastic shell a pale, nauseating, orange colour. Rodgers wrinkled his nose in distaste. He had a healthy aversion to capsules of whatever size or colour. He shut the box, then opened it again and sniffed. Apart from the somewhat sickly smell of the synthetic that made up the shell, there was the faintest whiff that seemed familiar and yet elusive. He shut the box again and handed it to Phillips.

"Right, let's get these to the lab at the double, although they're probably innocuous." He glanced at his watch: nearly twelve-thirty. He'd ring Rachel when they got back to the station. In the staff car he surveyed Phillips chunky profile. "Er, Phillips?"

"Sir?"

"How'd you like... er, to be a witness, at a wedding? As soon as we have breathing space?"

Phillips turned his head, shaken out of his customary stolidity. "You, sir? And Mrs Groome? Well, to think that life spare me to see the day." His eyes were back on the road in time to swerve and avoid a cyclist who was riding with one foot nonchalantly up on the cross bar.

"Watch it, Phillips — and don't put your mouth on life sparing," Rodgers exclaimed, then he poked his head through the window and swore at the cyclist in a mixture of Standard English and West Kingston expletives that left Phillips shaking his head in awed admiration.

"Quite a collection, sir. Would cost you a few hundred dollar in court."

Rodgers left Phillips to take the snuff box to the laboratory, then dialled Rachel's number. Ruel answered.

"Gone *out*?" Rodgers exploded.

"Yes, sir."

Ruel sounded thankful that he was at the other end of the line and not face to face with the not unexpected wrath.

"Where?"

"She jus' say she gone to see a frien'."

"Did she mention any names?"

"No, sir."

There was a short angry silence, then Rodgers said, "Right, Ruel. Have Miss Rachel call me as soon as she comes in. You hear, *same time*."

"Yes, sir."

Ruel breathed a sigh of relief as he put down the receiver. He was not too sure that he was going to like having the super around permanently. He heaved an elaborate sigh. "Life hard, fe true, y'hear," he informed the sleeping Bamboo.

Rodgers replaced the receiver and also sighed. He had told Rachel that she was not to go out unaccompanied. And now off she went without even leaving an address where she could be reached. God, he'd never change her; she'd always lead him a dance. The phone shrilled at his elbow. He picked up the receiver and barked, "Rodgers, here."

"Oh, thank goodness — I've been trying…"

"Rachel! Where are you? I told you…"

"Don't bark at me, darling, and don't be cross. I can't take any more."

There was a tremble in her voice that softened his own. "All right, sweet. I'm not cross — just worried about you. Now take a deep breath and begin at the beginning."

He listened intently as she told him, first of her fears regarding Celia Oxford, fears which were fully justified, how she found Celia almost too far gone, her battle to bring her back consciousness, and the telephone call. "I'm sure that it was Michel's voice, I could swear it," she ended. Then she added, "But, it wasn't Michel who spoke to me before."

"What about Mrs Oxford? Is she going to be all right?"

"I think so, she's asleep — but it is sleep and not a coma. It took me ages to get from her the address and the room number where she had to go."

She gave him the address and he recognised it as one of the other bachelor apartment buildings owned by the late Mantanios.

Rachel went on speaking quickly, outlining a plan that she had formulated. At one stage he gave a protesting, "No, I forbid it."

There was a short silence,then she said softly, "Don't be silly, darling, you can't forbid me yet."

Rowan tightened his lips at the implication. "Don't try blackmail on me, my girl…" he began, but she cut in:

"Darling, you've got to agree. It's after one now, there's not much time. It's too good a chance to miss." He hesitated so long that she said, "Rowan?" in that particular breathless way.

"All right, sweetheart, but for God's sake, be careful, and I swear, honest to God, that this is the last time… Rachel?"

But the line was dead. She'd made her point, got her way — why wait for more?

Rodgers scowled, smiled in spite of himself, then pressed the buzzer. "Sir?" Goodbody answered the summons.

"Is Mr Phillips back yet?"

"Yes, sir."

"Then get him, Pearson, and yourself in here at the double."

"Yes, sir."

One good thing that Goodbody was picking up from Phillips, was never to waste time in needless questions.

Then Rodgers laughed as he thought back over his recent conversation with Rachel — and its abrupt conclusion.

Chapter 24

As Rodgers finished giving the team detailed instructions there was a tap on the door. A uniformed constable entered, saluted smartly and handed him a brown envelope.

"Laboratory report, sir."

"Thank you, constable."

Rodgers scanned the report, his eyes narrowing. "Nothing but the usual combination of antihistamine and ephedrine, the normal prescription in allergy cases," he murmured. "But a faint trace of kerosene on the bottom of the box and on one of the capsules. Kerosene, that must be what I smelt, but couldn't put a name to it. Strange." He looked at Phillips, his eyes puzzled. "Why would anyone put kerosene in a box of asthma capsules?"

Phillips' expression was blank. "P'raps him just have kerosene on him fingers when him take one out," he offered without much conviction.

"Can you imagine Mantanios ever letting kerosene touch those pudgy, well-cared fingers?" Rodgers frowned. "It must mean something. Phillips, did you ever do any chemistry at school, or remember what you did?"

"No, sir. When I go to school, it just the three R's we concentrate on," Phillips said, content in the knowledge of how much more he had absorbed since those days.

"Goodbody?" Rodgers asked, not really hopeful of help from that quarter.

"Sir?"

"You do any chemistry at school?"

"Not much, sir, but what I did do, I liked."

"Pearson?"

"Little, sir."

"Well, can you recall any chemical that requires the presence of kerosene, for storage or what have you?"

The two young constables frowned in thought, then conferred briefly, then Goodbody's face lit up in a wide grin. "Yes, sir."

After the answer had been given, Rodgers said bitterly, "As obvious as that, eh? What a fool I am. It all adds up. But how was it done — and by whom?"

The 'how' could be worked out now, the 'who' was not so easy, although a possibility kept nagging insistently at the back of his mind. It was one that he would rather not dwell on, and he tried to push it still further back.

* * *

Celia Oxford's car was a veteran, but well cared for, Mini, circa 1976. The woman drove carefully, still feeling shaken after her ordeal, and the heavy make up had been put on with a hand even less steady than usual. The black hair was stiff and unnatural with lacquer, while the over-fashionable clothes made their habitual gaudy impact, screaming their unsuitability to the world. She kept her hands on the wheel, grasping it like a lifeline. Occasionally, when forced to stop at a crossing or a red light, she glanced at the package on the seat beside her, too big to go into the garish, shiny plastic handbag.

She was below Cross Roads now; the traffic was heavy, the end of the lunch hour. Music blared from sound systems and record shops, music that was harsh and raucous, which had lost any pretence to melody by excessive amplification. Idlers lounged against open shop fronts, tight pants or jeans, dirty merino tops or once brilliant T-shirts, which revealed bulging muscles, brawny arms and bare black chests. Beggars sat against crumbling walls, whining for alms from any passerby. Barefoot boys thrust grubby hands through the open car window at every red traffic light, and cursed roundly when the request : "Gi' me a five dollar" was not complied with. Higglers sat on the pavement, with goods of every description on offer: foreign shoes, dresses, anything that was hard to get locally. These higglers were more prevalent in the uptown plazas, which were dubbed the 'bend down plazas', but the occasional one was seen below Cross Roads, where she sat on the pavement, her wares piled beside her on a bit of crocus bag, making no effort at making a sale in the somnolent heat of the afternoon. Flies buzzed over heaps of garbage piled in the gutter, to be rifled by thin-ribbed dogs.

The squalor intensified as the woman turned the Mini into a narrow lane of mean little zinc-roofed houses, dirty surrounding yards with a dripping standpipe and a half-naked child chasing a scrawny chicken. These vignettes of a life, the existence of which she only half acknowledged, passed by the woman as she eased the little car through the piled refuse that desecrated the side of the narrow pavementless road.

She could feel the sweat breaking through the heavy makeup, runneling it to further incongruity, and dripping down her neck and between her breasts. Her hands grew sticky on the wheel and she wiped them alternately on her dress. It was with relief that she left the base little street and entered a wider thoroughfare, a backwater that once had an air of wealth and leisurely living about it, in the days when the clop of horses' hooves and the gentle roll of carriage wheels were the common form of transport, perhaps even, the wheels of a kitatereen of Lady Nugent's Day. Now the old houses had fallen into decay and disrepair. Some were already virtually demolished to make way for new buildings. She slowed down, uncertain, then saw what she as looking for — a white painted 321/2 on a high grey wall.

She glanced around in a sudden surge of fear. It was very quiet, even the constant roar of traffic from Slipe Road was muted. There was no one in sight as she turned into the open gateway and followed the drive round to the back of the building. A solitary car was parked by a flight of steps that led up to the back verandah. It was a dark blue Toyota, fairly new and well kept, unremarkable and able to remain anonymous in traffic.

She reversed and pointed the bonnet of the Mini towards the gateway. She locked the passenger-side door, but left the keys in the ignition and the driver's door unlocked. She got out of the car heavily and with reluctance, and went slowly up the steps.

The verandah was cool and quiet and quite dark. She hesitated at the entrance to the house, then walked with lagging footsteps along a corridor. The room at the end — that was her goal. The silence pressed in on her like a living presence and she glanced behind her, expecting, fearing to see she knew not what. She peered at her watch; it was difficult to read in the dimness, after the glare of the afternoon sun.

One minute past two.

She took a deep breath and pushed open the door. She left it slightly ajar as she stepped a yard into the room. A man was reclining on the bed. She turned so that her back was towards him and looked at half of the room reflected in a mirror in front of her. She heard the bed creak as he heaved himself to his feet and came and stood behind her.

"You're coy today, Celia," the hated voice said softly. "You've no need to be — they've got Stillman, damn them. You brought the money?"

She passed the package over her shoulder. He took it and went back to the bed. She moved slightly so that she could see his expression reflected in the mirror. He dropped the package beside him and took from his pocket a small round box. He opened it and she was galvanised into action.

"No, don't," she said as she swung round and knocked the box from his hand.

"Hey, what the... Hell, you're not..." Michel had lost both his carefully acquired Gallic accent and the nurtured, soft, caressing tone so that it was pure Jamaican that came out. Then his expression changed swiftly from amazement to anger and then to fear as he looked at the painted face of Rachel Groome.

She was a caricature of Celia Oxford as she faced him in the heavy makeup, stiffened, teased hair, and the padded too large garments. As he lunged towards her, she screamed, *"NOW!"* The door burst open wide and Phillips, Pearson and Goodbody entered, closely followed by Rowan Rodgers. The three overpowered the struggling Michel as he spat profanities and obscenities at them.

"Are you all right, sweetheart?" Rowan took Rachel in his arms, regardless of the others. She leant against him weakly, not caring that she was covering his shirt with makeup.

"Yes, but don't look at me — I look awful."

He laughed in relief. "You couldn't look awful if you tried; though I must say, I like your usual style better."

She pulled herself from his arms and bent to pick up the pill box and the scattered capsules.

"What's all this?" he asked.

"He was about to take one — tranquillisers, I think. I've seen him take them at The Looking Glass, but..." she faltered, then said hesitantly, "I knocked them out of his hand."

"Why?"

She avoided his eyes as she answered, "I suddenly remembered that in two recent deaths — capsules in some form or other were present."

He regarded her levelly. "You have either a greater knowledge of chemistry than I gave you credit for, or the old intuition's working overtime."

He turned away as Michel started to scream on a high unwavering note, and slapped him hard across the mouth. The screaming stopped and a keening wail took its place. "Shut up," Rodgers commanded, "or I'll give you something to really cry about." The wail became a gentle whimper.

Rachel bent and gathered up some more of the scattered capsules; she had seen three more on the further side of the room. "That seems to be all of them," she said as Michel was taken sobbing from the room. She handed the box to Rowan who slipped it into his pocket.

"I'll get them analysed, but first I'm going to take you home. Goodbody, follow in the Mini. We can get it back to Mrs Oxford later."

He took her firmly above the elbow and led her to the waiting Mercedes. She leant back against the luxury of the deep, leather upholstery, suddenly drained. She felt as if the exertions of reviving Celia, followed by the danger of the role she had just played had robbed her of all energy.

He slipped in beside her and said, "And I hope, woman, that this is the last time that you'll find yourself in such a place."

There was a knot of slatternly domestics grouped in the courtyard that served as a car park, gazing in muttering unease at the receding police car, the uniformed constables, and the big grey Mercedes. Rowan glared at them as he swung the car in a tight U-turn.

"I'll have this bloody place closed down," he murmured.

She didn't answer, but lay inert, her body giving in to the sway of the car. She felt his hand rest lightly on her knee, but was unable to acknowledge it, by either a tremor of thigh muscle or by lifting her hand to put on his. The car drew up at her house, and he helped her out and steered her through to the bedroom. He held her close for a moment and looked down at the strained face beneath the garish makeup. His black eyes were very tender.

"My poor sweet, you're exhausted. I'll get Ruel to bring in some tea, or would you prefer coffee? Or maybe a good strong drink."

She gave a deep sigh and spoke in a slow dragging voice, "I'm sorry — suddenly I'm so damned tired. I just need sleep now, coffee in an hour. And you?"

He bent and kissed her. "Ugh! It's so gooey — much nicer kissing just plain *you*."

He eased her back gently onto the bed. "I have to go back and see that slimy little Michel, or whatever the swine calls himself. He's been booked by now — I want a talk with him."

His eyes were hard now, implacable.

She reached up a heavy hand and touched his, "Darling, I don't like to..." She tapered off then almost whispered, "You *hit* him."

"You think that I'm in danger of becoming the brutal type you read or hear complaints about over the call-in shows? Don't worry sweetheart, that was a slap to stop hysteria. Not that I wouldn't like to rough him up a bit. Are you forgetting already the agony of mind that he's been responsible for in all those women? Believe me, the short agony of the body that I subjected him to, could never approach what countless women have gone through mentally — and he's morally responsible for a number of suicides. Don't forget that or feel sorry for him or for anyone connected with this racket."

She tried to smile, but there was pain behind her eyes. She turned her head on the pillow and asked, "The handbag that I had with me?"

"It's in the car. I'll get it."

He was back almost immediately with the shiny plastic monstrosity that Rachel had taken from Celia Oxford's cupboard. She took it from him and held it possessively. He quirked an eyebrow at the gesture. She didn't meet his eyes, then he bent and kissed her gently.

"You're so exhausted that I don't think that you need my stern injunction not to move from the house until I get back. I should be here at about five — six at the latest."

Then he was gone.

She waited until she heard the sound of the Mercedes being

put smoothly through its gears, followed by the receding hum of the engine, then with an exaggerated and heavy slowness, she opened the handbag and searched its unfamiliar depths. When she found what she was looking for, she contemplated it for a long time. The pain in her eyes intensified as she was forced to a conclusion that she was loath to accept.

* * *

Phillips greeted Rodgers as he entered his office a short while later, with a cheerful, "He's as guilty as hell, sir, bawling like a pickney that get a lickin'. It seems he knew that everything was over, with the arrest of Stillman and the death of Mantanios, so he came up with the bright plan to get on to all the women on the list and ask them to double up on the payments — to make a killing before the whole racket had to stop."

"Did you get from him how many he'd contacted?"

"He swore that Celia Oxford was the only one — he may be lying, but he's gone to pieces so badly, I don't think so."

"Get P.C. Browning and have her telephone all these women..." Rodgers began, then stopped as he remembered her personal involvement. "No, I'll do it myself. What about Stillman?"

"That is a tough one, sir. Act tough, is tough — but that Michel, he spill enough to convict them both, two times over."

"If it can be proven in court," Rodgers murmured. "We still won't be able to get anyone to testify."

"Stillman may take the rap for the murder of Veronica McCawly — if we can match up just one print from that window frame. His prints match those on the door of Mrs Groome's car. And Stillman can't get away on the charge of the abduction of Mrs Groome," Phillips reminded him.

"Unless I have a choice. I want to soft pedal that charge." Phillips was silent, and at last Rodgers burst out with, "Good God, Phillips, don't stand there like judgement. I'm not proposing to ignore the charge for personal reasons. It's just that I think that we've got enough on him otherwise."

Phillips nodded, his normally expressionless face suddenly compassionate. "Yes, Mr Rodgers, I understand how you feel, sir."

He picked up a file and went quickly from the office. Rodgers clamped his teeth on his unlit pipe. Of course, Phillips' unspoken criticism was justified, he was trying to shield Rachel from unwelcome publicity. Surely, after all that she had been through she deserved that consideration. He felt a sudden urgent desire for her, and shut his eyes as he tried it banish it.

This bloody case, riddled with sordid, sickening undertones, like a squirming nest of disturbed young drummer cockroaches, slimy, obscene, filthy. And to the end, the answer to the two deaths, of Therese and Mantanios, was not yet in sight. That of Veronica McCawly, there was no doubt of who bore the guilt for that. One down, two to go.

He pulled Rachel's list of the women's names found in Therese's notebook from the file, and dialled the first number. He was half-way through the list, a difficult yet welcome task, assuring worried women that it was all over, no more payments, no more waiting in fear for the telephone to ring. He assured them that their names would be forgotten, no records would be kept. He impressed them, by his voice, of his sincerity and integrity. He was about to begin on the second half, when Phillips entered the office. His manner was as usual, all trace of censure gone.

"Sorry to interrupt, sir, but thought you'd like to know right away. The capsules: one of the well-known group of the monoamine inhibitors, known to the man in the street as tranquillisers."

Rodgers grinned admiringly at the ease with which Phillips rolled the medical terms off his tongue, then his face hardened again, "And which any bloody fool can buy over the counter at some drug stores. I've said it before, and I'll say it again, that Sale of Drugs Law, has got to be enforced. There are still too many who flout it."

Phillips raised his eyebrows at his chief's vehemence. "Well, then it'll be up to us, won't it, sir?"

"I know — and we don't have enough men to do it, and more important things to do. But have we? Look what this unrestricted sale leads to — suicides and God knows what."

"Phillips waited, then said quietly, "That not all, sir. In the box was the very faintest trace of one of the distillates — kerosene, probably."

Rodgers became absolutely still.

He gazed at Phillips for a long moment, two pictures of recent events etched sharply in his memory. At last he said softly, "Was there, Phillips? Was there indeed?" He reached for his telephone and snapped at the operator who answered, "Get me Mrs Groome, 9992555, and *hurry*."

Chapter 25

After Rowan had left her, Rachel lay inert, absolutely still. Every part of her body felt leaden. She knew that her exhaustion was due in part to lack of sleep, in part to the emotional involvement she had with the case and the heavy responsibility she was under after her recent deduction. She drifted back to a childish game that she used to play when a schoolgirl: if I shut my eyes and go to sleep, everything will be all right when I wake up. But this formula didn't work — it never had in the past — there was the inevitability of the present, and the need for action when sleep was done. She sighed and felt her body become less heavy.

Unwanted thoughts crowded her mind. She had this vital knowledge — this awful certainty — what was she to do with it? Could she just ignore it? Just pretend that it wasn't there? And live with the knowledge for the rest of her life?

Her life— with Rowan?

There could be no life with Rowan if she said nothing. There would always be this between them. However hard she tried to conceal the fact, he would sense that some barrier was there. She stirred restlessly, each question and unsatisfactory answer chased round in her mind like a mouse on a wheel.

She pulled herself slowly to a sitting position. The enervating weakness was passing at last, thank goodness. She must get this ghastly dress off and clean the heavy, streaked makeup off her face. She wondered briefly how Celia Oxford was. Before she had left in her impersonation of Celia, Rachel had called Merton Oxford. He had been up at his house as fast as the traffic would allow, and she remembered his ravaged eyes as he had stood looking down at his still sleeping wife.

"Why?" he had asked in agony. "Why didn't she tell me? She means the world to me."

He had turned his eyes to Rachel as she had said softly, "Tell her that when she wakes up. It'll make it so much easier."

Now, sitting groggily on the edge of the bed, Rachel hoped that was true. She groped her way to the bathroom and washed her face, scrubbing with painful thoroughness to get off the makeup and the memories it conjured up. She had a shower, and was just stepping out of the bath, wrapped in a large towel, beginning to feel light and buoyant again, when the telephone rang in her bedroom. She padded in, leaving wet footprints on the tiles.

"Rachel Groome speaking."

"Rachel — I — Rachel..."

At first Rachel didn't recognise the voice, then realised that it was Margaret Cameron. "Margaret?"

"Yes. Rachel..."

"What is it? What's happened?" Rachel asked, alarm flaring.

There was a long pause; she could hear Margaret breathing painfully. She was either crying or fighting for control, or..."

"Margaret, what is it? Are you ill?"

"No, but... could you come up — now— it's Eleanore. She... she's dead."

* * *

As Rodgers waited impatiently for his call to come through, he looked with distaste at the contents of a folder that had been taken from Khylos Mantanios' safety deposit box. It was conclusive proof that he had organised the blackmail ring. There were pictures that made even the hardened and worldly-wise Rodgers' eyes gape when he realised who were the people involved. Slowly, and without further examination, he tore them into small pieces, then tried to erase the names and faces from his memory.

"See, personally, that these are burnt," he said to Phillips, then sat, head in hand, an expression of repugnance on his dark face.

Phillips watched him stoically. Lord, but he'd be glad to see the end of this case. Good thing when Mr Rodgers get married and settle. That Mrs Groome, she one nice little piece. Phillips thought of his own wife, Adassa — plump, complaisant, a good wife and mother — but sometimes a man want more than all that *goodness*... The buzz of the telephone broke into his musings.

"Yes?" Rodgers barked. "Ruel? Miss Rachel *what*?... but she

...*where?*... *when?* ... oh, God... No, never mind."

He slammed the receiver down in an uncoordinated jangle and rose to his feet at the same time, scraping back the swivel chair. "Phillips, get a staff car and follow me. No, on second thoughts I'll handle it alone."

His face was set in anger and another emotion, which if Phillips hadn't known his chief so well, he would have described as fear.

Phillips stood irresolute after Rodgers had gone, then decided to ignore the cancellation of that barked order. He hurried through to the Station Room,

"Goodbody? Ah, good. Come on, man, fast. Where's Pearson?"

"Here, sir."

"Come."

They raced through the Station Room, down the steps and were behind the wheel of a staff car as Rodgers' Mercedes disappeared through the main gates. There was a crescendo of sound from the engine as he went through the gears and a scream of brakes as he cut across a slower moving vehicle.

"Mr Rodgers goin' get tek up fe speeding, if 'im not careful," Goodbody observed, with a glint of anticipation, as if to say: That'll be the day.

"The bwoy who do that will have a hard time to make the charge stick," Phillips replied as he shot through the gate in a fair imitation of the chief's performance. "Hold on, bwoy, we got to move, even to keep him in sight."

The homeward-bound afternoon traffic was heavy and sluggish. Rodgers kept the Mercedes in low gear and overtook whenever he could, cutting in and out of the stream, oblivious of the glares and curses of other drivers. He handled the big car with impeccable skill, but the danger lay, as always, in the other driver doing something stupid. He was just above Cross Roads, overtaking a long, slow line, when he heard the whine of a traffic control motor cyclist. The man drew alongside.

"Pull over to the side, please, sir."

They were travelling parallel. Without slackening speed, Rodgers snapped, "Superintendent Rodgers, C.I.B. Move ahead and clear the way. Quick, man. This is urgent."

The patrol man hesitated, and dropped back a little. He'd heard of the redoubtable superintendent, but he head never seen him. He drew alongside again, to see Rodgers holding out his identification card through the window, still without any reduction in speed.

"Satisfied?"

"Yes, sir. Right. Where to, sir?"

"Get me as far as Papine. I'll take it from there."

The motorcycle shot ahead, siren wailing and Rodgers following close behind. Phillips, caught in the stream of traffic, and lacking the driving skill or sheer audacity of his chief, acknowledged defeat and settled for a slower speed.

* * *

As she turned right at Gordon Town, Rachel pulled over to the left and slowed down. There was no room on the narrow bridge for two cars to pass, and a big, low-slung American car was coming towards her. She recognised the driver as Dr Michael Lazarus. He half-raised a hand in salute as he passed, and intuitively Rachel was certain that he had just come down from Margaret Cameron's cottage. Why she should assume that, she didn't know, but it possessed her mind. All the way up the steep twisting road, that turned back on itself again and again, but ever sharply upwards, she tried to keep her thoughts grimly on driving. She kept hearing Margaret's voice saying: *she's dead.*

She's dead.

The words grew louder and louder in her mind, until they seemed to bounce back and forth between the encircling hills, like an echo that wouldn't die.

She's dead. *She's dead. SHE'S DEAD.*

She stopped the car on a slightly wider strip of road, a stony natural lay-by, and lit a cigarette to steady her nerves, then got out and stretched. The sheer beauty and green calmness of the deep valleys and high, wooded peaks acted like a sedative, and a light cool breeze, spiced with the scent of logwood blossom and wild vanilla, invaded her senses. The harsh chatter of an unseen parrot ousted the statement that had been repeating in her head, and she got back into the Metro, able to continue the journey in some degree of peace.

Margaret Cameron was sitting on the terrace, a glass in her hand, as Rachel braked the Metro to a smooth stop. Margaret didn't move, watching Rachel mount the shallow steps with dull eyes. She wasn't drunk, but she had obviously been drinking steadily. Rachel looked at her enquiringly, but the once fine, observant eyes seemed to be looking inwards.

Rachel sat down on a rocker. "Margaret, what happened?"

With an effort Margaret turned her head and focused on Rachel's face.

"She's dead."

"Yes — but how? Have you called the doctor?"

"Yes, he left — some time ago."

"Dr Lazarus." Rachel stated.

"Yes."

"Margaret, you asked me to come up. I'm here. So tell me what happened."

Margaret lifted the glass with a mechanical gesture and drank deeply. Then she put it down beside her on the table with exaggerated care, and for the first time looked at Rachel as if she really saw her.

"Eleanore — she had a haemorrhage — from the stomach. There was nothing that I could do. She was dead before the doctor got here."

Rachel's eyes dilated in sudden fear. A haemorrhage from the stomach! Again?

"What caused the haemorrhage?" she asked in a whisper.

The dull film left Margaret's eyes. "Why do you ask?" she asked sharply.

"Because you don't just have a haemorrhage for no reason."

"But there was a reason. She had been seeing Dr Lazarus about an ulcer. He was going to use this marvellous new treatment that was developed in Britain recently. He was waiting for a new shipment to arrive. He said that there was no doubt as to the cause."

Rachel's eyes probed the older woman's face, trying to read her expression. She saw a mixture of despair — and what? A touch of triumph?

Suddenly she had no doubts. "That was lucky for you, wasn't it, Margaret? I mean, that she did have an ulcer. The others didn't."

"The others?"

"Oh, come on, now. You didn't get me up here just to repeat what you said on the phone. Or have you changed your mind?"

"Changed my mind?"

Rachel got up impatiently. "Margaret, you're much too intelligent to go on repeating my words. Let me help you. Eleanore is dead: that much is a fact. She died from a gastric haemorrhage; that too is a fact. The doctor is satisfied that the death was due to natural causes, but we both know *that's* not a fact, don't we?"

An expression of relief spread over Margaret's face. "How do you know?" she asked in a voice that was nearly normal.

Rachel opened her handbag and took out a paper tissue. She opened it and held it out for the other to see.

"An unremarkable capsule."

"Where did you get that?" There was only academic interest in the question.

"Michel — whom I'm sure you know from The Looking Glass — was about to take a tranquilliser. I knocked the box from his hand. When I gathered them up later, I noticed that this one had no proprietary name on it, together with the faintest smell of kerosene. There have been too many instances of perforated stomachs lately, linked with capsules in some form. Did Eleanore take one or was she *given* one?"

Margaret got up and walked to the edge of the terrace. "I didn't give it to her. She went to my laboratory and helped herself, despite my strict orders to the contrary. She said that she had run out of her usual type. The point is academic though, for — sooner or later — I may have been forced to put one among the battery of capsules that she used for various ailments."

Rachel shuddered. This woman whom she had known and admired for so many years, just stood there calmly discussing murder in a dispassionate, scientific way. She forced herself to speak calmly as she asked, "So that's what you did, just slipped a prepared capsule among — your victim's ordinary ones?"

Margaret turned, her eyes were serene. "It was very easy. Everyone these days takes some form of drug. I was lucky that my victims, as you call them, took theirs in capsule form. During my visit to The Looking Glass, it was easy enough to put one among the girl, Therese's. She often left the box lying around. The same with Michel. I knew from long ago that Khylos Mantanios kept his capsules in snuff boxes — one on the dash board of his car. So on my visit to The Black Crab I left one for him. I knew that sooner or later the right one would be taken. It was just a matter of time."

Rachel reached shakily for a cigarette. "How can you stand

there talking so calmly about people you've — murdered."

"Murdered? I don't look at it like that. I brought them to justice. They were beyond the reach of the law, as no one would testify against them. It was my duty, as I knew those who were responsible for the misery of untold women — a misery that would go on and on until the day when suicide was the only answer."

"But you can't play God. If you knew who these people were, then it was your duty to expose them, not to go around dispensing your brand of justice."

"And if I exposed them, what then? Not one of those women would have come forward with any evidence."

Margaret's voice had lost for a moment its cool detachment and had taken on a note of biting scorn. Rachel gazed at her helplessly. "But what will become of you?" she asked.

"It doesn't much matter what becomes of me now. Eleanore is dead. I've no one else."

"What about your work? All you research — wasted, for what?"

"Not wasted; no research is ever wasted. Someone else will pick it up, where I leave off. And for what, you ask. For the peace of mind of an uncounted number of women, most of whom I do not even know."

"But, Margaret, what about your peace of mind? How can you live with the knowledge of what you've done?"

Margaret regarded Rachel pityingly.

"I thought better of you than this, Rachel. Peace of mind is something I have not known for a very long time, and as for living with the knowledge of what I have done — good God, girl, if one has the courage to do certain deeds, one has to have the courage to stand by those deeds."

Rachel didn't attempt to argue the point. Either Margaret was quite mad or more sane than anyone she had ever known.

"You still haven't explained why."

"You still don't see that — that scum — had to be removed?"

"You must have had a driving force — a triggering off — not just an altruistic impulse to suffering womanhood?" Rachel insisted.

"Yes, I had a driving force. I should have thought that your agile mind would have discovered what that was," Margaret said sarcastically. She was quite in control now, all trace of sorrow and the effects of alcohol gone. She returned to her chair almost briskly. She lit a cigarette, picked up her glass and said, "I'll get you a drink. You look as if you could use one."

While she waited, Rachel tried to arrange her chaotic thoughts and emotions. The revelation that Margaret Cameron could not only contemplate but accomplish another human being's death, and then talk about it in a cool, detached manner as if it were a scientific problem, left her doubting her own sanity. That she had feared something like this was not the point: having her fears substantiated by confession created new problems. She raised her head as Margaret came back and handed her a glass.

"Whisky all right?"

"Fine." Rachel gazed at the amber fluid and the moving ice cubes, then took a deep drink. "Please go on," she said.

Margaret remained standing, her back to Rachel, looking towards the shadowed hills and the soft rose tinted clouds of approaching sunset. She began to speak in a flat monotone.

The impersonal monotone, Rachel realised, was a self-imposed barrier between her repressed emotions and the events that she was recounting. She turned on Rachel and asked, "Can you understand? You, with your complete and utter femininity? You've had a husband — and, I suspect, as many lovers as you wanted or had the time for. You've always basked in male adulation, and even managed to keep a few women friends. Can you even begin to realise or imagine what it would be like to be cut off from all that? And to have no recompense?"

Rachel was silent, then Margaret said quite quietly, "I'm sorry, you can't help what you are, as I can't help what I am. None of this bothered me very much. I had my work, I was good at it. I was absorbed, I didn't need anything else. And then I retired and came up here to live. I have my research project, it keeps me occupied, but I was lonely after the bustle of life at the university — the student body constantly changing, the visiting bigwigs. So, I asked Eleanore Tarrant to come and share my life."

She fell silent, looking inward and back to the past. When she spoke again, there was pain in the fine, dark, hooded eyes, and the curving nose was pinched at the nostrils. "You must realise that to me Eleanore was just a friend. She'd been divorced from her husband years earlier — I'd known her on and off. I was fond of her

— in a purely platonic way. It wasn't until she was installed here that I discovered what she was — and why her husband had divorced her. She drank steadily — those migraines were nothing more than hangovers. Then, she began to make advances towards me and when I showed no interest, she looked elsewhere, and found what she wanted. The Looking Glass crowd soon saw what she was — and catered to her needs. Pictures were taken..." Margaret shut her eyes in pain. "And through them she was being blackmailed. She had no money — so I paid."

"But, why?" Rachel burst out. "Why didn't you tell her to go to hell? You had done nothing to warrant blackmail!"

"How could I? Nobody would believe that I wasn't guilty — as she was. We lived together, alone, remote. It would have been her word against mine. And she was vindictive enough, because of my coldness towards her, to lie to the hilt."

"And she threatened you with that?"

"Oh, yes. She paraded before me the publicity, the shame, the degradation of my good name in the scientific world, in he social world. She banked on my — fanaticism — my family pride. She knew that I was the last of the Camerons. I can trace my ancestry back to one of D'Oyley's officers, and to the chieftain of a Fulani tribe. I am equally proud of both lines of descent, and I would never allow my name to be besmirched."

"So she was being blackmailed for what she did, and you paid for what you are. Oh god, Margaret — but how did you discover who was behind this racket?"

"It wasn't all that difficult. I had The Looking Glass as a clear lead. Eleanore boasted of her association with the women she was introduced to by Therese, and where they met. The apartment houses — I have my contacts. It was fairly easy to discover that Mantanios owned them and The Looking Glass. I already knew him as the person who had bought my father's old house up near Swain Spring. And when you described your abduction, I recognised the place. That confirmed it for me."

Rachel asked after a silence, "What did you use?" She glanced round for the box which held the capsule which she had brought with her, but it had gone.

Margaret watched her with a smile. "I took it away, when I went to get the drinks. After all, it's the only bit of evidence against me, isn't it? Can't just leave it around — for your policeman friend to find."

Rachel got to her feet slowly, for the first time it hit her fully that she was alone with a self-confessed murderess — that she alone knew all the circumstances. No, not quite all. She tried to keep her voice steady, as she asked again, "What did you use?"

"So simple. The sort of knowledge that every schoolboy who does chemistry forgets by the time he's fourteen. So very simple — just metallic sodium, a small amount of metallic sodium, transferred to a capsule. I admit, I did have problems keeping the substance stable in the capsule, and not exploding. I don't suppose you know the properties of metallic sodium?"

Rachel shook her head. She was becoming steadily convinced that she was in some sort of waking nightmare.

"I thought not. Well, it has to be kept in an inert fluid, such as kerosene or naphtha, so I had to devise a chemical way to overcome that. That way is my secret. Then, place a treated capsule among the victim's usual supply of pep pills, tranquillisers, allergy or asthma controls — what have you, everyone takes something these days."

"But, wouldn't the — person — know from the different colour — or size — of the capsule?"

Margaret shook her head, "No, I've watched these people, they don't look. They just open the bottle, or whatever, shake one out and pop it into their mouth."

Rachel was appalled at revelations she had only guessed at. She asked faintly, "And then?"

"You wait," Margaret said calmly. "Just take your time. Eventually, the capsule is taken. In about half an hour the outer coating melts, the metallic sodium mixes with any watery fluid in the stomach — and poof! an explosion occurs, followed by haemorrhage, followed, even if help is available, by death."

"It's horrible!" Rachel felt physically nauseated. "It must be terribly painful."

"Oh, yes." Margaret's manner was that of the lecturer, pressing home the salient facts. "But I didn't think that a few minutes' pain, however intense, was enough for the weeks and months of mental anguish that they had made others suffer."

"You mean that you would have welcomed even more suffering for them?"

Margaret nodded.

"Why..." Rachel fought to keep down the waves of nausea that threatened to engulf her, "...why wasn't this — sodium — discovered during a post mortem examination?"

"That's the beauty of it. When it mixes with the stomach contents, it produces sodium hydrochloride, a normal constituent of the stomach. The metallic sodium disappears completely, and if the sodium hydrochloride count was a little higher than normal, it would be virtually impossible to detect, as the explosion would have — scattered the contents, shall we say?"

Rachel wanted to rush down to the Metro and drive fast down the hill, to the safety and sanity of Rowan's arms, but Margaret Cameron stood between her and escape, and was looking at her intently as she asked, "And now that you know the *why* and the *how*, and you're the only person in the world who does know, beside myself, what are you going to do with that knowledge?"

She advanced towards Rachel. Suddenly Rachel saw the folly of her coming on her own to confront Margaret with her suspicions. Margaret Cameron had become something other than the trusted old family friend. Rachel backed away, then felt nothing underfoot. The thought flashed through her mind, "What a fool I am," as she stepped back over the edge of the steps into space, hitting her head a glancing blow against the railing as she fell.

Rachel's last view as she fought enveloping waves of blackness, was of Margaret's face swinging closer to hers as she slowly slipped to the ground: it seemed to hang over her, becoming larger and larger, then disappearing as the blackness engulfed her consciousness.

Chapter 26

From a long way off, Rachel imagined that she heard Rowan say, "Not the only person in the world, Professor. I know too."

She opened her eyes with difficulty and the fear rushed back, until she realised that the arms holding her were Rowan's. She was leaning against him as he sat on a long couch, her body reclining, her feet up. She tilted her head back and looked up at him. To her surprise he was relaxed and smiling.

"All right?" he murmured against her hair. "You were knocked out for a moment, you know." She gave a nod, then stiffened as she saw Margaret Cameron seated opposite.

"Rachel," Margaret's voice held incredulity, "You didn't think that I was going to harm *you*, did you?"

Rachel kept silent and Margaret made a helpless gesture.

Rowan's arms tightened. "Whatever she thought, it's over now."

Rachel twisted away from him and sat up. "You heard? How much?"

"Enough," he said briefly.

"What are you going to do?" Rachel asked. She glanced at Margaret who sat silent, watchful yet serene.

"Do? There's nothing I can do."

"You mean Margaret will go free?"

"Free? Hardly. She'll have to live with it for as long as she does — live."

The words hung in the still evening air. Rowan's eyes met Margaret's. "You knew this could never get to a trial, didn't you? No doctor on earth could swear that those deaths were caused by other than natural means. There is no evidence."

"But Rowan, she *told* me. You *heard*."

"Do you think that that would stand up under cross-examination by a clever lawyer? Without the medical evidence, it's purely theoretical. It would be dismissed as hearsay — your word against hers. All that would come out would be the besmirching of those very names that she tried to preserve."

Rachel got up and walked unsteadily to the edge of the terrace. "You mean that you are going to let her get away with the murder of two people, an attempt on a third, and the death of Eleanore?"

"Wasn't that in your mind when you hid the capsule you'd found?" he asked sternly. She didn't reply and he turned to the still figure on the chair. "So, you played God — what now?"

There was still pride and strength in the tilt of her head, and her voice was firm as she answered him. "I had the courage to play God, as you put it. I must now have the courage to live with the past. I still have research to do."

* * *

Rachel sat close to Rowan on the drive down the hillside. They'd left the Metro to be picked up later. The hills closed in round them, friendly again in the darkness, for now the brief tropical dusk had made its swift change into night. A faint breeze riffled through tall pines, bringing that sharp clarity and crispness that was alien to the plains, still far beneath them.

"Rowan," she said at last. "Was that true — about not being able to make the charge stick in court? Or were you…?" she tailed off, unwilling to put her conviction into words.

He didn't answer for a long time, then said softly, "Being a policeman is not an easy job. Sometimes we have to decide when to play God. And when to abide by that decision."

"But why," Rachel asked after another long pause, "why did she tell me about it? If she was convinced of her rightness and her safety from the law?"

He slid the car to a stop. The harbour lay still and changeless three thousand feet below them. A few lights twinkled and the night sounds were all about them.

"That was her one weakness. She couldn't bear the guilt alone, so she wanted you to bear it with her. How long she will be able to live, alone with her memories, will be the test of her strength. Maybe we haven't yet seen the last of suicide related to this case."

He drew her towards him in the soft warm darkness. "And now you and I, my love, have got to get on with the business of living. And *now* is as good a time, and *here* is as good a place as any — if only this blasted gear stick wasn't in the way."

"Well, there is always the back seat," Rachel murmured into his shoulder.

ABOUT THE AUTHOR

Jeanne Wilson was born in England in 1920, but has lived in Jamaica since 1944 and became a Jamaican citizen immediately after Independence in 1962.

Mrs Wilson is a novelist, playwright, book reviewer and columnist for *The Gleaner*. Her publications include *No Justice in October* and *A Legacy for Isabel* (one-act plays — Evans Bros. [London], 1969); *Weep in the Sun, Troubled Heritage, Mulatto,* and *The Golden Harlot* (historical novels — Macmillan [London],1976-80, with editions published by Evans [New York], Arrow [London], Pocket books [New York] and St Martin's Press [New York]); and *The House That Liked To Travel, Holiday with Guns* and *Flight from the Islands* (children's books — Macmillan, 1977-78). *No Medicine for Murder* and *Model for Murder,* the first two of a series of six whodunits, were originally published by Ward Lock [London] in 1967-68; and were republished by Kingston Publishers in 1983 and 1993 respectively.

Mrs Wilson is a member of the Society of Authors of the UK, a Life Fellow of the American Biographical Institute, and a Deputy Director General of the International Biographical Institute, Cambridge. For eight years she was asked by the Swedish Royal Academy to nominate candidates for the Nobel Prize for Literature.

She acted on the local stage and radio for about twenty years, was in over one hundred radio plays and was involved in the School's Drama Festival, as sole adjudicator or committee member, for many years.

She was awarded the Institute of Jamaica Centenary Medal in 1980 and the Prime Minister's Medal of Appreciation in 1983.

She is married to the former Chief Medical Officer of Jamaica, Dr Jeffrey Wilson, and they recently celebrated their fiftieth wedding anniversary, having been married in 1943. They have one son, Roger, who lives in Canada.